DEADLY CURIOUS

Also by Cindy Anstey

DEADLY CURIOUS

CINDY ANSTEY

Swoon READS

New York

THIS BOOK IS DEDICATED TO MY WONDERFUL FAMILY, ESPECIALLY
MIKE, CHRISTINE, DEB, AND DAN, AND NEW MEMBERS
OF THE CREW, IAN, NICOLE, AND PRECIOUS SCARLETT.

A SWOON READS BOOK
An imprint of Feiwel and Friends and Macmillan Publishing Group, LLC
120 Broadway, New York, NY 10271

Our books may be purchased in bulk for promotional, educational, or business use. Please
contact your local bookseller or the Macmillan Corporate and Premium Sales Department at
(800) 221-7945 ext. 5442 or by email at MacmillanSpecialMarkets@macmillan.com.

Library of Congress Control Number: 2019932723

ISBN 978-1-250-25227-2 (hardcover) / ISBN 978-1-250-25226-5 (ebook)

Book design by Kathleen Breitenfeld

First edition, 2020

Before

He lounged under the ancient elm tree as dusk painted the sky a soft blush. Yawning, he tugged at the fob of his silver pocket watch and confirmed that he had waited well past the usual meeting hour. With a shake of his head, he stood, smoothed the wrinkles from his trousers, and started toward the path.

An unnatural stillness settled throughout the forest; the howling wind was muted, the leaves no longer rattled, and the birds were silent. Frowning, he squinted into the shadows all around him.

Deliberate, stealthy footfalls crunched through the rough grasses.

His heart quickened, and he swallowed in discomfort. Discomfort was soon replaced by fear.

This is ridiculous, he chided, giving himself a mental shake. There was no reason to be afraid. And yet this logic did nothing to stop the fear from growing.

"Who's there?" he called out.

He received no reply.

A twig snapped close by, and suddenly, he was running. He raced for the path at the edge of the glade, the fastest way out of the woods. And then he stumbled, tripped by an animal snare. He fell to his knees, struggled to untangle the wire—

A sharp, intense pain under his ribs stilled his hands. He felt a warm cascade spill across his gut and he tilted, slowly collapsing to the ground.

As he lay in a puddle of blood, a figure stood over him.

"Why?" he managed with his last choking breath.

The figure did not answer, and the silence of death filled the glade.

CHAPTER ONE

Investigating Murder and Mayhem

July 1834

As she had hoped, Sophia Thompson found the Risely Hall library empty. Choosing the settee closest to the window, she dropped onto it in an unseemly sprawl. Quickly breaking the seal of the letter, she turned it toward the light and prayed for good news.

But it was not to be.

Dearest Cousin Sophia,

While I would like to talk of pretty dresses and my newest pony, I can't. Other, much more weighty matters possess my every waking thought—besides, my dresses are still in the planning stage and the new pony is a plodder—hardly exciting, at all.

You were <u>wrong</u>! Life has not returned to normal! Nearly a year since Andrew's murder, and the tension in the manor increases daily. The family is in danger of shattering into a thousand pieces.

I cannot ease the anxiety that eats at every person in the house. I have tried . . . distracting Mother with conversations about the neighbors, pestering William with sisterly fun, and talking to Father about field rotation (whatever that might be). Nor can I unravel the purpose behind Andrew's killing.

And to make matters worse, there are rumors that Constable Marley wants to close the case, and is looking to accuse someone, anyone, of my brother's murder—even Father! It makes no sense. Why would Father kill his son and heir? Really, there is no logic in some people!

As you see, we are <u>desperate</u>! Andrew's murder must be solved quickly and the villain brought to justice before Constable Marley locks Father in irons or an angry mob burns down the house. Perhaps I exaggerate a trifle, but there is no telling what will happen in these unsettled times. I have no faith in Constable Marley's ability to solve the mystery of Andrew's death. What if the murderer still has his sights on the rest of the Waverley family? One day, we might all wake up dead.

By now you must realize the purpose of my letter. We need you! Yes, we need you and your inquisitive mind. You love puzzles and mysteries—the very reason you wish to be a detective. This case would go a long way to recommend you for training as a police investigator . . . if you succeed, of course. But I have far more faith in your clear thinking than the little minds around the town of West Ravenwood.

You must come to Allenton Park straightaway! And
while you are here, we will prepare for a joint coming-out.
Yes, I know it is a trivial consideration in light of Andrew's
death, but I need to escape this eternal dread somehow.

Please help me. I am in desperate need of a friend—
someone I can trust. I have no one else to turn to.

Be sure it is your papa you ask about a visit. I'm not sure
that your mama thinks kindly of this side of the family.

Please hurry. Time is running out.

Your loving cousin,
Daphne

Sophia frowned at the letter as she reread it. She was almost sick with worry when she read the letter a third time. Such hysteria was not like her cousin Daphne at all.

Giving her head a shake, Sophia tried to stave off her worry. She must think logically . . . as a Bow Street Detective would do. Logic and calm!

Holding up her fingers, Sophia took a deep breath and counted off the oddities of Daphne's letter and why they bothered her:

One. While Daphne had a tendency toward melodrama, this was excessive, and her cousin's call for help, uncharacteristic.

Two. Daphne was close to her brother, William, and yet he had warranted only a passing mention.

Three. Daphne had spoken of her coming-out in such a way that it almost equaled her concern about her family.

Four. Daphne mentioned, almost casually, that Uncle Edward could be arrested, accused of Andrew's death.

What was going on in West Ravenwood?

Sophia gulped a deep breath of air, calming her racing heart, and turned her eyes to the window.

Andrew's death had affected them all; although over time, the great sorrow of his loss had tempered into a dull ache of sadness. While alive, Andrew had been . . . difficult. His teasing often had a nasty edge, and he showed no interest in his sister or cousin's conversation, interrupting or walking away midsentence. It was most irritating but not unexpected, for Andrew was well aware of his exalted position as son and heir. But since his murder, Sophia had come to appreciate those few—too few—memories of when Andrew had shown her kindness.

Sophia shook her head, trying to clear her thoughts. It did not matter what type of person Andrew was—he had not deserved his fate. The mystery of his death needed to be solved. The murderer had to be found and punished. And if the constable in West Ravenwood was unable to do so without throwing out false accusations, then someone else was needed. Yes, perhaps even a green girl with an ambition to be a Bow Street Runner.

The Waverleys needed her. Daphne needed her.

Were she able, Sophia would have raced upstairs, grabbed some clothes, and set off on the high road, rushing north to West Ravenwood that very moment. But Sophia was not equipped to dash off by herself as of yet. At eighteen she needed funds and parental permission. Not to mention a horse, carriage, maid, a satchel . . . Dashing off was not as quickly achieved as it was so often stylized in fiction.

But Daphne needed help, and as quickly as possible.

Looking toward the door, Sophia imagined her mother in the morning room across the hall, a scowl on her face as she sat surrounded by overstuffed pillows. She knew her mother would not agree to a hurried journey north, but as Daphne had suggested, her father might.

Jumping to her feet, Sophia raced into the hall, hurrying across the tile on tiptoes, trying to make as little noise as possible. It was fortunate that her father's study was closer than the morning room, and Sophia ducked in without encountering her mother.

Papa sat in a wingback chair by a partially open window, well away from the insipid fire that Mama insisted upon. He had a calm disposition, gray curls to the nape of his neck, and a Vandyke beard of brown, black, and gray.

Lowering his newspaper, he looked over the edge at her. "Nothing to do today?" he asked, staring at her with a quizzical expression.

"No, actually. I have come about a request from Cousin Daphne," Sophia said offhandedly, hoping to get approval without having to produce the overly dramatic letter. Father thought little of high emotions and would not be swayed by them. "She has requested a visit, a distraction from the upcoming anniversary of Andrew's death."

"Really? I have had no letter from your aunt Hazel." Papa shrugged. "Your mother will not wish to travel so far."

Then, as if no more needed to be said about the matter, he shook his paper straight, hiding behind it once more.

"It is barely a two-day ride," she countered. But her words were quietly spoken. She did not wish to be disagreeable; it would not serve her purpose.

"You know it's not the distance, Sophia," Papa said from behind the newspaper, as if aware of her inner protest. "Your mother expects to be treated poorly now that her brother has been sent to the penal colony in Australia. She has no faith in the kindness of others."

"No one has said a word, Papa. They wouldn't dare. And really, one cannot help the follies of one's family. She is not to blame for Uncle Gilbert's behavior."

"I quite agree. Still, there is no convincing her."

"But, Papa, Daphne is all but begging me to visit. She sounds plaintive, and Daphne never sounds plaintive." *Melodramatic, yes, plaintive, no.*

"Does she? That's unfortunate. Well, I will speak to your mother . . . but, Sophia, don't get your hopes up."

"I won't," Sophia said, getting her hopes up. "We need not *all* go. I could travel to Allenton Park on my own—with Betty," she added. "In a hired coach."

Papa shook his head, his expression sour. "I will *not* see you in a hired coach."

Brushing her hands down her wrinkled gown, Sophia nodded, returning to the library. She shifted one of the settees closer to the window and dropped onto it once more, lifting the letter from Cousin Daphne. By the time she had read it a fourth time, Sophia knew that she had to find a way to get to West Ravenwood as soon as possible. She *had* to help her cousin!

———————

Sophia stared at the small puddle on the white marble floor of the grand hall and frowned. Dropping to her knees, she looked closer. The liquid was not tinged yellow, therefore not a "contribution" from one of her mama's two pugs.

For the better part of three days, Sophia had marched through the halls of Risely, begrudging every moment not spent speeding to Daphne's rescue. With no sign from either of her parents about the possibility of a journey to West Ravenwood, her anxiety and concern for Daphne had soared.

Hearing approaching steps, Sophia jumped to her feet. Fortunately, it was not Mama who breezed into the hall but Betty, one of the housemaids.

Sophia huffed, impatient with passing time, herself, the maid, even the puddle on the floor. "Betty, there is liquid of a mysterious nature on the floor. Do you know what it is?" she asked, being blunt on the advice of a book she was reading, *Investigating Murder and Mayhem: A Runner's Journey*. She puzzled a moment longer, thinking about the instructions in the book. "Or how it came to be here . . . there?" She pointed needlessly.

Betty barely glanced at the puddle. "Oh, never you mind. Just some drops of water from the vase when I moved it into the dining room. I'll get it up in a jiffy."

"Oh." Sophia huffed again—still frustrated with the puddle. Not mysterious after all. Just a bit of water spilled from a vase. Really!

"I have something for you," the maid said, flapping a paper in the air. "Your father collected the post again this morning."

With a squeal, Sophia snatched the letter from Betty. She recognized the handwriting: Cousin Daphne. Perhaps all was well and resolved? Sophia needn't commandeer a coach and rush to West Ravenwood, risking her reputation and parents' wrath? She held the letter tightly, wishing to break the seal and read it right there and then, but decorum prevailed.

"Where is Mama, Betty?" Sophia asked, casually glancing toward the smaller corridor leading to the back of the house. When Betty waved in the general direction of the morning room,

Sophia turned toward the library. Her fingers picked at the edge of the letter as she walked.

She had almost made it to her sanctuary when the hall was filled with the echoes of running feet. Pivoting, she watched Henry—her fifteen-year-old brother—land on the bottom step of the grand staircase. He sprinted across the entry and yanked the front door open before the footman could reach it.

"Henry, where are you—" she began, but her words sputtered to a stop. Henry had not so much as hesitated at the sound of her voice, racing across the threshold and ignoring her completely.

Through the door, Sophia could see his friend Walter Ellerby pulling under the portico. His curricle halted only long enough for Henry to jump in. The boys were off on another adventure; Sophia nodded for the footman to close the door.

Sophia sat seething with impatience, tasting little of the meal in front of her. She had tried to broach the subject of visiting Daphne just after the soup had arrived, and again when the eel was brought around.

Her cousin's latest letter did not bring happy news. Instead, Sophia had been bombarded with escalating distress about the family's imminent downfall. Daphne's pleas for help bordered on desperation. She seemed convinced that Andrew's death was merely the beginning of their trials and tribulations, that the entire family was in danger. *Soon to be murdered in their beds* was how she had put it. It was possible that Daphne's fears were exaggerated, but Sophia would only know for sure once she got there and investigated with her own eyes.

As dinner progressed, it became more and more difficult to

hold her tongue. Waiting for the exact right time to bring up the subject of Allenton Park was a challenge. First, the conversation centered on Henry's latest adventure with Walter Ellerby, riding around Welford Mills. It lasted for several minutes—several *tedious* minutes. When the subject turned to a harvest fair that was coming to a neighboring village, Sophia's patience disappeared entirely.

"Salisbury is about halfway to West Ravenwood," she blurted.

She would commandeer the family coach—and the coachman, Mr. Bradley, to drive it—if she must. The Thompsons seldom used it anymore; Mama might not even notice it was gone.

Sophia was about to say as much when Papa interrupted her.

"I have had a letter," he said, giving her a measured look before continuing. "From my sister. We are invited to Allenton Park for a month or two."

"Oh my, that is a shame," Mama said, signaling the footman for another serving of eel. "Offer my apologies."

Sophia frowned, staring at the end of the table. Her mama, hidden behind the frills and flounces of her yellow dinner gown, waved her fork in the air as she spoke. It was a face similar to Sophia's, especially when she frowned. They had the same wavy dark hair, wide mouth, and oval jawline, though Mama was corpulent and going gray.

"I will do no such thing," Papa said, smiling to nullify the harshness of his words. "I have instructed Mr. Bradley to be prepared by Thursday."

Mama opened her mouth, but Henry spoke first. "I would prefer to stay in Welford Mills, Papa. Walter will be heading back to school soon."

Papa chuckled. "Mischief and frivolity still to be had?"

"Exactly, sir."

"There. We cannot quit Welford, Mr. Thompson." Mama looked relieved and sat back in her chair. "It would not suit Henry."

"But, Mama, it suits me," Sophia protested. ". . . and Daphne."

"That is of no never mind, Sophia." Her mother lifted a shoulder in a casual shrug. "Your brother is happy to stay. Besides, the Waverleys are still not over Andrew's death yet. It would be a dreary visit indeed."

"One doesn't *get over* a murder, Mama," Sophia said, trying to control her tone of voice, though a smidgeon of anger snuck through. "And entertainment would not be the purpose of the visit but rather to lift their spirits."

And solve the crime. But Sophia was hardly going to advertise her true intent to her mother.

Andrew's death had been horrific, and to dismiss it so casually was cold and cruel. Sophia had not been at Allenton at the time, but Daphne had described the scene, including some of the more unpleasant details. Andrew was found in a puddle of blood in Glendor Wood just west of the Allenton manor. He had been stabbed in the gut—up under his rib.

"So, the question is settled." Papa nodded sharply, glancing at his wife. "You, my dear, will remain in Welford Mills with Henry while Sophia and I visit my sister and her family to distract them from their melancholy . . . if possible." He turned toward Sophia as Mama spluttered in protest at the far side of the table. "We will leave at ten sharp, Sophia, Thursday morning. Bring Betty as your lady's maid. Your mother will require the services of Laura."

Sophia gulped in relief. "Of course, Papa."

Thank the heavens. It truly did sound as if nothing worthwhile had been done to find Andrew's killer, and if the murderer was not found soon, all evidence and memories of that day would be lost. The tragedy of Andrew's death would be compounded without any answers.

Daphne would be vastly relieved with their arrival at Allenton . . . as would Sophia. Actually, the thought should have made her feel much better. However, as Sophia listened half-heartedly to her mother's complaints about being left all alone—with her son and eight servants—she realized that getting permission to visit Allenton Park had been relatively easy compared to everything else she would have to do once she arrived.

She had to clear her uncle's name, soothe Daphne's fears, and—most importantly—discover who had killed Andrew a year ago. It was an impressive list and a great deal to accomplish . . . especially with her lack of experience.

Sophia squared her shoulders. This was the new way of things—Sophia's *new* life. Marriage was no longer on the horizon; she had to make the future her own, untraditional and yet fulfilling.

What else does one do when all plans go awry?

Sophia had been greatly disappointed by the cancellation of her Season, though not for the usual reasons. Not a romantic sort, Sophia had seen the traditional process of husband hunting as a step toward independence. Uncle Gilbert's incarceration had put an end to her aspirations of finding a suitable husband. The Thompsons could not show their faces in London, let alone throw balls and invite eligible bachelors to dine. The Thompsons were no longer socially acceptable—they were related to a felon.

Sophia would be Miss Thompson forever, at the beck and call of her mother, unless she found some other means of establishing her own household. She had thought on the problem for months until she decided that she needed a career. Ever curious and a great reader, Sophia had come across a book in the library. No, it wasn't merely a book: It was a beacon of inspiration.

Sophia nodded to herself; *Investigating Murder and Mayhem: A Runner's Journey* would have to come with her to West Ravenwood. She would reread the list of devious behaviors; that should help pinpoint the appearance of a cold-blooded murderer and how such a person acted. She would discover the name of the villain and see him brought to justice.

Not only would her investigation help her cousin's family regain their peace of mind, but it would also go a long way toward establishing Sophia's credentials in the art of detecting— something that would be required, if she was to convince anyone of her skill.

Sophia would be the very first female investigating officer for the London Bow Street Runners. All she had to do was catch a killer.

CHAPTER TWO

Defective Detective

Mr. Jeremy Fraser, newly appointed trainee of the Bow Street police force in London and—some would say more importantly—fourth son of a minor baron, leaned closer to the coach window to stare at the scenery flashing past. They were coming into West Ravenwood.

Reaching across the opposite seat, Jeremy slid the driver's speaking window open, and he shouted over the sound of the pounding horse hooves and their jangling equipage. "I'm told Allenton Park is on the far side of town, Stacks—beyond the bridge. But best to ask."

Hal Stacks acknowledged Jeremy's statement with a nod and an unintelligible comment.

Jeremy sat back, trying to collect his thoughts and ease his nerves. He had been told the situation at Allenton Park was urgent—involving a murder. He had then been rushed out of the Bow Street office and into a carriage before he could ask any questions. Why the great hurry was necessary he could only guess, but Jeremy was fully aware that this was a test. He was on his own to sink or swim. This, his third case, could bring him either accolades . . . or his termination papers.

There had been a murder in West Ravenwood, and he had been sent to find and capture the culprit. And yet . . . he was certain there was a twist to this story. Sir Elderberry had smiled slyly when he had given Jeremy the address and sent him on his way.

Shaking his head, Jeremy wondered if he was riding pell-mell into a prank. Would he get to West Ravenwood and find that the deceased was a cat, or that there was no place called Allenton Park after all? The more seasoned officers loved to "initiate" new recruits with such schemes.

Still, he had no choice; he had to treat this so-called "murder" as a valid case until he learned otherwise. If it was to be a sink-or-swim situation, then Jeremy had every intention of swimming . . . metaphorically speaking, of course.

As the carriage slowed to allow for other traffic, Jeremy noted that West Ravenwood was fairly sizable—definitely more of a town than a village. The steeples of at least four churches were visible towering above the chimney pots of the cottages, and the high street was lined with shops offering fine cheeses, lace, and millinery.

A quick conversation with a man on the side of the road established the location of Allenton Park. Stacks guided the horses up over the short bridge that spanned the narrow River Coope and then turned uphill.

The approach to Allenton Park began with an impressive carved gate depicting rearing unicorns and snarling dragons, followed by a steep drive lined with majestic oak trees. The sizable manor that crowned the hill was of the style built a century earlier, with various juts and add-ons to accommodate the changing needs of the family. The cut masonry of the facade showed varying shades of gray with touches of ochre. Chimney pots abounded, as did oriel windows. Substantial and imposing, Allenton Park offered an air of elegance and authority; formal flower beds accented the flagstone path leading to the main entrance.

No sooner had Stacks pulled the horses to a stand than the front door flew open. A young lady of seventeen or so stepped out and then frowned at his carriage. She shifted, as if she were about to return to the house.

"Excuse me," Jeremy called as he opened the carriage door and stepped onto the flagstones. He signaled for Stacks to stay on the driver's bench. "Is this Allenton Park?"

The girl hesitated as if unsure of the answer or of her duty to reply. With a flip of her long dark hair, she frowned at Jeremy. "Yes, it is."

It appeared as if she wanted to say more, but she clamped her lips tightly together. Then she lifted her gaze over his head, past the coach and down the drive.

Jeremy swiveled to identify the cause of the sudden clatter coming up the hill. It was another coach—dusted with the dirt of the road—and four horses, looking tired and in need of hay and a brushing.

"Excellent!" the girl said to . . . no one. Then she turned toward the still open door. "They're here!" she shouted with great enthusiasm.

A footman—or so Jeremy assumed by his attire—leaned past the threshold for a peek. He frowned at Jeremy and was about to say something when a voice called from inside the manor. The footman turned and nodded to an unseen person.

Suddenly the entrance was filled with people. A tall bespectacled gentleman with his hair brushed away from his face stood leaning on a cane next to a woman of a diminutive stature; she had surprisingly short grayish-brown hair and a Grecian nose. A young man, likely Jeremy's age of twenty, with a half-grown Vandyke beard joined them. They all shared the same oval-shaped face and deep-set eyes as the girl, obviously her family. Accompanying them was a thin older woman, looking prim and proper with her gray hair pulled tightly into a bun at the nape of her neck and an unadorned black gown; she had the aspect of a housekeeper. Added to this mixture were the footman, and a stodgy-looking man that was very butlerlike in his appearance and demeanor.

Clearly, Jeremy had arrived at an inconvenient time. Some sort of arrival was imminent and questions about a murder were entirely out of place. Looking from one eager face to another, Jeremy was quite certain that he had indeed been the victim of a hoax after all. Yes, Allenton Park existed, but there had been no murder.

The footman stepped around the motley collection of souls, opened the door of the newly arrived coach, and handed out a young lady—a rather attractive young lady with black hair swept up under a wide-brimmed straw bonnet; she had a lithe physique and dainty features. Following on her heels was a gentleman with gray curls and a broad smile.

As the crowd gathered to greet the newcomers, Jeremy tried his best to fade into the background. He kept stepping backward until he encountered a solid wall. Only, the wall was in fact a person.

"And who might you be?" a deep masculine voice asked.

Jeremy turned to face the gentleman he assumed was Mr. Edward Waverley.

"I do beg your pardon. I arrived just before your guests. I'm here . . . I was sent here by Sir Elderberry of Bow Street." Jeremy tried to sound confident despite being anything but. He attempted a smile but knew it was weak at best. "I'm a Bow Street Runner . . . or will be soon enough. An . . . investigator."

"I have sent many a letter to Sir Elderberry about a number of things. You'll have to be more specific."

Taking a deep breath, Jeremy straightened his waistcoat. Now was not the time to let his insecurities get the better of him. "I am here about the murder, Mr. Waverley."

Silence. Sudden silence.

Each word resounded and echoed beneath the overhang of the entry.

The reaction was more dramatic than he anticipated. Mr. Waverley turned red in the face and then lost all color. Mrs. Waverley slumped, leaning heavily on the arm of the gentleman by the coach, and the younger members of the family gasped.

Only the young lady in the straw bonnet reacted in a sedate and reasonable manner. She lifted her brow at Jeremy. "A police investigator?"

———•———

"Shall we start with your name, young man?"

Mr. Waverley strode across the floor of the dark wood-lined study—the cane in his hand more of an affectation than a need. He gestured toward a chair sitting in front of a substantial mahogany desk. The gentleman's complexion had returned to a more normal hue, and the wary look had disappeared from his face—though Jeremy was not sure that irritation was a promising alternative.

Jeremy stood in the doorway, ignoring the chaos in the entrance hall as the family exchanged greetings and the staff took hats and traveling cloaks.

"Principal Officer Fraser—"

"Yes, yes. You are one of John Fielding's men. A Bow Street Investigator."

"Indeed, sir."

"Come into the room, young man, even if you have no wish to sit!" Mr. Waverley shook his head, muttering to himself for a moment before continuing. "And you are here about the murder of my son."

Jeremy frowned. He stepped closer to the desk, ignoring the chair, and huffed a sigh. "I was under the impression—obviously a mistaken impression—that you requested assistance in the investigation and hired the Runners."

Mr. Waverley laughed. It was not an amused laugh, though, but one of scorn. "I have been trying to get the attention of Bow Street for many months. Why have they finally deigned to send an investigator?" He dropped into the chair behind the desk and stared at Jeremy with a look of hostility.

"I couldn't say, sir."

Mr. Waverley shook his head again. "So you are a Bow Street Runner—a green one by the looks of you—and you have come regarding the murder, which took place nearly a year ago. I have long since given up on the local constabulary, but I had expected better of the Runners."

"I know nothing of that, Mr. Waverley. I was assigned to the case three days ago."

"Bow Street sent you with little to no information. Really! That is most unimpressive—as is your youth. An experienced man would have been more to my liking. Is this your first case?"

"No, indeed not," Jeremy was hasty to reassure, while not admitting that the number was all of three.

"I don't need eager enthusiasm; I need someone who knows what they're doing. This is *not* a trivial matter. We are talking about the murder of my son, and I want *justice!*" Mr. Waverley, in his apparent grief, seemed to be spoiling for a fight. "I've been privy to a discovery—a development, if that is the right word," the gentleman said. "Of which I informed Bow Street *months* ago."

Jeremy reached into the breast pocket of his jacket and pulled out a pad of paper. From his hip pocket, he drew out a pencil. As he prepared to record the details of the crime, he allowed a smidgen of his tension to waft away. He had not been sent on a wild goose chase after all. Though now he understood Sir Elderberry's smirk. He had sent Jeremy into a tense situation without any warning.

"About three months ago," Mr. Waverley began, "I was searching Glendor Wood, as I have been doing almost daily since last Michaelmas—"

A loud burst of nervous laughter echoed into the room. Mr. Waverley leaned to the side, looking around Jeremy and out into the hall.

"Searching Glendor Wood . . . ," Jeremy prodded.

As much as he tried to hide his "youthful eagerness," as Mr. Waverley had labeled his fixed attention to his duties, Jeremy *was* eager. He was energized by the hunt: ferreting out clues and bringing justice to victims, and this was his first *murder*. He was on his own, and outside London in an area of the country he had not traveled before. It was the perfect proving ground.

"Yes, indeed . . ." Mr. Waverley blinked at Jeremy, visibly trying to collect his thoughts.

Another burst of laughter crashed over the threshold, startling them both.

Mr. Waverley lifted his chin in a clipped manner. "You have arrived at a most inconvenient time." He flapped his hand as if shooing a fly. "This crime should have been solved long since. I have waited and waited for help to arrive. Now *you* will have to wait as I have a duty to greet my guests. Go. Take a place in West Ravenwood; there are several inns. Come back tomorrow."

Mr. Waverley stood, pushing his chair back behind him. "This crime needs to be solved quickly or it will never be solved at all. Someone must pay for what they did to my son."

These proved to be Mr. Waverley's final words on the subject, for the gentleman marched across the room and out the door without waiting for Jeremy to comment. Jeremy hesitated a moment, and then, with a shrug, he stuffed the paper and pencil back in his pockets, and he stepped into the hall.

His footsteps echoed throughout the grand two-story entrance as Jeremy made his way to the front door. He was about to signal the liveried footman to open it when another set of footsteps caused him to turn. Jeremy scanned the marble entrance hall and then up the twin staircases on either side of the room.

Two young ladies stood on the balcony between the staircases looking down at him—another footman stood nearby, valises in hand.

"The Unicorn and Crown is better than The Black Cat," the younger girl said. Then she pivoted, disappearing down the corridor with the footman at her heels.

A frown flashed across the face of the girl in the straw bonnet. She tipped her head as she briefly met his gaze.

"Curious," she said in a near whisper, though her words were clearly audible in the large, empty room. Then she, too, turned and hurried down the corridor.

Jeremy glanced at the footman feigning disinterest by the front door. "The Unicorn and Crown?" Jeremy asked.

"An inn in West Ravenwood, sir," the man replied helpfully. "It's a tad more costly, but The Black Cat has bedbugs."

"Good to know. Thank you . . . ?"

"Darren, sir."

"Thank you, Darren." Jeremy stepped out the now-open door and then turned back. "Where might I find the parish constable, Darren?"

"That be Mr. Marley—Constable Marley. And being that he has the haberdashery, he keeps an office in The Pins and Needles on the high street."

Giving Darren his thanks once more, Jeremy climbed into his carriage and directed Stacks to find the Unicorn and Crown. He would drop off his luggage at the inn and then set off immediately for Constable Marley's office. If he couldn't get the details of the case from Mr. Waverley, he would get them from the constable.

———⊷—⊷———

Jeremy arrived at the inn to claim the last available room, and Stacks was relegated to the common space above the stables. After depositing his cases in the room, Jeremy rushed over to the haberdashery only to find that Constable Marley had gone on a delivery and would not be back until morning.

And so it was that Jeremy Fraser had rushed from London, conscious of the ticking clock, worried that he would not arrive in a timely manner, only to sit in a pub, twiddling his thumbs in complete ignorance of why he was there.

"It might not be wise," Stacks said, pushing his dinner plate away from him. He was a thin man of thirty years or so, with a square chin and a shaggy mop of reddish-brown hair. He had come with the carriage: vehicle, horses, and driver hired for the time it would take to see this case through. Apparently, it was not the first time Stacks had assisted the Runners; he was rather opinionated.

"What might not be wise?" Jeremy asked, glancing around the crowded pub of the Unicorn and Crown. He sighed heavily, wondering if the abysmal day could possibly get worse.

"Not wise to put it about that you be working for the Runners. There be plenty what don't appreciate such an association."

Jeremy scrunched up his forehead and pinched the bridge of his nose, feeling a headache coming on. "Stacks, I really don't understand what you're trying to say. Please explain."

"You don't know if this be one of those towns what has gone ahead with the enclosures."

"No, and I'm not sure of the relevance."

"Well, you see . . ." Stacks sat back in his chair with his arms folded behind his head. He smiled a cat-in-the-cream grin, clearly pleased to be the one explaining the lay of the land to a Bow Street trainee. "Common land is no longer for common folk."

Jeremy nodded in agreement.

"In places like these—" Stacks glanced out the multi-paned

window overlooking the main street. "Most of the land belongs to the big estates. Common people used to hunt rabbits and the like, to help get by in the hard times, but a law were passed against the common use of land; landowners are putting up fences and hedgerows to stop what they say is poaching now. And if you be caught *poaching*, the punishment be harsh. Prison, transportation—even hanging."

"And how does that relate to my position as a Runner? I'm not here looking for poachers."

"Anyone in authority is seen as a threat, Mr. Fraser. A Runner, an officer of the law . . . he's dangerous, even if he says he's trying to solve a murder."

Jeremy sat up straighter, swallowed in discomfort, and looked at the other customers of the Unicorn and Crown. "But I'm here to investigate a murder, not haul anyone up before a judge because of a brace of hares."

Unfortunately, Jeremy in his anxiety spoke louder than was necessary, and his voice carried across the room. He sighed deeply when he saw heads turn and the hostile expressions that accompanied the glances.

"They's not likely to believe you, Mr. Fraser. If I were you, I would not advertise your association with the Runners. It might get you killed."

CHAPTER THREE

Let Sleeping Dogs Lie

The next morning, Sophia paced the entrance hall while her cousin fetched her bonnet. They were off on an errand: Aunt Hazel had mentioned that a pendant was due to be retrieved from the jeweler, and Daphne had been quick to volunteer their help.

Sophia chewed at her lip as she paced. Daphne had yet to say anything about the matter that had brought Sophia racing to Allenton Park. It left Sophia wondering if her concerns for her cousin's welfare had been misplaced.

Striding back and forth across the hall, Sophia tried to devise a conversation that would lead to the subject of Andrew's murder and the concerns Daphne had mentioned in her letters. She spun at the sound of an approach above her and watched as Daphne skipped down the stairs, skirts in hand.

Near the bottom, Daphne's step hitched and she pitched forward. Without a thought, Sophia rushed to the stairs, catching her cousin as she crashed into the handrail. They landed together in an ungainly heap on the floor, thoroughly mussed but unhurt.

"Are you all right?" Sophia asked, her heart pounding.

Daphne gasped for air, a hand pressed to her bodice. "I think I tripped," she said needlessly, clambering to her feet and straightening her gown.

Sophia did the same, tugging the bows at her elbows into place. "I have not known you to be clumsy before."

Daphne's hand paused halfway across her skirt. "It wasn't me. I tripped over something." She turned to look up the stairs.

Just above her, the culprit lay on its side, its head hung over the tread. "There. See, it wasn't my fault. I tripped over a toy horse."

Sophia frowned and then leaned closer, slowly reaching to pick up the toy. "Seems a strange place for this. You could have had a bad fall. Broken a limb or cracked your head."

"True, absolutely true." Daphne stared at the thing, taking it from Sophia and slowly turning it over, as if mesmerized by it. "It should be in the nursery . . . Someone could have been seriously hurt if they tripped and didn't have a cousin to catch them." Daphne's complexion became ruddy and her breathing shallow.

"Nothing worthy of concern," Sophia said quickly. "I'll mention it to your housekeeper, Mrs. Curtis."

"Come to think about it, the nursery was cleared out years ago. This must have come from the attic. Why is it on the stairs?" Daphne's tone was suddenly high and squeaky. "Someone put this toy here deliberately. Only the family uses these stairs. Someone *tried* to cause an accident!"

Sophia stepped to her cousin's side, taking her arm, and

propelled her toward the door. "Shh," she murmured. "There is an explanation—a nonlethal explanation. We just need to ferret it out."

Daphne pulled Sophia to a stop. "Someone just tried to kill me."

Sophia thought her cousin was being a tad dramatic, but an investigator should not jump to conclusions. "I'm sure there are other possibilities."

Daphne hesitated, then nodded. "Of course, there are . . ." She paused, waiting for Sophia to supply all those other possibilities.

"Um . . ." Sophia hesitated. "The footmen were transporting donations to the church, and the horse fell out of the box. Or perhaps Aunt Hazel offered it to one of the staff's children . . . Um . . . or . . ."

Daphne shifted, dropping the toy horse on the table by the door. "Or someone tried to *hurt* me."

Sophia noticed the substitution of the word "kill." Daphne clearly saw that stating she had been subject to a murder attempt was a bit excessive. But why would someone wish Daphne permanent harm? Sophia was fairly certain that there would be a logical explanation for the toy being on the stairs; she just hadn't thought of it yet.

"Let's not think on it for a few minutes." She hoped the respite would allow Daphne the time to get her thoughts together.

Sophia took a deep breath of fresh air as soon as they stepped through the door, and watched Daphne do the same. They both needed to find calm in order to think clearly.

"Let's head into town and fetch the pendant for your mother."

Distraction was a good way to comfort a witness; Sophia had read the comment in *Investigating Murder and Mayhem*.

It seemed as good a plan as any.

"Odd. All very odd," Daphne said as the front door closed behind them. She hooked her arm through Sophia's and they started down the drive, matching their paces. All was calm.

And yet, Daphne did not avail herself of the calm. "This past year has been dreadful," she said before they had taken more than ten steps. "I'm so glad you're here. I have been living with an all-consuming fear the entire time with no one to talk to." Daphne's tone was slightly theatrical. "The murderer is still here. *Here*, in West Ravenwood. Biding their time, preparing to strike again." She paused and turned to Sophia, eyes wide with panic.

Had Sophia been of a more susceptible nature, the pronouncement would have caused her great concern. She patted Daphne's hand to offer comfort. "Tell me why you think so," she said, trying to adopt a mature, worldly tone.

Sophia gave her cousin's arm a squeeze and they continued to walk, nodding to the gardener as they passed him trimming the hedges.

"Father said as much to Constable Marley. He insisted that the constable redouble his effort to catch the killer, said time was running out."

Sophia nodded, agreeing internally that time was indeed of the essence. Memories were fading and the scene of the crime would have altered. Clues would be few and far between, disappearing under the weight of time. Still, to say as much to Daphne would be unkind—her cousin was already in such a state.

"That is rather ambiguous, Daphne. Uncle Edward might have meant that time was running out for the discovery of Andrew's murderer, not that there would be another victim."

Daphne furrowed her brow and twisted her mouth. "Yes, I suppose that is true . . . but we still have cause for concern." She took a deep breath and swallowed visibly. "Constable Marley came to see Father again yesterday, before you arrived. I didn't hear what was said as the interview took place behind closed doors in Father's study . . . But I could tell they were shouting at each other."

"Shouting? Uncle Edward?"

"Yes, exactly. Father seldom shouts. I snuck up to the study door for a listen, but Mother caught me and I had to return to the library. And then when the constable was leaving, he yelled back at my father from the entrance hall. Heard him plain as day."

Sophia waited for Daphne to continue, but apparently she thought her explanation complete. "What did he shout?" she asked, guiding her cousin through the gate and onto the main road.

Daphne blinked and looked around as if suddenly aware of her surroundings. She increased her pace, pulling Sophia into a quickstep. "He said, 'If you keep it up, you will be arrested.'"

Sophia startled. "*Arrested?* That is a rather odd threat. Uncle would never break the law; Constable Marley would have no cause to arrest him. A man—particularly a gentleman—cannot be brought before a judge without a valid reason."

"How do you know that?" Daphne asked, tucking a strand of hair under her bonnet ribbon.

"I read it somewhere," Sophia replied vaguely. She could have been more exact—Chapter Seventeen, page 231 of *Investigating Murder and Mayhem*—but as much as Daphne knew of Sophia's interest in detecting, she didn't really *understand*.

"So I need not worry that Father will be taken away," Daphne said, brightening. "Excellent." She sighed with relief. "We have more than enough to worry about."

Sophia clamped her mouth shut. Innocent men had been accused before. She would not know if the threat to Uncle Edward was real until she met the constable herself. Most such appointed men were reasonable and clear thinking, but there were others who enjoyed their power a bit too well and liked to throw their weight around.

Sophia let her cousin's fears settle down for some minutes before asking, "What other worries?"

Daphne stopped walking, pulling Sophia to a standstill with her. "I told you, Sophia. Father's temper is on edge over the least little thing. Why yesterday, I rode Misty, my thoroughbred mare, through the upper field, and Father berated me in front of William. Really, I only knocked down a row of barley . . . maybe two. But he scolded me for ten whole minutes! And when I returned from my afternoon stroll about the garden with Miss MacIntyre—my governess—my skirt hem was rather muddy, which is not to be wondered at as it had rained the day before. Still, he blamed Miss MacIntyre and sent her packing! Can you imagine? Seeing my governess off because I got my skirts a little dirty!"

Sophia opened her mouth to respond, but her cousin was not done.

"He's not quite right, Sophia," Daphne said, gesturing toward her head. "And I can only say this to you because you are family . . . I would never say such a thing to someone like . . . Charlotte. No, Father is not acting like Father. He hides in his study scribbling on paper, muttering to himself.

"And then there is Mother. She's so easily distracted. We'll be talking, discussing important matters—such as the color of my next ball gown—and Mother will turn to me and say 'Would Andrew like a puppy?' My dead brother! Would my *dead brother* want a puppy? Really?!" Daphne shook her head vehemently, knocking her bonnet askew. "You see what I have to put up with. And then William snaps at me for singing in the garden—says it disturbs the bees. I can't do anything right. I can't say anything right."

She looked near to crying and Sophia reached out, pulling Daphne in for a cousinly hug.

Squaring her shoulders, Daphne swallowed and then straightened her bonnet. "I have started restricting my conversation. Talking about the weather or what's for supper. Voicing my opinion on *anything* gets everyone's back up and so I say nothing. Well, I might mutter under my breath, or write a letter to you or talk to Charlotte or cry on Miss MacIntyre's shoulder . . . which I cannot do anymore.

"And all the while, I keep thinking if only we knew what happened to Andrew. Why he was killed, who killed him. Then we could put him to rest, get on with our lives. Father would stop trying to solve the mystery, Mother could remember she still has another son and a daughter, and William could stop blaming me for *everything*!" Daphne turned to face the road once more. "Everything," she whispered, then continued to walk.

Sophia stared after Daphne for a moment before hurrying to catch up. She put her arm through her cousin's and gave her an affectionate squeeze.

Daphne did not realize that she was acting out of character as well—anxious and troubled. The whole Waverley family was in desperate need to know what had happened to Andrew. And yet, as Sophia strolled down the road toward the market town of West Ravenwood, she found herself momentarily distracted by a simpler question.

Who is Charlotte?

"He was rather handsome," Daphne suddenly said with great enthusiasm.

Sophia startled, surprised by the abrupt change of subject and mood of her cousin. "Who?"

"The Runner. Dreamy blue eyes."

"Were they?" Sophia asked. She supposed the young gentleman's eyes were engaging, his expression approachable . . . Perhaps that was what Daphne meant by dreamy. But more importantly, the Runner was a *Runner*! It was most exciting to see a detective in action . . . well, sort of in action.

Uncle Edward had made short shrift of his arrival, practically giving him a heave-ho out the door. She would have loved to have been there while the Runner had asked his questions. To talk to him about his approach to solving the murder of her cousin nearly a year after Andrew had been killed. There was so much she could have learned, speaking to this officer of Bow Street.

Still, all was not lost. He was not gone but was staying in West Ravenwood, meeting Uncle Edward this afternoon. She would make certain she was nearby during that meeting. But before their meeting, she would talk to Constable Marley and get the unemotional story behind Andrew's death.

"Is the haberdashery near the jeweler?" Sophia asked.

"Down a block and on the other side of the street. Did you need some fabric or needles?"

Sophia lifted her shoulders in a lackluster shrug. "I wish to talk to the constable about Andrew." She was not sure what

Daphne's reaction would be. Daphne knew of Sophia's aspirations to be a detective, but did she really wish for Sophia to investigate her brother's death, or had she simply wanted a companion with which to commiserate? "Constable Marley runs the haberdashery, I believe."

"Yes, he does. That is an excellent idea. Perhaps you can help each other solve the mystery, although, Constable Marley has become rather prickly about the subject. We can stop by the haberdashery after we pick up the pendant." Daphne grabbed Sophia's hand. "The Runner might be there."

"Mr. Fraser?"

"Yes, him."

The sound of an approaching coach sent Sophia and Daphne to the side of the road; they watched it pass and then stepped back onto the gravel. Within a block they had passed the Unicorn and Crown, and Sophia found her thoughts wandering to the intelligent blue eyes of one Mr. Jeremy Fraser.

———— ⋅•⋅ ————

The haberdashery was a narrow sewing notions shop squeezed between a dry-goods store and a stationer on the main road. Crowded with wares, a restricted aisle to the back office was where Constable Marley ran the policing of the town. Sophia and Daphne were forced to wait while a sour-faced woman and her daughter finished purchasing a set of colored pencils. Once the girls had maneuvered their way to the back, they stood before a closed door, listening to loud but indistinct voices on the other side. Sophia lifted her hand to knock, hesitant to interrupt.

Suddenly the door was flung open to reveal a large man with

jowly cheeks and small eyes. Constable Marley was showing Mr. Fraser out of his office.

"What you fail to realize, young man, is that it is an insult. Yes, an insult. Asking the Bow Street Runners for assistance while I be handling the case is the same as saying that I'm not doing me job!" An angry flush climbed up Constable Marley's face. "You will have to get your information elsewhere. Mr. Waverley has no business interfering."

"It is very much his business! What father would not try to discover who had killed their child?"

Constable Marley harrumphed—a raucous clearing of his throat. "That gives him no right to consult the Runners without notifying me!"

Mr. Fraser, who was facing the door, glanced out the opening and met Sophia's questioning gaze. His expression cleared almost immediately, and he smiled in a way that left Sophia slightly breathless and confused. Then he returned his attention to the constable. "I believe there are others who wish to speak to you, sir."

The constable whirled around, lifting his lips into a smile—with no true benevolence—in the girls' general direction. "Young ladies, what can I do for you?" His eyes lit on Daphne with recognition, and he nodded with a modicum of respect.

Sophia took the lead, stepping slightly forward. "Good day, Constable. I am Sophia Thompson, cousin to Miss Waverley. My father and I arrived yesterday at Allenton Park. We, or rather I, was hoping to discuss the progress of my cousin Andrew's case. I understand that there has been a development—"

Constable Marley held up his hand, silencing her with a look.

"No. I will not discuss this case with you or Mr. Fraser. You can discuss it among yourselves if you like, but I will not participate. I am tired of the whole mess. There are no answers to be had. The only person acting out of order, in a suspicious-like manner, is Mr. Waverley. Sneaking through the underbrush, poking at the shrubberies. And I will not be party to finger-pointing without evidence. I've better things to do."

"But—" Mr. Fraser began.

"Off you go." The constable shifted out of the doorway. "I'm sure Miss Thompson will be able to fill you in. If not, Miss Waverley will do the job."

Sophia offered Constable Marley a lackluster smile. "We can hardly walk down the street together, chitchatting as if we had been introduced when, in fact, we haven't." She waved her hand in a circle between Daphne, Jeremy, and herself. "Might you do the honors, Constable?"

After chuntering for several moments, the constable did just that. Both parties bowed or curtsied. And then, without so much as a "Have a nice day," they were escorted out of the store.

Out on the street, Sophia looked at Mr. Fraser with curiosity, ignoring the other pedestrians jostling past. There was nothing about him that declared his association with the famed police force of Bow Street. He wore no uniform, but rather the usual gray jacket and waistcoat of a gentleman; a watch fob hung from his pocket. His expression was kindly, his eyes intelligent, and he projected an air of strength. It was all very reassuring . . . until he spoke.

"That didn't go as planned." Mr. Fraser chewed at the corner of his mouth. "I am as uninformed now as I was when I arrived." He glanced at the girls, focusing on Daphne. "I don't wish to be indelicate, Miss Waverley, but would you be willing to discuss the death of your brother? Constable Marley told me Andrew was the victim, but little else."

Daphne tipped her head and nodded. "I find the whole thing distressing, Mr. Fraser; discussing it will not change that. However, if you are going to walk up to Allenton Park with us, could we discuss the murder in the privacy of the upper road?"

"Absolutely." Mr. Fraser gestured forward and they stepped into the crowds, strolling at a comfortable pace past the busy shops. As promised, they stayed away from the topic of murder for the time being. Their discussion comprised, instead, observations about the weather. It was not particularly scintillating conversation, and the topic was happily dropped upon venturing past the last house of West Ravenwood.

The road was dappled with sunshine as they walked along under the tall elms. Bees chased the wind and birds filled the air with melodies. Daphne was quiet for some minutes before Sophia realized that her cousin was deep in thought about Andrew.

"There was no hint," she said eventually. "His death changed our lives forever, and yet we had no warning. The sun came up at the expected time. Cook burned the toast, Father hid behind his newspaper at breakfast, William had gone for a ride, and Mother was still abed. All very normal." She kicked a rock further up the road. "Nothing prepared us for the horror."

Sophia blanched and stepped closer to Daphne. She wanted to offer some words of comfort, but everything had already been said, many times over.

"We were told that his suffering would not have been long due to the depth of the wound. I suppose that was some comfort. The underbrush was well and truly trampled. Constable Marley decided that it meant Andrew had been waiting for someone, likely pacing."

Mr. Fraser tsked appropriately and made sympathetic noises. He hesitated for a moment and then squared his shoulders. "Do we know who that someone was? Whom he was waiting for? Actually, let's go back. I have none of the details.

"When was your brother murdered, Miss Waverley? Is there an estimated time? Who found his . . ." He hesitated once more. ". . . his body?" He cleared his throat and continued. "Where was he found? Who examined the body? Were there signs of a struggle such as premorbid wounds or bruising? Was the time of death determined? How would someone with murderous intentions know where to find Andrew—alone and vulnerable?"

"Stop, Mr. Fraser, please! Give me time to answer." Daphne took a deep, ragged breath. "Andrew was found by one of the groundsmen, sent for that purpose, and he was killed in July of last year. Mr. Reyer, the village surgeon, examined Andrew's body. He had been stabbed. Bruising was not mentioned within my hearing, and as to the killer finding him—" Daphne laughed; it was an abrasive sound, not at all jubilant. "Andrew was a ladies' man, and a man of habit. It was likely a common meeting place for a romantic rendezvous."

She swallowed convulsively and Sophia knew her cousin to be struggling with her emotions.

"You keep saying 'man,' Daphne," Sophia chimed in. She wanted to give her cousin a breather, a break from the horrendous memories. "Mr. Fraser might get the wrong impression." She turned to the Runner with a troubled expression. "Andrew was but three and twenty. Still quite young."

"Indeed. Twenty-three is young; though three years older

than I am at present, Miss Thompson." Thoughts of a puzzling nature flit across his face until he returned his gaze to Daphne. "Please, continue."

"There is not much more to tell. The knife was not found. Animal traps and snares were discovered in the vicinity, lending to the theory that Andrew happened upon a poacher and was killed by him for fear of being revealed. That was the motive Constable Marley suggested. But the case has gone nowhere." Daphne blinked rapidly, and then continued quickly to hide her discomfort. "Most people think it was an accident. But how can someone be stabbed by accident? It was a deep wound; it would have required a strong thrust. And then, Constable Marley insinuated that Father had something to do with it. That made no sense at all."

Lost in thought, the three continued to walk down the road in silence. The whinny of a horse in a nearby field brought them back to the here and now.

"But that can't be all, Miss Waverley?"

"How do you mean?"

"Something *has* happened. There's been some change— Mr. Waverley referred to it and Constable Marley implied it. I would not have been called in otherwise."

"Unless Uncle Edward was getting frustrated and wanted fresh eyes," Sophia said.

"Yes, true enough. And yet, I'm convinced that there was a new incident. What could that be?" Mr. Fraser shook his head, a thoughtful expression etched into his handsome features.

"New?" Sophia turned to stare at Daphne as she came to an abrupt halt. "Do you know?"

"There was something," Daphne said, swallowing convulsively.

"Something awful. I could hardly believe that Father carried it into the house, let alone crowed with pleasure at his find."

Sophia touched her cousin's arm. "What do you mean? What did he find?"

"The knife. He found the knife that killed Andrew in Glendor Wood."

CHAPTER FOUR

Listening at the Door

The silence between them was deafening, and the day suddenly darkened as the sun slipped behind a cloud. The half light augmented the strained atmosphere, and the steep climb to the manor became a challenge.

"Where did he find it? And why does your father believe it is the knife that was used to kill your brother?" Mr. Fraser asked with careful diction, as if he were weighing the value of each word.

"Yes, evidence," Sophia said, pleased to recognize the tactics that were being adopted by the Runner. "What evidence was associated with the knife to make Uncle Edward believe it to be the . . . one that—?"

Uncomfortable with the direction of her thoughts, Sophia broke off. She was being too blunt, too cavalier about Andrew's death. Andrew had been a bully, and quick tempered, but his sister had loved him.

Sophia should think before she spoke. It would be a lesson well learned.

Fortunately, Daphne was too lost in her own thoughts to realize that Sophia had been tactless.

"I really don't know why he thought so, but he was convinced of it." Daphne stopped walking and turned toward Sophia. "Things are not as they should be, Sophia, not at all. We are still at sixes and sevens; I was not exaggerating when I wrote." After taking a ragged breath, she continued. "I'm scared," she said without a quiver of emotion in her voice—no melodrama.

Such stoic conduct from her cousin was more unnerving than tears. "What are you scared of, Daphne?" Sophia asked, trying to sound unruffled and in control of her own fears.

"I think someone is trying to kill me," Daphne added in a whisper. Then, glancing at Mr. Fraser. "It's likely nothing," she said with a false laugh. "Just accidents, mistakes, lapses in judgment . . . nothing at all."

Mr. Fraser frowned. "Accidents? What accidents?"

Daphne's face puckered as she considered. "I tripped on a toy horse that had been left on the stairs," she said. "Nearly tumbled down to the tiled floor of the entrance hall, but Sophia caught me." She turned to Sophia, giving her a warm look of appreciation.

Mr. Fraser blinked in surprise. "A toy? Are there children at Allenton Park?"

"Exactly. You see the problem." Daphne nodded with approval. "No, no children at Allenton. There haven't been for some years. The toy came from the nursery, which hasn't been used since I was a tot."

Sophia had tried to find a reason for the toy being on the stairs but had yet to devise an alternative theory. She had questioned the butler on the way out the door, and when receiving no new information, she had questioned the footman. All to no avail; everyone was puzzled as to how the toy came to be on the stairs.

"And then last week, just before I wrote to Sophia—the *reason* I wrote to Sophia—a box of sweets arrived as a mysterious gift; the donor was not identified. They were placed on the front step with my name. Mrs. Curtis—our housekeeper—" she explained, "brought them up to me. I quite enjoyed the treats . . . but they made me sick as a dog. The physician thought that they might have gone off or been poisoned. Mother spoke to Constable Marley but he did not investigate—just suggested that we don't eat anything left on our front step again." She rolled her eyes.

"Weak advice. Not in the least helpful," Sophia said, making a conscious effort to smooth her furrowed brow. She was rather put out with Constable Marley and his cavalier attitude.

"Why would anyone try to poison you?" Mr. Fraser asked. His tone was even and professional, but his eyes were stormy.

Sophia gazed up at the sky, paying little heed to the placement of her feet. "Did the box have a manufacturer's label? We could find out who sells those type of sweets in town. They might be able to say who bought them. A description, at least, would be a start."

Mr. Fraser leaned forward to look at Sophia. He tipped his head and frowned as if surprised by her question. "Excellent idea."

Sophia smiled warmly at the young gentleman, inordinately pleased by the comment and his look of admiration.

"Yes, indeed, it is a good idea," Daphne said as she shook her head. "But unfortunately, the box was thrown out long ago, and I didn't notice anything on it before it was trashed. Just a plain white box with a blue ribbon."

Once again, the three lapsed into silence, their footsteps in unison as they trudged up the hill. As they came to the crest, the whole of Allenton manor was laid out before them. The wide drive circled around a colorful bed of dahlias in the center of the lawn and continued up to the front door. The *opening* front door.

A female figure emerged, wearing a yellow day dress embroidered with winding leafy vines and small roses. Her full sleeves were cuffed at the wrists, and had flounces around the neckline. It was an elegant display that surprised Sophia; the ensemble exhibited a sophistication seldom seen outside London.

Daphne stiffened and then dragged in a heavy breath. "Charlotte is here."

"Ah, so this is Charlotte," Sophia said. "You've mentioned her several times but I do not recall who she is."

"You've met, though I believe it would have been several years ago," Daphne said, speaking quickly. "Last time you were in West Ravenwood, Charlotte would have been away at finishing school in Bath. She is Mrs. and Reverend Dewey's daughter, but she has become quite attached to Mother. They plan charity events and the like throughout the year."

Daphne's voice became harsh and her steps slowed. "We are not particular friends. Though, as I said, she is great company for Mother."

Sophia glanced in Mr. Fraser's direction. She was not surprised to find that he was absorbed by the approach of Charlotte Dewey; Charlotte was a handsome young woman. Her features were striking—reddish blond hair, blue eyes and a wide mouth that dimpled under her cheeks. Looking demure and biddable, she bobbed a shallow curtsy when she reached the trio in the center of the drive.

"Hello, Charlotte," Sophia said to fill the conversational void; it had suddenly gone silent. "It's been a long time. I didn't recognize you."

"A long time, indeed, Miss Thompson," Charlotte agreed, and then turned to Mr. Fraser. "Mr. Waverley is expecting you. That is . . . I mean . . . you *are* Mr. Fraser, are you not?" She continued after seeing his nod. "He is waiting in his study." She moved to the side, allowing him space to step past her.

"Shall I do the introductions?" Sophia asked quickly, trying to smooth over the awkward moment. She didn't want to see Mr. Fraser rush off right away.

After the presentations were complete, Sophia made certain to include Mr. Fraser in the niceties of health inquiries and weather comments before he decided that he would leave them to their chat. He offered a backhanded wave as he entered the manor, and the door closed behind him. Sophia was disappointed to see him go but turned back to Charlotte with a smile.

"I didn't know you were coming today," Daphne said. Her expression more than her words offered the question: *Why are you here?*

"I came by to visit with your mother, Daphne." Charlotte flapped her hand over her shoulder in a wide swoop to indicate Allenton manor. "Mrs. Waverley wants to hold a charity event— something to benefit the poor of the parish. We've been considering a booth at the fair, a gala party, or contest of some sort. The funds would go toward the parish children's education. It is most generous of her to take the time to organize such a thing."

"Yes, Mother does enjoy helping the less fortunate." Daphne glanced at the front door and took a half step in that direction. "And what did you decide?"

Charlotte's brow furrowed, and her expression was pained. "Nothing yet. Our meeting has been postponed. Mrs. Waverley is distracted—rightfully so, but distracted nonetheless, by your father, Miss Thompson." She glanced at Sophia.

"Aunt Hazel has not seen my father since Andrew's funeral last year," Sophia said. "They have much to discuss and news to relate."

"That was certainly evident." Charlotte gave a half laugh . . . almost a giggle. "They were rather animated, guffawing and talking over each other. Splendid to see after so many months of brooding." Charlotte glanced toward the door as if she could see through the wood. "The distraction is just what your mother needs."

"Yes, indeed," Daphne said with a frown, likely not appreciating the familiarity of the reverend's daughter. "I'm sure you will be able to discuss the charity event with my mother soon enough. You need not despair."

"I certainly hope so," Charlotte nodded, mistaking Daphne's commiseration for support.

———————

Once inside the grand entrance hall, Daphne headed down the central corridor to the drawing room to return the repaired pendant to her mother. Sophia headed to her uncle's study near the foot of the staircase. She hoped that she hadn't missed too much of the meeting between Mr. Fraser and Uncle Edward. Rapping on the door in a firm but nondemanding manner, Sophia stood back waiting to enter. She had heard the murmur of voices as she had approached the door, but they broke off as soon as Sophia's knuckles brushed the wood.

"Yes." Uncle Edward pulled the door open, exposing a medium-size but comfortable paneled room, sporting hound and horse paintings on the walls as well as four wingback dark leather chairs in the center of the room. An ornate George III desk sat against the far wall.

"I was wondering if I might sit in on your meeting, Uncle? Daphne has asked me to help with the investigation."

Uncle Edward chuckled. It was not a happy sound, but one that was forced and grated her nerves. "Has she? Teasing you, I think. What a suggestion." He continued to chuckle until he noticed that Sophia had not returned his smile. "Certainly not! What was she thinking? What are *you* thinking? Young ladies do not involve themselves in murder! It's . . . it's . . . it's *unnatural*." Uncle Edward turned an unusual shade of red as he huffed and stammered.

A squeak and a tap on the floor tiles behind her alerted Sophia to someone's approach. Shoes or boots scuffed across the porcelain.

"What would your father say if he knew?" Uncle Edward pounded the floor with his cane.

"Knew what?" Sophia's papa asked, peeking his head over Sophia's shoulder. "Are you causing problems again, Sophia?" He patted her arm with affection.

Sophia pivoted to look at him. He grinned at her, looking more relaxed than he had in months; the lines around his mouth had all but disappeared and his folded brow was . . . well, not folded. Getting out from under the oppression in Welford Mills had done him a world of good.

"Warren, please talk to your daughter," Uncle Edward insisted. "It is most unseemly for a young girl to want to involve herself in murder. Unseemly and vulgar. Yes, yes, quite out of good character. This is a case for the professionals to investigate." He started to close the door. "If she needs something to do, there are ladies' magazines in the drawing room, with dress patterns and hair . . . suggestions." And with that final condescension, he closed the door—rather firmly.

"But, Papa," Sophia began, turning to face her father. "I'm not interested in dress patterns."

"Yes, I know, my dear. But I have been instructed, as you heard, to tell you that it is most unseemly for a girl to become involved in murder—"

"He said, for a young girl to want to involve herself in murder." Sophia curled up the corner of her mouth, preparing to debate the issue. "*Unseemly and vulgar.*"

"Yes, yes, too true. He did say that. And apparently this is a case that requires professional investigation." He waved at the footman, standing stiff and straight by the front door. "Could you bring us a chair, please?" He turned back to Sophia. "And you should know there are ladies' magazines in the drawing room, with dress patterns and hair . . . suggestions. Did I get it right that time?"

"Yes, but—"

"Right there." Papa pointed the footman, who now carried a Chippendale chair with a green seat cushion, to the right side of the study door. "Now sit, Sophia."

Sophia sat with a very ungraceful drop and offered her father a scowl.

"Excellent. Now, I direct you to sit here, thinking about everything we have just discussed. You will have to be quiet for a fairly long time. You might hear voices coming from the study . . ."

Sophia sat up straight and leaned to the left, closer to the door.

"But you will have to ignore everything that is being said within the study and contemplate dress patterns and—"

"Hair suggestions?"

"Exactly." Then lowering his voice so that only Sophia could hear, he asked, "What are you doing, by the by?"

"I am hoping to help Mr. Fraser solve Andrew's murder." Then she touched her father's arm and met his gaze. "For a purpose, Papa. Not idle curiosity or a burning desire to be a busybody. I must find an occupation, now that my marriage prospects are near zero. And after a great deal of reflection, I have decided that I would like to be an investigator. A Bow Street Runner."

"That is a rather odd choice, Sophia. For one, you are a young lady, and ladies do not work. And for another, there are no women investigators employed by the Runners, my dear," her father said quite reasonably. "Your mother would have an apoplexy at the thought." He chuckled.

"I will be the first," Sophia said with more conviction than she felt.

"Well, indeed . . . yes, it's good to have an ambition." Sophia's father patted her shoulder, kindly done but a touch patronizing. He straightened and then he glanced around. "Hmmm, I seem to have lost the drawing room."

Sophia pointed toward the back of the manor.

"Yes, excellent," he said as he began to walk away. "You have always had a head for direction. That might be of some use in sleuthing . . . and the like."

Sophia shook her head as she watched her father disappear into the drawing room. She knew it was going to be a chore convincing her parents—not to mention the Runners themselves—to give her a chance, to try her hand at investigating. She would need to prove that she was capable, talented, in the ways of detecting . . . lawks, she had to prove it to herself, too. Rereading *Investigating Murder and Mayhem* was a must. Perhaps if she used words like "larceny," "apprehend," or "judicious," she would be taken seriously.

"What are you doing?" Mrs. Curtis asked some fifteen or so minutes later. She clicked her tongue in disgust. "That chair belongs in the dining room."

"It's just temporary, Mrs. Curtis." Sophia addressed Miss Curtis as a married woman in the usual tradition for upper servants. She lifted her finger to her lips. "I'll have it returned as soon as I'm done."

"And what exactly *are* you doing?"

Sophia straightened in her chair. She had heard dribs and drabs of the conversation through the crack in the door; Uncle Edward had a loud voice. However, the occupants of the study had been silent for some moments, leading Sophia to believe that it was time to move away; the meeting was over.

"I'm thinking, Mrs. Curtis, as my uncle directed me to do . . . about ladies' magazines . . . with dress patterns and hair suggestions."

Sophia stood and smoothed her skirts, contemplating her next course of action. She wished to talk further with Mr. Fraser, of course. "But it is now time to commune with nature. Some fresh air." And with that, Sophia walked across the entrance hall—just in time.

The brass handle rattled as it was turned and the study door opened.

Sophia stood on the threshold of the front door for some time, listening to Mr. Fraser as he made his goodbyes to Uncle Edward. It was a stiff dismissal on the part of both gentlemen and fairly lengthy, as Uncle seemed determined to advise Mr. Fraser on how to go about his business. Sophia could imagine how well that was appreciated.

Taking the opportunity to slip further down the drive, Sophia half walked, half ran to the other side of the flower bed. It would appear—or at least she hoped it would—as if she were taking a walk in the garden and just happened to bump into Mr. Fraser as he was leaving.

She knelt beside a dahlia, appreciating the plant's symmetry. She was waiting, breathing deeply, trying to calm her pounding heart, and chastised herself for her overexcitement when she heard *it*.

It was the sound of stealth. Someone walking slowly and cautiously in her direction.

Sophia gulped and stood slowly, resisting the urge to whirl around. Footsteps were not unusual; this was an active manor with plenty of men and women in service inside and outside the big house. The sound of movement was nothing to cause fear. It was only the appearance—or rather the impression—of stealth that made her uncomfortable. Turning slowly, Sophia looked for the cause of her discomfort.

The soft early afternoon light was dappled under the oaks lining the drive; the lawns and garden beds were lush, well-manicured, and deserted. Nary a soul wandered down the drive.

No one raked the lawns or clipped the hedges. There seemed to be no one about and yet . . . the shadows under the third oak looked somewhat misshapen.

As if someone were crouched behind the large trunk, trying to hide.

A sudden bang jerked Sophia's gaze to the manor. A multitude of windows stared back, and she was suddenly aware of being clearly visible to anyone within those walls. A blurred shape passed in front of one of the open windows on the second floor, and Sophia squinted at it, trying to understand what—and likely who—it was.

And then Sophia swallowed her nerves and chuckled in self-deprecation at her overly active sense of fear. The bang was undoubtedly the noise of the window being opened—certainly no cause to panic. Giving the window one last glance before walking away, Sophia was pleased to note that there was *nothing* to see.

She would have to keep her fears in check, if she were to make a career of investigating. Jumping at every little noise and shadow would not do her any good.

With a casual glance over her shoulder, Sophia stepped away from the manor and then stopped abruptly. Slowly, ever so slowly, she pivoted until she faced the manor once more. And there she stood motionless, except for a wildly beating heart, barely breathing.

A face—there was no doubt of its nature this time—stared down at her from the second story. It had a surreal quality, as it was all that stood out. Eyes, mouth, and nose, the rest was cloaked in shadow. It was far enough away that Sophia was not provided with a gender or an identity, but the face was clear enough that

Sophia could see the downturn of the person's mouth, the folded brow, and the piercing gaze.

In an attempt to hide her dismay, Sophia lifted her hand in greeting. The eyes continued to stare straight at her, projecting revulsion and disgust.

CHAPTER FIVE

Fear and Loathing

Jeremy frowned at the chair sitting next to the study door. It looked better suited to a dining room than the grand entry of a manor. Of more significance, it hadn't been there when Jeremy had entered the room to talk to Mr. Waverley.

With a mental shrug, Jeremy returned his thoughts to the more important dilemma of Mr. Andrew Waverley's untimely demise. Mr. Waverley had not been brimming with additional information; Jeremy knew little more now than what he had gleaned from Miss Thompson and Miss Waverley.

However, Mr. Waverley had bestowed upon him the possible weapon used by the murderer; Jeremy clutched it protectively, wrapped up in his handkerchief. *If* it indeed was the instrument of murder . . . Jeremy had been with the Runners long enough to take nothing for granted.

Nodding to Darren, the footman, Jeremy stepped outside the manor and took a deep breath of fresh air. Oh, how he missed the tranquility of the countryside. London was active and exciting, but also noisy and dirty. This was a welcome respite.

Shifting the knife to his left hand, Jeremy stared out across the front lawn; it was thriving and appeared lush in its summer finery. The central flower bed was resplendent in bright globes— flowers with red petals in a round shape, adding a cheerful splash of color.

And standing next to the bright red flowers was a lovely young lady. Jeremy smiled . . . until he remembered the seriousness of his visit. He could not—*should* not—be distracted by the entrancing character of one Miss Sophia Thompson. Still, he need not be rude and ignore her presence, either.

"Hullo!" he called quickly as Miss Thompson looked to be turning away; it would deprive him of the pleasure of her company.

She glanced toward him with a frown. It was not the friendly greeting that he had been expecting. Granted, he had only been out of her company for thirty minutes or so. But she looked more than unfriendly. She seemed . . . agitated. Could *he* have done something to cause this unexpected reaction?

"Is all well, Miss Thompson?" he asked as he stepped closer, concerned more than he should have been to be on the outs with the lovely young lady.

Still looking up at the manor, Miss Thompson nodded in an absentminded manner. "Hmm," she said, confusing Jeremy entirely.

"I beg your pardon?" he asked.

"Oh! I apologize." Turning to face him once more, she blinked as if only just realizing where she was. "I had the strange sensation that I was being watched."

"That would not be a surprise, Miss Thompson," Jeremy said with confidence. "A pretty young lady wandering about is sure to attract attention. You are standing before countless windows."

Miss Thompson looked at him for some moments, a frown growing increasingly deep on her forehead. "No," she said eventually, with a shake of her head. "It will not do."

"What will not do?"

A grin replaced her frown. "Flattery. It will not dissuade me. While I appreciate the compliment, it will not distract me. Though you are right about the windows—many face this direction and any number of persons might be looking out. But what about the drive?"

"The drive?"

"Yes. Moments ago, I had the sensation that I was being observed from the drive as well. You know . . . tingles on the back of your neck and a mysterious discomfort." She pointed toward the third oak.

"Behind that tree?" Jeremy started forward as soon as Miss Thompson nodded. He marched to the tree with every intention of giving the person responsible for Miss Thompson's discomfort a good dressing down. He was most displeased that someone, anyone, would make Miss Thompson uneasy.

However, upon reaching the tree, he found that there was no one behind it. The grass was slightly trampled but there was no telling when that occurred. "Not to worry, there is no one—"

Off to the side, the bushes shook, and out slunk a large gray cat. Jeremy heard a distinct giggle from behind him.

"Oh dear." Miss Thompson laughed. "And here I was certain that I was being watched."

"You were . . . by a cat."

"Rufus."

"I beg your pardon. You were being watched by a Rufus." He returned to Miss Thompson's side.

"Would you care to take a turn about the garden?" she asked. "Not at all appropriate to be seen chatting on the front lawn."

She gestured to the side of the house and Jeremy fell into step. "Was there something you wished to discuss?" he asked, seeing her attempt to begin their conversation several times.

Miss Thompson grinned in a charmingly mischievous manner. "Well, yes. I was hoping you could explain a few things to help me understand. If you don't mind."

"If I can, I would be pleased to do so."

The path they had chosen widened out and wound past a bed of roses. He offered his arm so that they could stroll and converse comfortably.

"Excellent. Then perhaps we will start with explaining the object in your hand," she said. "What it is and why it is swathed in a handkerchief."

"Ah." Jeremy held up the knife, though he would admit that it looked nothing like a knife, wrapped up as it was. He kicked at a rock, sending it skittering across the path. "Why do you wish to know, Miss Thompson? It is not a pleasant object. Are you prepared for that?"

"I am indeed prepared, Mr. Fraser. I wish to be party to the investigation. Two heads are better than one, don't you think?"

Jeremy tripped, jerking them both forward. With an apology, he stopped to pick up an unremarkable stone and dropped it at the edge of the path as if had been the culprit of his trip. Taking Miss Thompson's elbow again he led them forward. "*Why* do you wish to be involved in the investigation?"

"I feel an obligation to Daphne and my aunt and uncle to help if I can. I know West Ravenwood and its people; my insight could be of great use."

Jeremy paused. "Is that all?" he asked, certain there was more—something was hanging in the air, unaddressed.

Flushing prettily, Miss Thompson dropped her gaze to the stones beneath their feet. "I thought it might be good training."

"Training?"

"I would like to become a Bow Street Officer," she said quickly. "A Runner."

Had they been walking still, Jeremy would have tripped again. Her answer was completely unexpected. "It is an . . . unlikely outcome, Miss Thompson. There are no female Runners and, most would argue, for a good many reasons." Emotions were on edge, criminals were often violent, and Runners saw a very seedy side of life—all of it not suitable for a gently brought up girl.

But even as his mind rejected the idea, he met her piercing gaze and noted her emotionless expression; there were some at Bow Street who had not mastered as much. And while he knew the majority of Runners would not welcome the assistance of a woman—a young woman at that—Jeremy knew the value of a different opinion.

"It's not a safe or comfortable career, Miss Thompson. I would hope to change your mind."

"You can't," she said in a clipped voice. "So, what is it in your hand?"

Jeremy looked skyward for a moment, thinking. "Yes, of course . . . This is . . ." He cleared his throat. "Mr. Waverley gave me a knife—one that he believes was used in the murder of your cousin. He has been searching Glendor Wood for several months. I would have thought clues to be few and far between at this late stage, but apparently while his search of the lower path—leading to West Ravenwood—was of no value, he did discover this knife under a bush on the upper path. The one that apparently leads to Savor Road and eventually Allenton Park." He looked at the object in his hand and then dropped his arm, effectively hiding the knife from her sight. "It's not a common knife. The carving on the handle is of Middle Eastern or Asian design."

"Can I see it?" Sophia slowly held out her hand, looking reluctant to touch the knife despite her request. Once it was in her hand, though, she unwrapped it and stared at the carving with intensity. "Curious. It has a strange primitive style, predominantly black with bright splashes of color," she said. "And I wonder what this is supposed it be? Are the figures sitting in a boat, perhaps? An indication that the artist is from an island of some sort? I know none of this affects the investigation, but it might be an indication of the type of person we are looking for. Yes, quite unusual and appealing . . . in a dangerous, murderous way."

She slowly turned it over, assessing the underside. "There seems to be an artist's mark on the blade." Straightening, she handed the lethal object back. "It should not be hard to find the owner. The knife is unique."

"I quite agree," he remarked with a nod of approval. He was impressed with her observations. "I will start my investigations with the knife merchant in town. The people at the inn will be able to direct me to his shop."

"Excellent idea, but the merchant is unlikely to know anything about it."

"Really?" Jeremy lifted the corner of his mouth in a half smile. "You think it might have come from elsewhere? Perhaps it was bought while the owner was on a tour abroad, or some such?"

"Yes, there is that. You would have to talk to the surgeon about the size of the wound in Andrew's chest—to establish that this might be *the* knife—otherwise it is just a knife hidden in the woods. But I was thinking more in regard to Mr. Tilter, the knife merchant. He is a quiet, withdrawn sort of person and easily annoyed. Repeated questions are bound to cause him a great deal of irritation. He will deflect and show you the door."

"Why would he be dealing with repetitive questions? I imagine Constable Marley spoke to him months ago. Surely that would not set him off."

"Not Constable Marley, me. *I* intend to speak to Mr. Tilter as well. I cannot investigate without asking questions."

"But you will not have the knife to show him."

"No, but I can describe it fairly accurately. And I already know where his shop is located, so I will reach him before you."

Jeremy frowned and huffed in frustration—disappointed somehow that Miss Thompson intended to thwart him. His appreciation of her person dipped slightly. "So, you intend to interfere."

"Not at all, Mr. Fraser. I intend to *investigate*."

Her expression brightened, and Jeremy's appreciation bounced back up again.

"I suggest that we work together. There is no need to plague the townspeople—or each other—more than necessary." There was a hint of amusement in her voice. "I'll bring Betty."

"Betty?" He started to stroll again, pulling Miss Thompson forward with him. "Who might she be?"

She smiled. "Betty is my maid. You and I cannot wander about without a chaperone, after all. It would cause a great fuss—concern about my reputation, and such. So, that then is settled. We will work together." She went on quickly when Jeremy opened his mouth to disagree. "We'll need to learn where Andrew was found—the exact place. Was the ground trampled? Did it look like more than one person was in the area? Did said person lie in wait? Was anything usual found at the scene? I'm thinking of something besides the knife . . . poacher's traps, a mysterious glove or an incriminating button."

"Incriminating button?" Jeremy repeated dubiously. "Incriminating? Where did you hear that word?"

"I may have read *Investigating Murder and Mayhem*," Miss Thompson said airily, raising her chin. "And, Mr. Fraser—" Her brow furrowed. "Why did it take Bow Street so long to react? My uncle has been asking for help for months— quite willing to pay the Bow Street fees."

Jeremy dragged in a deep breath, as if he had been the one talking. "Great heavens. So many questions." It was clear that Miss Thompson *had* been doing a lot of thinking about the case.

She said nothing and continued to stare at him with a raised brow, likely waiting for Jeremy to explain why the Bow Street Runners had been negligent. As Jeremy had no idea why they had taken so long to respond, he thought avoiding the topic altogether was preferable to admitting ignorance. He tried to focus on the topic at hand and ignore the fact that Miss Thompson was staring at him and standing quite close. There was something rather appealing about the young lady—in an intellectual way, of course—and it was difficult to concentrate on murder and knives when her perfume wafted in his direction.

Shaking his head, Jeremy frowned. He could not allow distractions of any sort. He was a Bow Street trainee, and if all went well, he would be a Bow Street Investigator in short order. Distractions had to be ignored!

"I'm not certain of the location of the murder," Jeremy explained after clearing his throat. "I will have to have someone show me where it occurred. I'll get a sense of—pardon?"

"I said 'us.' Someone will have to show *us* the location."

"That's not a good idea."

"Of course it is. Don't worry, I'll bring Betty there, too."

"I wasn't thinking of propriety."

"What then?"

"Would it not be emotionally draining to go there . . . to where your cousin was murdered?" He watched her complexion turn pale.

"I don't really *want* to go there. I think it will be horrible." She drew in a ragged breath. "But I also believe it is necessary, to get a complete picture of what happened. Especially if I am going to be of assistance."

———•———

Jeremy left Miss Thompson after having established a mutually convenient time to visit the knife merchant. While he was reluctant to lean on Miss Thompson's good name within the town, he had to admit she was right. Being a Runner—even one still in training—would not win him any points in a town harboring poachers. Few would be comfortable with his questions, particularly if Miss Thompson had been there before him. He just hoped that Miss Thompson had the mental fortitude to deal with an investigation of this sort. He would have to watch her closely for signs of distress . . . a chore that would not be laborious.

Jeremy sauntered down the drive through the dappled light of the trees. His thoughts were focused—not on Miss Thompson's numerous questions but on what the answers would have been, had she insisted on a reply.

Where was Andrew found, exactly? Jeremy would have to get that answer from Mr. Waverley, for it was doubtful that Constable Marley would lead him to the murder site. And once there, all evidence of the violence would be gone; too much time had passed. Jeremy would only be able to get the lay of the land, see its proximity to paths and houses, and imagine how the murder had taken place. There were often many possibilities.

And then there was the matter of the "incriminating button." He laughed to himself. Where had that possibility come from? Jeremy was almost certain that Miss Thompson had been teasing.

A strange sound caught Jeremy's attention—a rustle in the bushes on the right side of the drive. A twig snapped and then a rock rolled across the dead leaves beneath the brambles. Something was moving through the shrubbery, but it was hidden behind the large leaves of the pink flowered bush.

Was that darn cat following him? But even as the question formed in his mind, Jeremy dismissed it. The creature causing the commotion was bigger than a cat. There was too much of a disturbance.

With long, hurried strides, he rushed toward the flowering shrub. "Come out from there!" he shouted. "Show yourself!"

Nothing moved. Jeremy slowed his steps, feeling rather foolish. He was jumping at shadows. This would not do. Runners were made of stronger stuff.

He glared at the shrub, ready to accuse it of playing him false when one whole side of the plant shook as if it were being pushed aside.

"Come out!" he shouted, although with less ferocity than he had bellowed moments earlier. He was suddenly very aware that he was alone here; the nearest people were strangers uninterested in his welfare—except for the possibility of Miss Thompson.

He took a deep breath.

"Reveal yourself!" Jeremy said to the shrub, keeping his voice firm but even. "Step forward!"

This time, a figure stood. Cloaked and in shadow, there was no clue to their identity. Even the deep chuckle of mockery offered no gender. Jeremy reached into the flowering shrub, grabbing at the fleeing figure, but the shrub prevented him from getting close enough to grip the cloak.

Then, in a flash, the figure hightailed it, running toward the woods.

Jeremy tried to yank his arm clear, but his jacket sleeve caught on the hooklike branches. It took some minutes—and various curses—to free himself from the plant.

By then the cloaked figure had slipped into the dense forest and disappeared.

CHAPTER SIX

Between a Whisker and a Squeak

"But we've only just arrived, Papa," Sophia said sulkily, chewing at the side of her mouth. "Mama must have written the day after we left. It's hardly fair."

"Hardly unexpected, either." Papa lifted one shoulder in a casual dismissal. "I will go back early—"

"But, Papa—"

"*I* will go back early, as I started to say. But there is no need for you to be deprived of your cousin's company. Your aunt Hazel has commented on Daphne's behavior; she is laughing again and teasing William. You are good for her." He smiled affectionately. "Doesn't surprise me in the least. No," he continued with a deep sigh. "I will go back, but you can stay. I'll return in a few weeks to take you home. Still, there is no need for me to hurry away. I will write your dearest mama and let her know that I will be along eventually."

Sophia jumped to her feet, racing around to the other side

of the breakfast table. "Thank you, Papa!" she said with a broad grin, hugging him across the shoulders.

Patting her arm, Papa nodded, and then returned to his morning newspaper.

Sophia slipped out of the breakfast room, her mind a jumble of questions. First and foremost was her concern about timing. Would a few weeks be enough? Could she find a murderer within that time frame? The constable had not been able to do so in a year . . . but he had not had the benefit of *Investigating Murder and Mayhem: A Runner's Journey*! Well, she assumed he hadn't. The man did not look like a reader. Though, as soon as that thought crossed her mind, she began to wonder what a reader looked like.

Still, all these extraneous points were moot. Sophia had something to prove; she had to excel above the ordinary if she ever hoped to see inside the Bow Street Headquarters. However, Papa could only delay her mother for so long; Sophia would be carted back to Welford Mills eventually.

So, time was of the essence. They had to visit the knife merchant, and by *they*, Sophia meant she and Mr. Fraser . . . and, of course, Betty. Then off to see the murder site, and . . . well, she would think of something else as she proceeded. Perhaps she would ask Mr. Fraser his thoughts on the subject—or consult *the* book.

Yes, that was a better idea. She would not look quite as naive if she had a framework of questions and ideas of how to proceed. A few minutes studying the advice of an expert would not be out of place. And no time like the present; she had an hour or so before she and Betty needed to set off for West Ravenwood to meet the appealing Mr. Fraser. But on second thought, Daphne might wish to come.

Sophia skipped up the stairs and headed toward her cousin's room.

A horrendous, piercing scream filled the corridor.

It was coming from Daphne's room.

Lifting her skirts, Sophia raced to the end of the hall. Heart pounding, she flung open the door.

"Daphne!" she shouted. "Are you all right?"

It was a ridiculous question, as Daphne would not be screaming if there were no problem, but Sophia was finding it hard to think clearly.

Daphne was not fending off a gang of kidnappers, she was not being attacked by a bear, nor had she fallen and broken her ankle. No, indeed.

Daphne was standing—hopping actually—on her bed, pointing at the floor. Her mouth was agape and there was a very real possibility that she would scream again.

"Daphne! That's right, over here. What's wrong?" Sophia was suddenly seized by a fit of laughter, but suppressed her giggles as best she could. Daphne looked rather silly, flapping her arms around like a berserk chicken.

"A monster!" her cousin shouted. "It's huge! Gray and furry . . . it has gigantic red glowing eyes. It was going to attack, tear me to shreds. Look, there it goes!"

Sophia turned in the direction of Daphne's pointed finger and swallowed her amusement with some difficulty, trying to hide her surprise.

An adorable mouse scampered across the carpet, more frightened than Daphne, and out into the hall.

"Hardly a monster, Daphne. Your greatest danger might have been a little nibble." Sophia turned and offered her cousin a hand down from the bed. "I can hear people coming. You might want to get down," she said quickly. "Your mama will be here soon—"

"I'm already here, Sophia." Aunt Hazel breezed into the room. "Why were you screaming, Daphne?" she asked her daughter with a weary sigh.

Sporting a vibrant tangerine day dress, Aunt Hazel could pass for ten years younger than her actual age, until one met her eyes. Then she seemed ten years older.

"A mouse, Mother! Big enough to be a rat!" Daphne said as if no other explanation were necessary. And apparently, she was right.

"At this time of year? How very odd. I'll have Mr. Strate bring the cats back in from the barn."

Daphne shuddered. "You know how I hate rodents, Mother."

"*Everyone* knows how you hate mice, Daphne, dear. I'd best warn the staff that there is a mouse on the run," she said as she half turned toward the door. A new scream could be heard echoing through the hallway, and it was joined by a shout of surprise. "Oh, it won't be necessary. They've seen it."

Sophia snorted, catching her aunt's eye.

"Yes, I agree," the older woman continued. "When one lives in the country, one should be used to things such as mice and spiders." She frowned at Daphne, looking her up and down. "That is a most unappealing gown; it will not be coming with us to London," she announced with authority and then pivoted, marching out the door. "Even a good pressing will not help it."

"A fact of which I am well aware!" Daphne said sharply, but in a near whisper. Waiting for a moment, likely to ensure that her mother was gone, Daphne stomped over to her wardrobe and threw open the door. "I have three good dresses. Yes, three." She held up three fingers to clear away any doubt. "Only these three are worthy of my coming-out; that is all. Mama has not ordered any others."

As she spoke, Daphne drew out one of the gowns she had indicated. A swath of peach silk slipped off its hanger and fell to the floor in a puddle of ruffles. Daphne scooped it up, held it out arm's length, and then gave a strangled gasp of surprise. "Oh no!" she said. "It's ruined!"

Daphne had not exaggerated. The beautiful gown was a shattered mess. The bodice was crisscrossed with slashes, the material barely held together by threads. The skirts were as bad if not worse—dismembered bows and ruffles rained down, covering the rug at her feet. There would be no patching this gown.

"What a shame," Sophia said, knowing a ruined dress would be devastating to Daphne. She watched as her cousin continued to rummage through her wardrobe, pulling out two more dresses. Fortunately, they were undamaged, and she quickly returned them to the confines of the wardrobe. But the ruined gown could not be returned; it was nothing but rags. "I am so sorry. What happened? Was it the mouse?"

It seemed a lot of damage for such a small creature but what other explanation was there?

Daphne whirled around, shaking the material at Sophia. "Look at this mess!"

Sophia frowned and leaned closer. She lifted one part of the skirt to look at the cleanly sliced edges. "This was not chewed." She shifted her gaze to the bodice. "It's been cut. Someone took a knife or a pair of scissors to your gown. Why would they do that?"

Not only why, but how? A stranger could not wend their way

through the halls of the manor without being seen. A stranger would not know where Daphne kept her dresses. Who had access? Family members, visitors, and staff . . . And the gown was ruined beyond repair—there was a spiteful air to the damage.

Sophia swallowed carefully and held her tongue. She avoided voicing the most obvious observation so as not to frighten Daphne further: There was a malicious soul in the manor targeting her cousin.

Daphne's eyes grew wide and she swallowed visibly. "Now I have only two gowns to take to London," she said, as if that were the important conclusion of the incident. "Mother will not be happy. She'll accuse me of being petulant and ruining the gown so that I could have another."

Sophia shook her head, certain that Aunt Hazel would think no such thing. "That would be quite an expensive display of selfishness."

Daphne looked dazed and more than a little frightened. "Sophia . . . ," she began and then crumpled in an indelicate drop to the floor. The ruined material fell with her. She sat slumped, legs crossed, tears forming in her eyes.

"Sophia, this is a disaster. You have to find out what is behind all these . . . these . . . vicious attacks. I know it all stems from Andrew's murder. You have to find out what happened. You have to stop this." She swiped at the mess in front of her, scattering the bows across the floor. "Someone is after *me* now. I'm in danger, and I have no faith in the authorities to protect me. Mother and Father don't see the danger. They're so very wrapped up in their own . . ."

"Their own sorrow," Sophia completed for her cousin.

"Yes." Daphne nodded. "True enough." She shook her head

slowly and deliberately. "Someone has to figure this out. You, Sophia, you can do it. You *have* to do it."

Sophia squatted beside her cousin and put her arms around her shoulders. "I'll try, Daphne, and I will keep on trying until we know what's going on."

It was a promise that Sophia intended to keep.

It took a good half hour to calm Daphne back down. While Sophia silently puzzled out the purpose of the ruined gown— it smacked of jealousy: vicious and mean and very personal— Sophia's conversation stayed away from all things mysterious. She knew it would be impossible for Daphne to put aside her emotions and adopt logic until after the shock of the mouse and peach dress had lessened. Sophia, instead, concentrated on Daphne's favorite topics. They discussed Daphne's pony, her appreciation for pie, and the prettiest flowers in the garden. Eventually the conversation returned to the *beau monde*.

"Mother says my new gowns should be made in London, but there are no plans to go to town. She spends all her time organizing charities of one sort or another with Charlotte. My Season should be a priority!"

"Your mother is still dealing with the events of last year, as we all are, and she is keeping herself busy by thinking of others."

"I'm an *other*." Daphne stared at Sophia wide-eyed, her mouth pinched and mulish.

"I meant those less fortunate."

Daphne frowned. "Oh, I see." She closed the doors of her wardrobe with a little more force than was necessary. "Very worthy of her." She groused quietly and then ambled over to her window, looking out at the tranquil, lush grounds. "But I do not want to be stuck in dreary old West Ravenwood. And if I do not find a husband before I'm twenty, I'll be here for eternity! All will be lost." She turned back to Sophia. "An old maid!" She huffed, forgetting that Sophia was looking at a similar fate.

"You could always find something to do," Sophia said helpfully.

"Perhaps I'll be an investigator, like you," Daphne said as if it were the easiest thing in the world.

Sophia was rather put out by Daphne's suggestion; it rankled, though she did not quite know why. "I'm sure you'll enjoy sifting through clues, studying the inner workings of difficult personalities, and understanding criminality."

Daphne shook her head, her long dark hair swaying back and forth. "No, indeed. You're quite right. That does *not* sound enjoyable. I'd much rather *you* do all that and I'll go to balls and concerts and impress society with my poise." She smiled, unaware of the needling effect of her words. "Besides, you have to be brave to chase down a murderer," Daphne continued. "And I am not in the least brave, Sophia. In fact, I would rather not go anywhere until that foul murderer is found. We are being watched. I know it. It's worse outside the gate, of course, but even here, in the manor." She glanced at one of the peach bows that had escaped their tidying. "Here, in my own room there is no safety."

"Well . . . not for your dresses."

Daphne snorted a laugh and then her face grew serious. "You might make light of it, Sophia. But we both know that this is a grave matter. Someone is watching and waiting and threatening our well-being, and we don't know when they will strike."

"Or why," Sophia added with a deeply folded brow. "I keep wondering *why.*"

"Why?" her cousin asked.

"Yes." Sophia dropped onto the side of Daphne's bed, bouncing slightly from the force. "Andrew was a young man. Only twenty-three. Why would someone want to kill him? He had barely started life—though he seemed quite the expert at making girls fall in love with him. I think every girl within a hundred miles dreamed of marrying him."

Daphne's eyes had taken on a glassy look.

"*Why* was Andrew killed?" Sophia asked, feeling heavy as the enormity of it all hit her again. "Andrew angered someone, or scared them, or discovered something that would cause the murderer grief, or had something that someone wanted."

"A theft?" Daphne latched onto the least disturbing possibility. "The murderer stole something from Andrew?" She sounded affronted; then she paused for a moment, staring at the carpet. "If the murderer stole something from Andrew—then the villain should be happy. He got what he wanted. He would leave the rest of the family alone. But he hasn't. No. Accidents and incidents follow us around. The villain didn't get what he wanted, did he?"

"That's a likely possibility. And it brings us back to the question: Why?" Sophia picked up a bonnet that had been tossed onto the window seat. She poked and fiddled with it, lost in thought. "In fact, *why* is the most important question. To know why is to know *who* . . . or, at least, to have a better idea of who."

"There are too many whos," Daphne complained.

"Yes, I had best make a list. I don't know why *Investigating Murder and Mayhem* did not mention that, but I believe a list of suspects would be rather handy."

"Girls? Are you coming downstairs?" Aunt Hazel's voice drifted through the open door, and then her disembodied head popped across the threshold. "Is there a problem—another one?"

"Daphne is worried she won't be prepared for her coming-out," Sophia said quickly. She did not want to discuss Andrew's death with her aunt in front of Daphne. And to mention the peach gown when Daphne was still riled up would just be inviting trouble.

"Oh, Daphne, I have told you, there is plenty of time. If your dresses are made too soon, they will be last year's colors and styles. You would look horribly out of date. It would not do. No, we must wait until the winter. We will take a journey to town just before Christmas." Aunt Hazel sighed, almost a soulful groan, as she stepped back into the room. "We could bring Charlotte. I'm sure she would know what would best suit. She looks so elegant these days."

"What a splendid idea, Mama," Daphne said with no little sarcasm. "Dress advice from the reverend's daughter."

"She might be your sister-in-law one day, my girl. We thought Andrew had caught her eye but it seems she's had a change of heart." Aunt Hazel giggled in a girlish manner. "I believe William is quite taken with Charlotte now and she tries to be helpful," Aunt Hazel said. "In fact, she will be here soon to discuss the charity booth we are planning for the county fair. Would you and Sophia like to join us?"

"Thank you, no." Sophia shook her head with perhaps a little too much vehemence. She did not want to be distracted; she had to concentrate on her case. It sounded so official when she called it a case! "I'm going to West Ravenwood to . . . do a little shopping."

Folding her pixie face into a well-defined frown, Aunt Hazel shook her head. "Not a good plan, Sophia. Best stay nearby. There is a restlessness about town that does not bode well."

"Not to worry, Aunt, I will take Betty," Sophia said casually, joining her and Daphne in the corridor.

They waited for Sophia to grab her bonnet and gloves from her room, and then they strolled to the front of the house and down one of the wide staircases. Charlotte was announced just as they reached the bottom, and Sophia decided that it would be best to hurry on her way before being caught up in the machinations of the charity booth; she would reread the Runner's book and start her list later.

"I didn't expect you'd be needing me for another half hour, miss," Betty moaned about being summoned early. "I hadn't finished me morning tea."

Mrs. Curtis stood, the epitome of prim and proper, in the entrance by the front door, having fetched Betty from the kitchen. "There will be tea aplenty when you return," Mrs. Curtis reassured the disgruntled maid and signaled for the footman to open the door.

"All this rush and hurry," Betty continued to grumble. "Is we avoiding something, miss? Or someone?"

Meeting Mrs. Curtis' inquisitive glance, Sophia smiled. "A very good possibility," she said when Mrs. Curtis returned her smile with a shrug. "Shall we get a wiggle on? Mr. Fraser will be waiting for us."

"What? The Runner?"

"Yes, indeed." Sophia was excited about the prospect, even if Betty wasn't. Jeremy Fraser was hard to not appreciate.

Jeremy, as Sophia was now calling him in her mind, was already waiting at the corner of Rover and High Street when they arrived. His handsome profile attracted a fair number of glances, from ladies young and old. He smiled, rather broadly, when he saw them across the street.

Sophia was somewhat surprised to find that her heart beat faster as they approached, and she was quite out of breath, though there was no reason; she had not been hurrying.

———•———

Jeremy reentered the weapons store, The Cutting Edge, on the main street of West Ravenwood with Sophia on his arm. It was an orderly shop, with glass cases lining the perimeter and one down the center. Knives of all shapes and sizes sat in straight rows on the shelves, shining brightly as if just polished.

The proprietor watched from a dark corner in the back. The man leaned more than sat upon a high stool, watching with great intensity.

Jeremy had come earlier than arranged, planning to slip into the store and ask his questions before the agreeable Miss Thompson appeared. He hoped to prove Sophia wrong, to demonstrate that the inhabitants of West Ravenwood would not be uncooperative if they "investigated" separately. A Bow Street Runner was usually granted respect. Unfortunately, the memo had not made it to The Cutting Edge.

Mr. Tilter was, indeed, a crusty sort, gruff and prickly, ready to take offense at the least provocation. The conversation had not made it past introductions and a general observation of it being a lovely summer day: Mr. Tilter had thought it would rain, citing the cool breeze as a telltale sign; the streets would turn to mud and Mr. Tilter suggested that Jeremy head straight back to the inn, collect his belongings and set off for the coast. Mr. Tilter believed it was always sunny and warm by the sea.

Jeremy, who had spent many a summer in Weymouth with his family, was hard pressed to agree.

And so, upon Jeremy's entering the second time, Mr. Tilter acted as if they had never met, even allowing Sophia to introduce them. He smiled broadly—at Sophia—greeting her by name and made light conversation. When Jeremy brought out the knife that Mr. Waverley had found in the woods, Mr. Tilter nodded and laid it gingerly on the case in front of him. He ignored Betty, who wandered around the front of the store staring at the varied blades and stylized hilts. The man focused his attention entirely on the eight-inch blade and the carved and painted ebony handle.

"Ah yes, it's been a few years since I have seen this beauty but it was indeed one of mine." He peeled back the handkerchief a little further. "Beautifully carved. Made on one of the islands in the Dutch East Indies. Don't know what these creatures are supposed to be but they are rather menacing. I bought the knife from a sailor coming off a Balinese ship in London. It's a shame the wood has weathered and this"—he lifted the knife, using the handkerchief to wipe away the dirt caught in the crevices—"has been ill used, I believe." He clicked his tongue in disapproval. "I thought Mr. Dankworth would know better."

Jeremy straightened. "Mr. Dankworth? Who is he? Why would this knife mean anything to him?"

The merchant continued to buff the knife as if deaf to Jeremy's words.

Sophia looked back and forth between them and then smiled at the merchant. "Why would Mr. Dankworth be involved?"

Mr. Tilter laughed with little amusement. "Fancies himself a collector, Miss Thompson. Lives down by the river, on the other side of town. He's got knives, shields, lances, and even a sword or two."

"You sold this knife to him?" Jeremy asked. He waited for

the man to answer but he did not . . . until Sophia repeated his question.

"Yes, indeed, he did buy it from me. Got it for a bargain, too. Surprised it was left in the woods, though. Thought he'd treated his weapons better than that." He glanced at Jeremy. "Collects unusual ones, you know."

"Thank you, Mr. Tilter," Sophia said warmly. Jeremy could feel her excitement. "We appreciate your help."

"No *we*, about it. You! I helped you, my girl. Don't you go around tellin' people that I helped *him*." He jerked his head in Jeremy's direction. "A Runner. Lordy, that would make a swarm of angry bees. No! Police persons are not welcome in this part of the country."

And with those words, Mr. Tilter shooed them and Betty out of the shop. He closed the door so quickly that Sophia's skirts were caught in the doorjamb and Jeremy had to give them a good tug to get them free.

"Great heavens! This is scandalous!" a voice said from behind. "Get your hands off my cousin's skirts, Runner!"

Jeremy whirled around to find William Waverley and Miss Charlotte Dewey behind them. However, despite the young gentleman's words and predatory stance, Jeremy could see that William was trying not to smile.

"Really, William. People are going to stare if you make such remarks," Sophia huffed, pushing past the newly arrived couple while shaking out her skirts. "What are you doing here?" she asked, her eyes on Charlotte. "Were you not going to discuss charity with Aunt Hazel?"

"Your aunt was not feeling quite up to snuff—something about a mouse—and so dearest William here"—she squeezed dearest

William's arm—"thought to take a walk." She glanced up at him and batted her eyes; it was the type of look that made Jeremy want to laugh. It was part flirtation, part adoration, and part nonsense. Still, William seemed to take it in stride and appeared flattered.

Shaking his head, Jeremy allowed his eyes to wander further up the street only to find that he was under scrutiny. Actually, they all were.

Waiting at the next corner, staring with no attempt to disguise that fact, Constable Marley watched them all—even Betty. There was no hostility in his stare, just curiosity. But it felt intrusive and irritating.

It was also clear that the constable, for whatever reason, thought their behavior was irregular. In fact, his posture was more of a chastisement than that of a protector. There was no support or commiseration in his stance. There would be no sharing of information.

For good or ill, this was truly Jeremy's investigation; Marley's theories were at odds with his. Jeremy was on his own.

A tinkle of laughter drew his attention and Jeremy turned toward Sophia. She was teasing William with cousinly banter. Their eyes met and he held her gaze for a fraction of a second longer than was necessary. When she smiled, Jeremy knew he was *not* on his own; he had Sophia Thompson by his side.

CHAPTER SEVEN

Dark Corners of Forgotten Spaces

"I shall see Mr. Dankworth on my own," Jeremy stated more firmly than he had intended as he walked with Sophia back up to Allenton Park. Betty trailed behind, looking bored to distraction.

They had left William and Miss Dewey to stroll the main street, window shopping and chatting about important matters—such as Charlotte's new horse and William's appreciation of roast beef. It had been at Charlotte's prodding that the group had separated. She had not welcomed the serious tone that Jeremy and Sophia had inserted into their conversation. Frivolity seemed to be the order of *their* day.

Sophia, however, took the state of affairs seriously. "See Mr. Dankworth yourself? Or *by* yourself?"

Jeremy considered the semantics of the question. "Well, if Marley . . . Constable Marley is inclined, he might join me."

"I'm sure he will be disinclined to assist," Sophia said. "The constable seems to have taken a dislike to you, I believe, Mr. Fraser. I'm sure you have noticed."

Jeremy nodded. "I have indeed. But the point I was trying to make is that while I see no peril to you while we are inside a shop on the main street of West Ravenwood, visiting a private residence on the other side of the River Coope might be . . . ill-considered."

"Scandalous!" Sophia laughed.

"Actually, I was thinking dangerous. The man, Mr. Dankworth, owns the knife that killed your cousin. Until I take his measure, I do not know what he is capable of."

Sophia laughed again. "Oh dear, poor Mr. Dankworth. He'll be puzzled by the insinuation."

"Pardon?"

"You see, Mr. Dankworth is not your murderer, my dear Mr. Fraser. While I've never met the gentleman myself, I have heard of him. A kindly, well-educated elderly gentleman confined to his home. He is infirm, you see, and therefore could not have wandered through the woods last year, let alone stabbed my cousin with enough force to kill him."

"Bedridden?"

"No, I believe he uses a chair. Again, hardly suitable for navigating over the roots and through puddles of a forest. Besides, he has nothing to do with the family as far as I know . . . except, apparently, owning the lethal weapon that dispatched my cousin."

"Yes, I see the problem."

"Indeed. While Mr. Dankworth will be able to discuss the weapon, being the murderer or even helping us catch him is highly unlikely. I'll meet you by the front gate around two—no one appreciates an unexpected visit in the morning. We wouldn't want to start out on the wrong foot. And no need to announce our intentions to the family, I think. It would merely cause them concern. I'll bring Betty again."

Jeremy looked over his shoulder quickly enough to see Betty's grimace. "If your family would object, I can go on my own, as I said."

"My extended family is not aware of my plan to be a Bow Street Detective. They're going to have to come to terms with it eventually. I've only discussed my interest with my papa and Daphne as yet."

"I imagine your papa is enthused and looking forward to announcing your occupation to the world."

"Hardly. He thinks I'll grow out of it. Find a husband, settle down . . . you know, the usual."

"You are nothing like the usual, Miss Thompson."

"Thank you, Mr. Fraser. I will take that as a compliment."

"Exactly as it was intended," he said with a smile. And then he stopped, shook his head to clear his thoughts, and looked up at the sky. "Most young ladies would prefer to marry, have children, and run a household."

"I no longer have that option," Sophia said, and then explained the situation with her mother's brother. "Were I the marrying kind, this would be devastating. But I'm not, so it isn't."

Rather confused, Jeremy nodded as if it all made perfect sense. Coming up to the intricately carved entrance gate, Jeremy bowed, offering a perfunctory farewell—after all, they would see one another in four hours—and he turned, heading back into the lively metropolis of West Ravenwood.

In the end, Sophia did not meet Mr. Dankworth that day, and neither did Jeremy. The elderly gentleman was feeling poorly, and his housekeeper—more of a dragon than anything else in Sophia's mind—would not let them past the front hall. They would have to return some other time and continue their investigations along a different path until then.

Returning to Allenton Park without having advanced the case whatsoever was most disagreeable and made Sophia peevish. Fortunately, Daphne was tied up in her own woes and was blithely unaware that her cousin was smoldering with frustration.

"Charlotte came back with William, and she and Mother have been in the drawing room for the better part of two hours—making *important* decisions on the color, size, and purpose of their booth. I hope the homeless children appreciate their efforts because I certainly don't. It's tedious and repetitive. Boring, boring, and then again boring!" Daphne huffed. "She is a flatterer. Every suggestion that Mother makes is either *brilliant* or *amazing*. Really, I can't stand to listen to them anymore. Even Mrs. Curtis nodded when I said as much, and she's not known for being critical."

"Once they've made their plans, do they need help manning the booth?" Sophia asked, trying to diffuse Daphne's tension.

The girls were relaxing on their favorite bench in the bright afternoon sun of the conservatory, hidden from the door by the ferns. The air smelled sweet and earthy, a soft breeze wafting through the open windows. It was a tranquil setting, greatly appreciated by Sophia and hardly noticed by Daphne.

"Help at the booth? Oh, quite likely." Abandoning her slouch, Daphne straightened. "You weren't going to offer, were you? Please say you're not. If you do, I'll be expected to do the same. I would much rather wander about the fairgrounds—it's going to be held in the north field—and chat with any young gentleman who might happen to attend."

Sophia looked up in surprise. "Are we talking about anyone in particular?"

Daphne grinned. She pulled a leaf off the closest fern, trying to look nonchalant. "Dylan Crewe might be there. You remember him. The one with blond hair and blue eyes, cute dimple on his right cheek . . . or is it his left? Anyway, he—Dylan Crewe—is home for the summer. Been in Cambridge at the university all year!"

She flounced back against the white wicker bench. "But he won't be at the fair if Andrew's killer has not yet been found. No one will." She shook her head. "Andrew would have a laugh if he saw me now, all tied up in knots, worried about being murdered in my bed. He loved to be amused, loved to ride pell-mell down the south field, and loved to ride the hounds. He was too loud, too saucy, and too vain, but he was young. I'm sure he would have become a fine human as he aged. But he didn't have a chance to grow old. And now, because of Andrew's murder, I'm worried about going to the fair. Our own fair!"

Sophia ignored Daphne's assessment of her brother's character. She did not see Andrew through loving eyes, as did his sister. Andrew had made Sophia miserable with his mockery and critical comments. She would learn who had killed him because it was wrong and the killer should pay for such a foul deed. Success here was her proving ground—entry into Bow Street—not a sentimental journey of revenge.

"You needn't worry about being killed at the fair," she said, sounding far more confident than she felt. "Murder is done in dark corners of forgotten spaces. No witnesses," she said, staring out at the lawn.

"That was a very dramatic turn of phrase," Daphne said, giving her cousin her favorite compliment.

"Thank—"

The air was suddenly full of glass, and their ears were battered by a loud crash. Daphne shrieked and Sophia gasped, throwing her arms up over her head for protection from the shards.

It was over in a flash but in that time, Daphne was cut across her cheek and Sophia's arm was sliced, blood dripping onto her skirts.

"What was *that*?!" Sophia cried, staring at the mess of glass shards strewn across the tiles.

Shaking the glass out of her hair, Daphne stared past Sophia's shoulder at the window.

Sophia pivoted and frowned. She reached across to the window but her hand slipped through the frame. The glass was gone, broken at their feet. Had a rock gone through the glass? A branch? Or . . . had someone *shot* through the window?

"Get down!" Sophia shouted, suddenly fearful.

She grabbed an embroidered cushion off the bench and swiped it through the glass, making a patch for them both to hunker close to the floor without being cut further. She pulled a wide-eyed Daphne down beside her and then lifted her finger to her lips.

A rhythmic pounding echoed in the silence, growing louder. Sophia swallowed her fear and fought to regulate her breathing. She looked around at the potted plants, searching for something to use as a shield.

Just before slipping behind a dwarf palm planted in a strong brass pot, Sophia realized the cause of the thumping—feet, running feet. She sat back on her heels and breathed a deep— very deep—sigh of relief. The sound was coming from inside the manor. Within moments, Aunt, Uncle, Papa, and a collection of servants burst through the conservatory door.

"What was that?" Papa asked immediately. He saw Sophia and Daphne hugging the floor, and ran across the tile to help them up, kicking aside glass as he did so.

"Are you all right?" he asked. His expression was fraught with dismay.

"What a mess!" Uncle Edward said, stating the obvious. "What were you young ladies doing to cause such destruction?"

Sophia stood, straightened her shoulders, and glared. "This was not our doing." She did not appreciate the inference!

"The window smashed on its own, Father," Daphne said, supporting her indignant cousin.

"Nonsense. Windows do not spontaneously break into"— Uncle Edward glanced around—"a thousand pieces."

Staring at the collection of servants crowding the doorway, he frowned. "Mrs. Curtis!" he bellowed. The crowd parted but Mrs. Curtis did not step to the front.

"Oh bother and blast!" Uncle focused on the butler standing by Cook. "Benton, get this cleaned up." Uncle Edward pointed at the glass with his cane as if there would be some confusion if he did not specify. While the servants organized the cleanup, Uncle harangued Sophia for her carelessness and not taking responsibility for her actions.

Papa tried to interject a voice of reason, but Uncle had worked himself into a frenzy; it was best to let him vent before trying to set him straight.

Sophia huffed, ignored her uncle's temper, and shifted her gaze to one of the wooden columns that supported the glass roof. It was some time before her adrenaline eased and her eyes cleared of their anger. But when they did, Sophia noticed something odd.

The support column was marred—not by the glass at its base but by an embedded lead ball. The force had splintered the wood. The lead ball was mere inches from where they had been sitting.

Someone *had* shot through the window. Someone had tried to kill them.

———•———

"No one would shoot through a window on purpose, Sophia. That's dangerous. Could have hurt anyone—even killed them. No, no, it was an accident." Aunt Hazel nodded, agreeing with herself.

They were waiting in the drawing room, dressed in their finest, ready to go in to dinner. Daphne's cheek bore evidence of the day's upset: a thin irregular red line of a cut that was thankfully not deep. Sophia had donned a long-sleeved gown to hide the bandage on her arm, but her wound was also not deep.

"Hunters nearby . . . or someone cleaning their rifle without care. Yes, indeed, there are countless possibilities," her aunt continued.

Sophia glanced at her father and shook her head. No, not

countless. Two. Aunt Hazel had mentioned *two* possibilities—and they were flimsy at best.

Uncle Edward glared at the unlit fireplace, as if blaming it for the upheaval. When he spoke, it was more bluster than conversation. William glanced around the room with a bored expression. He was not concerned in the least, nor was he interested in the company or the topic of discussion. Daphne appeared to have come to terms with their assault in the conservatory. She smiled in return to Sophia's furrowed brow and lifted her shoulder in a halfhearted shrug.

However, Papa casually, too casually, sauntered to Sophia's side.

"I think I'll stay a little bit longer," he said quietly, giving her a look rife with meaning.

"The most important question here seems to be, 'Why?'" Sophia said, noting it was becoming a recurring theme. "I'm not at all certain it was an accident. And if the shot was *not* an accident, why did someone shoot into the house? Was the rifle aimed at Daphne and me? Though we were hidden from the door into the house, someone outside would still have known that a person sat on the bench. And if it was Daphne or me . . . why? I think I'd better start my list."

"What list?" Aunt Hazel asked, scratching at her neck.

"I thought I might make a list of everyone who is here now and was also here at the time of Andrew's death."

"Andrew's murder." Aunt Hazel swallowed with difficulty and then continued. "Might as well call it what it is, Sophia."

"Yes, and speak to Marley about your whys and suspect list." Uncle Edward had turned to face the room again. "He's the one to help you."

"Actually, Uncle, I was going to ask Mr. Fraser's opinion."

"Yes, you could, but do not use up too much of the Runner's time. He is on a mission and a commission, you know. He was hired for one purpose and one purpose only: to find Andrew's murderer. Don't distract him."

"I was hoping to help."

"Wonderful sentiment, Sophia. Just don't get in the way." Uncle nodded as if something had been decided, though his tone was one of doubt. "Excellent. Now, let's talk of other things."

Despite his words, Uncle Edward did not look relieved. "Haunted" was the word Sophia would have used to describe his expression.

Jeremy was in a terrible state when he learned of the accident . . . incident . . . shooting, whatever it was going to be called. He had spent the evening writing up a list of suspects, jotting down his impressions, and condensing his notes from his interviews, completely oblivious to the harrowing scene being played out in Allenton Park. He would not have learned about the smashed window and its cause had he not overheard a conversation at breakfast at the inn.

Jeremy could barely breathe until he learned that Sophia was going to be fine—a few cuts and bruises, but otherwise fine. It was miraculous that Daphne suffered no major ill effects, either, of course.

Stacks, without any diplomacy, suggested that the news of the young ladies' injuries was the true cause of Jeremy's distress, not being left in the dark about the shooting. Jeremy did not like his driver's reasoning but upon examination, he realized, it was true.

As a result, Jeremy had left Stacks at his breakfast and hurried to the main road out of town. He wanted to see Sophia—and Daphne, of course—to verify that they were as hale and hearty as the rumors said them to be.

When he arrived, Allenton Park looked none the worse for wear. No blood spatters on the front door or bodies piled up under the ornamental shrubs. His knock was answered within a reasonable amount of time, though the butler did give him a strange look. Still, there was a blanket of normalcy wrapped around the manor and Jeremy breathed a sigh of relief . . . until the grandfather clock in the grand entrance chimed nine in the morning.

Horrified, Jeremy stared at the clock. He blinked, willing the short hand to move to eleven or even twelve, but it did not cooperate. Jeremy felt a sudden flush of heat race up his cheeks as they turned bright red.

He had arrived early, much too early to demand an audience with any members of the family without prior arrangement; they were likely still abed. He could throw his weight around, demand to see Mr. Waverley—after all, he was a Bow Street Runner here on business. Social niceties did not always fit within the time frame required of an investigator. Still, needless antagonism was not required, either.

"I shall examine the conservatory from the outside," Jeremy said to the butler, Benton, trying to hide his faux pas. He pivoted, leaving Benton on the threshold of the front door, staring after him.

As he rounded the corner of the east side of the house, Jeremy could see the glass roof of the conservatory. A lovely, tall wrought iron fence prevented him from continuing next to the wall. He followed the perimeter of the fence, around various plants and trees, never getting any closer. He spent the better part of fifteen minutes—he had checked on his watch—looking for the gate. The lovely wrought iron fence was looking less lovely by the minute.

"Just there, Mr. Fraser." A voice drifted over Jeremy's shoulder.

He turned to see one of the gardeners pointing at a shrub with clippers in his hand. Dressed in browns and sporting a thick bushy beard, the man was almost invisible against the flora.

"What is?" Jeremy frowned, uncomfortable with the idea that he had been concentrating too hard. He hadn't seen the man halfway up a ladder trimming one of the hedges.

"The gate, sir. It's hidden back there. You wanted to get to the conservatory?"

Jeremy smiled. "Yes, indeed. Thank you." His expression might have been brighter than necessary, as he was not used to helpful treatment; most folks in West Ravenwood had been downright obstructive.

Pushing back the branches of the indicated shrub, Jeremy found the gate and the latch. The hinges were well oiled and the gate opened soundlessly. Once inside, the shadowed light gave way to a brighter, open space. There were no formal gardens on this side of the house; lawns, ornamental trees, and shrubs were the decorations of choice. The area was expansive, far larger than he had expected.

Jeremy could now see into the conservatory. Other than a missing window, it looked normal. He continued to scan the scene. On closer inspection—squinting—he could see a post behind the empty glass frame where an embedded lead ball had splintered the wood. Just as he was about to approach the glass-framed extension, Jeremy heard a rustle in the bushes next to him and a soft female voice from deep within.

"Let go," she whispered, "or I will have to . . ." A branch snapped. "There, warned you." The bush shook. "Oh bother!"

"Miss Thompson? Is that you?" Jeremy asked. He took a deep breath, calming his suddenly stampeding heart.

"Oh, Mr. Fraser. How opportune." A branch shifted next to his head, and a face appeared. "I seem to be caught on something; a stem, a twig, an offshoot of some sort. It's . . . it's . . . well, it's caught *behind* me, and I cannot reach it. If I move forward the chance of ruining my gown is fairly high. Might you . . . might you free me? I would so appreciate it."

Although Jeremy could not yet see the offending branch, the way Sophia's cheeks turned a pretty shade of blush led him to believe that the treacherous branch was clinging to her skirts in the area of her . . . um, posterior.

CHAPTER EIGHT

Watching from the Shadows

S tepping forward, Jeremy parted the leaves of the . . . the . . .
"What kind of shrub is this?"

Sophia frowned, leaning closer to study a leaf. "Green," she said
finally with a grin. "I really have no idea. A knobby one with lots
of tangled branches that grab at you if you try to pass through."

Taking that as a hint to approach from the other side, Jeremy
rounded the plant and saw that Sophia's posterior was indeed
caught. He grabbed the branch at the base, bending it away from
her skirts and guided Sophia backward through the tangle.

"There," he said when she was free at last and her skirts were
undamaged. He watched as she brushed the dried leaves from
her gown, paying great attention to the front of her bodice. He
swallowed, and then half turned so that he was now facing the
conservatory. "Why, if you don't mind me asking, were you trapping yourself in a plant?"

"Believe me, it was unintentional. I was curious; I was looking for a place from where the rifle might have been shot. Where

the person hid before firing. I thought there might be some sort of clue."

"Such as?"

She pointed back at the plant whence she had come. "A bit of cloth caught on a branch. A trampled spot, a footprint . . . anything really. Anything that might inform us about the shooter."

Her list was very similar to his own. "And did you?"

"Did I . . . ?"

"Find anything?"

"No, and I was rather diligent. I searched every aspect of every bush and, as you saw, I even crawled inside a few . . . but nothing."

"Interesting," Jeremy said, for want of something better to say. He stared at the unoccupied conservatory, noting the position of the bench below the marred wooden post. "Has the bench been moved?"

Sophia, hand still swiping at her gown, stilled. She brought her eyes up and studied the placement of the furniture and potted plants inside the glass room, and then straightened. "I know the bench was moved for the cleanup, but it looks to be back where it was. Even the palm has been returned to its proper place."

"The bench is clearly visible from out here," Jeremy observed quietly. "Even with the plant partially blocking the view."

"Yes, the palm only hides the bench from the door to the manor, otherwise it is visible from outside at almost every angle. It is a private garden that requires little upkeep and affords the family lots of privacy . . . or so we thought. If, however, someone were within this enclosure, they would have had no problem seeing the occupants. And the shooting happened midafternoon—full daylight. I was dressed in a buttercup yellow gown and Daphne was in a soft pink. There would have been no mistaking that someone—two someones, actually—sat upon the bench. If it had been an accident, a rifle misfired from the woods or some such, then the shot would never have made it that far, let alone shattered the glass. And an *accidental* shooter would have rushed to verify that no one had been hurt."

"So the possibility that it was an accident is small."

"Very small." Sophia watched Jeremy pat at his jacket and then the sides of his pants. "What are you doing?"

"Looking for my journal and pencil. I think this discussion is worthy of jotting down." Jeremy pulled said objects from the pocket of his jacket, and then watched her frown and pat the sides of her gown.

"I have no pockets," she said. "But I can see how they would be useful. Best not rely on memory alone. Yes, indeed. I'll have to have the seams picked out of my gowns and pockets added."

"Pockets—especially pockets full of paper—will spoil the lines of your skirts."

Sophia turned to stare at him with an odd expression; it was part annoyed, part confused, and part surprised. "You think appearances matter while investigating?"

Now it was Jeremy's turn to be embarrassed. He could see how very serious she was about becoming a Bow Street Runner. He wished, for her sake, that her dream was possible.

"No, not important at all," he said, and then cleared his throat to hide his discomfort. "However, what might be of importance"— his segue was a bit rough but it served its purpose—"is that whoever shot out the window, had to know the manor and . . . Is it your habit to be in the conservatory at the same time each day?"

"No, not at all. Seldom, actually. I prefer to wander the gardens if I'm in need of fresh air."

"So, this is a crime of opportunity—one that had no time for planning. It cuts down the possible suspects considerably. How long were you and Miss Waverley seated before the incident?"

"Not long; we had only just begun our conversation."

"Interesting."

"Is it?"

Jeremy blinked in surprise. It was a word of habit; few called him out in it. He quickly continued. "Who did you see on your way to this room? Who saw you?"

"I'm not really sure . . . I wasn't paying attention; I was talking to Daphne at the time. I remember seeing the housemaid. Benton held the door for us to enter the conservatory, and Mrs. Curtis flit about, fixing the vases and whatnot. One of the gardeners was raking just beyond the fence. And . . . why are you smiling?"

Jeremy tried to wipe the grin from his face until he noticed that Miss Thompson was grinning back. "This is how you observe when you are *not* paying attention?" he asked with a laugh. "I believe you *do* have a head for investigation, Miss Thompson."

"I'm a natural," she said, trying to maintain a serious expression. "As I've been saying all along."

Jeremy glanced around the enclosure. "The shooter would have needed to be inside this enclosed part of the garden to have any expectation of successfully shooting through the window, and few people would know of the gate."

"Gate? What gate?"

"Exactly." Jeremy led Sophia to the gate hidden in the bush. "Even you, one of the family, was unaware of its existence. I shall ask Mrs. Curtis who knows about it . . . or would Benton be a better source?"

"I think the head gardener would be more informed about something on the grounds."

"Very good." He paused for a moment, thinking. "I don't believe you or Miss Waverley were the intended target, unless the shooter has terrible aim. You were visible and yet the shot sailed above your heads." The statement was meant to offer comfort, reassurance, but it brought to mind another question. "So then, what *was* the purpose of the shooting, if not to injure?"

Jeremy gazed at Sophia, seeing not the person but rather the horrible damage that could have happened, and he shuddered, swallowing against the lump in his throat.

"To scare us . . . and the family?" Sophia suggested.

"Quite likely. But if the intention was to scare *you*, Miss Thompson, was it to frighten you away or simply persuade you to stop investigating? Is this a serious threat, or have you merely stepped on the wrong toes and caused an affront?"

"Rather drastic to shoot at someone even if they have caused an insult."

Jeremy glanced at Sophia, noting her stiff stance and suddenly unanimated expression and quickly continued. "Or was Miss Waverley the target . . . to frighten her, to keep her at home? Though why, when she is not actively involved in the investigation remains to be determined."

"It might have nothing to do with Andrew's death or the investigation."

"True enough, but then what? A robbery gone awry? A secret admirer hoping to ride to the rescue?" He took a deep breath and continued. "Perhaps the shot was meant to scare you *both* and the family. A warning—do not venture further!" He said the last phrase in a deep booming voice, as if it were from on high. He was rewarded with a laugh—though it was slight and Sophia still appeared concerned.

"Really! That was rude!" a voice said from inside the conservatory. The tone was prickly with insult.

Jeremy nearly jumped out of his skin, but hid it with a quick turn of his head. Two faces with wide eyes stared back at him. "Ah. Miss Dewey and Miss Waverley, good morning," he said affably, stepping closer to the broken window, affording a comfortable conversation. "I was speaking to Miss Thompson and meant you no insult."

Charlotte harrumphed—actually *harrumphed*—and did not look mollified.

"It's early for a call, Mr. Fraser," Daphne said. "Even a business call." She blinked on realizing that she had just criticized Charlotte as well, but the reverend's daughter was distracted. She was staring at Sophia.

"You have leaves in your hair." Charlotte looked from Sophia to Jeremy, her cheeks growing red.

"Do I?" Sophia asked and then turned to Jeremy. "We really should not frolic in the bushes, Mr. Fraser. Apparently I have leaves in my hair. They gave us away."

Jeremy found it difficult to keep a straight face. "Perhaps not," he said when he had mastered his amusement. He reached up and pulled a curled leaf from the crown of her head and offered it back to Sophia with a deep bow—as if the object were a beautiful rose.

Playing her part, Sophia dropped into a deep curtsy. "Thank you, kind sir," she said, taking the shriveled brown leaf with reverence. But the act fell apart as her enjoyment won through.

With a laugh, she offered the leaf to Daphne and then Charlotte, and when neither took it in hand, Sophia tossed the leaf to the ground.

"Charlotte is waiting for Mother to finish her morning meal and requested a visit to the conservatory. Apparently, the shooting is being discussed all over town," Daphne explained in a rush; perhaps she was discomposed by the silliness. "She wished to see where we were nearly killed."

"Oh yes, I was so concerned," Charlotte said, clearly forgetting that she was supposed to be piqued. "Thank heaven you and Daphne are safe. Mrs. Waverley would have been so upset had something happened to either of you."

Jeremy nearly snorted at the understatement.

———•———

Lifting the paper off the small bedroom desk, Sophia sighed and shook her head. She had taken an hour to list all the people in and about the manor at the time of Andrew's death, as well as the present. The lists were almost identical. Sophia was a little light on the names of the servants and their roles within the house and required a consult. Charlotte might be gone by now, and so Daphne would be available and brimming with information, or so Sophia hoped.

Pushing away from the desk, Sophia rose. Investigating required a fair amount of questioning, thinking, and rethinking— mental exercises that she found invigorating. But there was a noble purpose to her questions now: solving a crime. What could be more rewarding than assuaging the pain brought on by the premature ending of a life? Yes, Sophia nodded to herself, she had found the perfect way to spend her days.

She glanced out the window just in time to see Jeremy disappearing down the drive. She watched for a moment, noticing his relaxed loping pace and his confident posture. She was strangely drawn to the young gentleman, and upon introspection, she realized it was not entirely his position as a Runner that quickened her heart. She was very much attracted to his smile and the mischief in his eyes when he teased.

With a heartfelt sigh, Sophia watched until Jeremy disappeared around the curve of the drive, then she headed downstairs. Unfortunately, when she stepped onto the main floor, the mixture of voices emanating from the drawing room told her that Daphne was still ensconced with Aunt Hazel and Charlotte. The consult would have to be postponed.

Stepping backward across the tiles, Sophia considered a chat with Uncle Edward as an alternative. She glided across the floor to the study and pressed her ear to the door. She could discern two distinct voices, but the oak muffled the sound, making the identification of said voices difficult.

Grabbing the door handle, Sophia thought she might open the door a crack—just enough to identify the occupants. Then she could decide on whether she was comfortable causing a disruption or if she would wait until later.

"What are you doing?" Mrs. Curtis asked. Her collection of keys jangled noisily as she traversed the hall, coming from the back of the house.

"I was hoping to get Uncle alone," Sophia explained. "But he seems to have company, likely my father. I was hoping to ask him—Uncle Edward that is—some questions regarding various . . . various members of staff. Oh wait. Mrs. Curtis, you are the very one I should talk to! You would know better than anyone."

"Know what?" the woman asked suspiciously. "What are you up to?" She frowned and ran her hands down her skirts. It was a habit that Sophia had noticed before.

"I'm making a list of Allenton Park occupants at the time of Andrew's death and those that are here now. I would like to compare and cross off names—there are so many."

"Suspects?"

"*Possible* suspects."

"It's not your job, Miss Thompson, and you should leave it to the professionals."

"I would like to *be* one of those professionals—a Runner—one day, Mrs. Curtis. I'm helping Mr. Fraser with the investigation."

Mrs. Curtis sputtered a laugh; it was full of disdain. Then she held out her hand, onto which Sophia placed the list. She kept her pencil at the ready for changes and alterations.

"Hmm. You've done quite well. Miss MacIntyre should be added to the first list—but not the second. The under-gardener's name is Glen— Glen Phillips."

"Tall man with a bushy beard?"

"Indeed." The housekeeper shifted, as if preparing to continue on her way. "Oh, and Marty Sneed is the new boot boy," she added, handing back the pages.

"Excellent. Thank you." Sophia clutched the papers to her bodice, pleased that her memory had served her well. She made the amendments and then, lifting her skirts with one hand, Sophia dashed up the stairs to her room. She grabbed *Investigating Murder and Mayhem* and tucked the list pages inside.

As she would be more comfortable waiting for Daphne in the library, Sophia started back down the staircase. Lost in thought, Sophia did not watch where she was going.

Her feet suddenly went out from under her, and she slammed down onto her posterior. Her book and papers fluttered to the ground. The hard landing jolted her, and Sophia squeaked pathetically, breathing deeply.

Shocked, Sophia frowned at her hands, now propping her up on the stairs, and tried to reason out what had happened. With a thud, Sophia slipped to the next step and so on down until she reached the bottom on her bottom.

Struggling to her feet, and very glad that she had not made any noise and drawn a crowd, Sophia dusted off her skirts, arched her back, and rubbed her posterior where it had come in contact with the steps. She turned to stare at the bottom step where the bright, cheerful ball that had caused her accident sat half inflated. It looked quite innocent, bright blue with a square of red and white candy stripes.

The fact that it was not in the nursery or the attic was odd— very odd indeed. Like the toy horse that Daphne had tripped over, it was out of place. There was nothing threatening about the ball.

And yet, situated as it had been in the middle of the staircase almost guaranteed that someone was going to step on it. Sophia was just lucky that she had fallen backward onto the most padded part of her anatomy. If she had pitched forward, she could have snapped her neck.

———◆———

Sophia was very attentive for the rest of the day. She watched her feet, her path, even checking around doors before entering a room. She was not afraid, really . . . just aware that someone at Allenton Park had bad intentions. Whether it had anything to do with her investigation of Andrew's death or was merely a grudge, Sophia could not say. Whether it was directed at her, she could not say, either; everyone in the family used the staircase.

Though, the same could not have been said about Daphne's ruined dress. That had felt personal, directed against Daphne. Informing her aunt and uncle about the destruction had elicited stoic silence from Uncle Edward and a sigh of weariness from Aunt Hazel. Neither was very helpful.

Sophia was left with even more questions. Was the villain a member of the staff or the family? Questions heaped high and wide with nary an answer.

It wasn't until the end of the evening that Sophia had a chance to speak to Daphne about the ball on the stairs; her cousin was more than a little disturbed.

"Last week, I stepped on a toy horse. This week you tripped on a ball. Someone is going to be hurt!"

"I think that is the point. The villain moves among us," Sophia said with unintended drama. "In the house, or at least has access to the house." She was beginning to share Daphne's sense of foreboding.

"Is this the same person who killed Andrew?"

"I don't know." Sophia gnawed at her bottom lip. "Poachers would not have access to the attic to grab a toy and the dress in your wardrobe . . ."

They were seated on Sophia's four-poster bed, having retired for the night. Betty was busy stoking the fire across the room and hanging Sophia's gown in the wardrobe. "I'm beginning to understand why you felt so desperate. It feels personal. And we're no further ahead in our search for the culprit."

"It feels as if someone is playing with us—trying to escalate our fears. Enjoying our misfortune." Daphne turned her face toward Sophia, distress written in every line. "What would cause such animosity that murder becomes a viable option?"

"Is murder the intent? Or is it merely harm: a broken leg here, a bundle of nerves there?"

"Andrew—"

"Andrew might be an exception," Sophia said.

"Do you think the poachers are trying to stop the investigation?"

Sophia stared at the carpet, considering. "I'm not convinced that poachers are involved. I could be wrong, of course. Enclosure has caused great trouble for many people, but if murder is the intent . . ." She swallowed the lump in her throat. "That line has already been crossed—why not . . . continue?"

Daphne grabbed Sophia's hand squeezing it tightly. "Are we going to be murdered, one by one?"

"No, no. I'm saying the opposite. The reason Andrew was killed might not be the same reason we're being threatened now. Might not be the same villain, at all." Sophia huffed. "Listen to me. I don't know what I'm saying anymore. Don't know what to think, except that I'm tired and keyed up. We need a good night's sleep." Sophia pulled her hand free and stood.

"Mr. Fraser is going to catch him . . . them." Daphne nodded with great intensity—looking reassured, for no reason that Sophia could discern.

"Of course, a devoted and able investigator." Sophia wanted to throw her name in the hat, too, but Daphne was looking for comfort. She would rest easier thinking that the fate of the Waverleys was in the hands of a Bow Street Officer and not a green girl who was making it up as she went along.

CHAPTER NINE

Called Back

Jeremy leaned his elbows on the table, trying not to look dejected. Apparently without success.

"The investigation not going well?" Stacks asked. He continued to fill his fork to capacity and popped it into his mouth with an audible hum of pleasure. "We're not heading back to London anytime soon?"

"No. Certainly not this week." Jeremy frowned. "Tell me, Stacks, you've been a driver for many a Bow Street Officer. How long does a case such as this usually take?"

"Well." Stacks pushed his empty plate to the center of the table and leaned back in his chair. "It takes as long as it takes. The villain don't normally stand up and wave."

"No, I hardly expected that."

"So, no idea who yer chasing as of yet?"

"Several ideas, actually, but none seem to pull all the threads into a tidy knot."

Enough time had passed since Andrew's murder that Jeremy

was dealing with clouded memories as well as missing facts. It was not surprising that Constable Marley was stymied and looking at Mr. Waverley with suspicion. The knife that likely killed Andrew—belonging to Mr. Dankworth—had been hidden in Glendor Wood and only found recently by Mr. Waverley himself. That discovery was very convenient and rather unlikely. And yet, Jeremy was not convinced that the gentleman had contrived the discovery or murdered his son, if for no other reason than a motive was missing—a significant part of the puzzle. Besides, Mr. Waverley had asked for Bow Street to investigate. He'd hardly be paying the Bow Street Runners to chase after himself.

There had been enough "incidents" since Jeremy's arrival that they could be taken as red herrings—diversions, misleading clues—making Jeremy think the killer was still active and trying to distract him.

Poachers were still on Jeremy's possibility list, as well. Poaching was a hand-to-mouth existence, trapping small animals to put on the dinner table. Until recently, it was lawful for the townspeople to trap. But the laws had changed, and those animals were now considered to be the property of the landowner. Now, tables were empty, children went hungry, and parents became desperate. Desperation could often turn to violence. Still, poaching did not explain the incidents inside the manor.

Jeremy had also learned that Andrew was not considered an upstanding citizen, often getting into trouble. Ruining seeded fields, knocking down haystacks, flirting openly with milkmaids, and generally causing mayhem. And if Andrew was not killed for something he did, perhaps it was something that he saw. He might have witnessed something that his companions did not wish to be known, like treason, theft, or embezzlement.

Jeremy straightened, pulling his elbows off the table. He needed a new approach. He needed help.

"Stacks, have you ever assisted a Bow Street Officer?"

"Grabbing a culprit or some such?"

"No, I was thinking of something more mundane. Doing some legwork. Talking to people."

"Ah yes." Stacks smiled a pompous sort of smile. "I did some o' that for Officer Jefferies. He were chasing down a thief in Brighton, an' he needed me to speak to the blacksmith on the sly. You know, quiet like."

"Yes, exactly. And . . ."

"And Constable Norris when 'e were investigating that fire in Manchester what took out the Hardy Factory."

Jeremy nodded, relieved. "I'm going to put you to work, too, Stacks. I need you to ask around, get the names of Andrew Waverley's chums when he was in West Ravenwood. Tradesmen, merchants, and the like will be more willing to talk to you. They don't quite know what to make of me . . . I'm straddling two worlds. Anyway, people are quite observant about the trouble-some antics of upper-class young men."

Stacks nodded. "Gets 'em riled."

"Exactly. But that anger imprints the mind." Jeremy rubbed his hand across his forehead, thinking. "Yes, you get the names and I'll interview his friends. I just need to know Andrew's cohorts—the ones he chased trouble with . . . Because that *is* something I've learned: Andrew Waverley was not an angel. Constantly pushing the limits of acceptable behavior."

Jeremy frowned at the table. "And not just the boys, ask after his lady friends, as well. He liked chasing skirts. I just need to know who to talk to, who to interview. I'm getting nowhere fast,

Stacks. I have a feeling that time is of the essence. I need another set of feet on the ground."

"Thought Miss Thompson were helpin' you."

"She is, in a manner of speaking," Jeremy said, not sure of the protocol. "We have to tread lightly and at the same time move the case along. I don't know how long it was meant to take—I was rushed on my way so quickly, I didn't think to ask—but I can't stay *too* long. It's already been two weeks since I left."

Stacks smiled and raised his shoulder in a half shrug. "I don't mind staying. I rather like it here."

Jeremy nodded, grabbing his journal from the table. He said farewell to Stacks, ignored the stares and dark looks of the other patrons, marched out of the inn, and was halfway to Allenton before he realized where he was going.

Drawn to the manor for the wrong reason—it, or rather she, being Miss Thompson. He had no real purpose . . . no, wait he could think of something. Yes, an excuse, a reason for disturbing the household this early in the day . . . again.

And the more he thought, the more he knew that he should view the Waverley rifle cabinet while there. He had dug the lead out of the conservatory post and would like to see if it matched any of the rifles owned by the family.

It was a valid line of inquiry; however, Jeremy was greatly disappointed—it would not require Sophia's company.

———•———

Sophia, too, was disappointed when Uncle informed her that Mr. Fraser had come and gone by the time she arrived at the morning room to break her fast. She had wanted to talk to Jeremy about the hazards around the manor. Just that. Nothing more.

Well, she might admit to enjoying his company . . . but only to herself. Yes, just talking and company. Although . . . even when focused on the serious nature of their investigation, Sophia quite liked the feel of his arm beneath hers as they walked side by side. Yes, just talking, company, and walking.

"He thought two of the half-dozen hunting rifles in my gun cabinet would have the capacity to spit out a lead the size of the one he dug from the post in the conservatory." Uncle turned to Papa, continuing his observations. "Though what conclusion he drew from that I haven't the slightest idea. Then, asked me . . . wanted me to accompany him to the murder site. Can you imagine? Really! That would not be pleasant in the least."

Uncle swiveled his head from side to side like a man watching a tennis match. "He could ask any of the servants. I'm certain they would know where it took place. I need not be the one to do the job!" Uncle's voice had gotten shriller and louder, swelling to a point just short of yelling.

The table of six souls was silent as Uncle's words echoed throughout the room. Chairs squeaked as bottoms shifted, and there was a general feeling of discomfort.

"That was a little inconsiderate of Mr. Fraser," Aunt Hazel agreed finally. "But I imagine he means to get a description of the day Andrew was killed and any observations that you might have made. He was not trying to upset you, my dear."

"He likely thought it would not be any more difficult than looking through the underbrush for the murder weapon," Sophia said, cross with the criticism on Mr. Fraser's behalf.

Uncle harrumphed.

"I'm going out for a ride this morning, Mother," William interrupted, oblivious to both the tension and the conversation.

"And then I'll pick up Charlotte for you and bring her back to the manor."

"Does her mother not need her at home?" Aunt Hazel asked. "Charlotte should not deprive Mrs. Dewey of her assistance."

"Charlotte and her mother are not on the best of terms, Mother," Daphne said, popping a piece of buttered toast into her mouth. "They spend as little time with each other as possible."

Aunt Hazel looked down the table, frowning at her daughter. "What does that mean?"

Daphne glanced at William before answering. "Charlotte is not interested in visiting the sick and elderly, nor playing the organ on Sundays. Mrs. Dewey was hoping for help in her parish duties, but Charlotte is much distracted."

William snorted a laugh and pushed back his chair. He sauntered out of the morning room with a swagger.

"No question of what is causing the distraction," Daphne said, staring after her brother.

"They, meaning Mrs. Dewey and Charlotte, are very dissimilar," Sophia observed, feeling her father's eyes. The same could be said about Sophia and her mother.

"It's not to be wondered at," Aunt Hazel said, as she, too, pushed back her chair.

Sophia watched her aunt leave the room, wondering why she should not be wondering. She frowned her question at Daphne.

"Charlotte's adopted," Daphne explained, and then dropped her voice to a whisper. "And rather spoiled because of it. I believe Mrs. Dewey would insist upon Charlotte's help otherwise."

Sophia nodded and turned her attention back to her breakfast.

That afternoon, Jeremy was passed two letters upon his return to the Unicorn and Crown. He was not surprised; he had sent regular correspondence to the Bow Street office, keeping them up to date on the progress of the case. This letter, however, was not in the hand of the clerk. The writing was much more precise, and the capital letters were formed with a flourish.

Jeremy found a free seat in the corner of the pub near an open window and broke the seal. It didn't take long to read; Sir Elderberry was not known to ramble.

It was as Jeremy had feared. He was taking too long. Sir Elderberry didn't say as much outright, but rather inquired if Jeremy was in need of assistance. The support of Edgar Jefferies was offered.

Jefferies, who had been a Runner since the days of the force's inception, was not Jeremy's favorite person. The officer was a braggart, impressed with no one but himself, and thought little of anyone else's contribution to law and order. Worse yet, the man was quick with his fists when asking witnesses for information. No, Jeremy didn't want the man anywhere near West Ravenwood. Time to put his nose to the grindstone and send a letter back to Sir Elderberry clearly stating that while he appreciated the thought, Officer Jefferies was not needed.

Turning to the second letter, Jeremy frowned. He did not recognize the hand. Once he unfolded it, he was rather surprised to see that it was an invitation from Mrs. Waverley to dine at Allenton Park that evening. It was to be a casual affair, an al fresco meal on the back lawn, as soon as the heat of the day ebbed.

She apologized for not inviting him sooner, but she had not realized that he was the son of Lord Nathan Fraser of Bath. It was so hard to keep track of the children of the aristocracy, she complained, especially the younger sons . . . and she hadn't thought to check her baronetage list. She did not mention that Mr. Waverley had been aware of Jeremy's social standing; her husband had clearly not shared this information with his wife. There was a slight tone of admonishment as if Jeremy's decision to find employment as a Bow Street Officer had contributed to her ignorance.

Jeremy was nonplussed. He didn't know whether to be insulted that the invitation was based on his family connections— something that was a gift of birth and not hard work—or be insulted by the patronizing tone regarding the Bow Street Runners. He chose neither, but instead asked for pen and paper from the innkeeper, and wrote out an eloquent acceptance. The note was sent up the hill with a message boy, and Jeremy sat back and ordered a dark ale.

"There ya be," a voice just over his right shoulder said.

Before Jeremy could turn, Stacks edged past the neighboring table and sat on the chair across from him. The man dropped a piece of paper on the table. "I took it upon meself to have Sandra, the barmaid"—Stacks looked across the room and winked at someone, likely Sandra herself—"write up the list, being as I cannot form me letters."

"Excellent reasoning, Stacks. Though, I should have asked if you knew how to write. My mistake."

"No problem, Mr. Fraser. It be a great excuse. I quite like spending time with Sandra. And now I got ya five names: three fellas and two girls. I had ta ask around a fair bit—got the cold shoulder from most. But the grocer, he knew what was what. Talkative, I tell ya! Had to tell me all about rotting turnips and potato eyes before I could get him to the subject of Andrew Waverley's friends."

Jeremy lifted the paper. "Todd Rummage, Baxter Temple, Gene Smith, Shirley Chips, and Audra Pratt."

"All from West Ravenwood—except Gene Smith, of course."

"Why of course?"

"Everyone knows that the Smiths are from Dorchester."

Jeremy snorted a laugh. "Yes, common knowledge."

"Oh, an' I didn't have Sandra write down Charlotte Dewey's name, as I believe you already know that Miss Dewey and Mr. Waverley were sweet on each other. They were often racing through town in his barouche, causing a fuss and scaring the chickens. There was talk of the two being . . . well you know, close. Met on the sly—which just means the family didn't know. Townspeople would see them coming and going."

"Miss Dewey has transferred her affections to the other brother," Jeremy observed.

"It be a year—or nearly that."

"You're right, Stacks." Jeremy sat back, tucking the folded paper into his jacket pocket. "Change of subject. I've been invited to Allenton Park for dinner, and I would like to arrive in the carriage."

Stacks nodded with approval. "Not a problem, Mr. Fraser. I'll run by the stable and get it arranged. I'll meet ya round front in an hour. That do?"

Jeremy smiled. "Absolutely." This dinner would be the perfect time and place to learn more about Andrew. And if it proved to be an uninformative evening, it would not be a complete waste of time, as he would have the opportunity to talk more with Miss Sophia Thompson.

A most enticing prospect.

"His father is a baron?" Daphne asked for the fifth—or was it sixth?—time as the girls dressed for dinner.

Sophia nodded yet again. "That was what Aunt Hazel said. Uncle Edward was not pleased to have him join us for dinner, but Aunt Hazel insisted."

They were in Daphne's room with her maid, Susan, and Betty. Sophia was putting up her hair—as dictated by her age—while Susan buttoned the back of Daphne's dress. Daphne's hair flowed prettily down her shoulders—as dictated by *her* age. One year made such a difference.

"Did you know?" Daphne asked, looking at Sophia in the mirror with wide eyes.

"No, but I'm not surprised. He is educated and mannered. We don't just talk of Andrew and the investigation, you know."

"Oh?"

"Oh" was a deceptive one-syllable word; it could have many meanings. In this case, was Daphne asking: "What else do you talk about when not discussing Andrew?" Or "Do you think I should be interested in him?"

Choosing to interpret Daphne's "oh" as the latter, Sophia laughed, turning in her chair. "Mr. Fraser is not for you, Daphne."

Daphne lifted her chin and sniffed defensively. "And why not?"

"Mr. Fraser is a *fourth* son. Required to work. You need someone who is footloose and fancy free, otherwise your parents would not approve."

With a short nod and a small giggle, Daphne agreed. "Yes, yes, indeed. I forgot about that part. Besides, I have Dylan to consider." She flicked her hand in Sophia's direction. "What about you?"

"What *about* me?"

"You and Mr. Fraser. You could work together. It would be so sweet."

Sophia bit her lip to prevent an impertinent remark. Daphne had not meant to touch a nerve, and Sophia was not even sure which nerve she had pricked. It could have been the word "sweet" and the condescending tone that accompanied it—or it might have been Sophia's realization that she had been thinking along the same lines. Though, she would never use the word "sweet" to describe the turmoil of happy and anxious emotions that Jeremy Fraser's presence invariably created.

Yes, the prospect of working in tandem with such a talented young detective was rather exciting—no, thrilling . . . no, nice. Yes. It would be *nice* to work with him. A partner. In the business sense.

Sophia watched as her cousin pinched her cheeks and wrinkled her nose at the image in the mirror. "I should probably warn you, Mother invited the Deweys to join us as well."

Sophia sighed silently and followed Daphne into the corridor.

CHAPTER TEN

Confusion and Convulsions

That evening, the weather was most cooperative. The temperature and humidity dropped to a comfortable level, and the threatening clouds meandered away. When Sophia and Daphne stepped through the French doors onto the patio, a long table covered with vases of flowers and sparkling silverware had been set up on the far side, overlooking the distant rolling hills and church steeples. Comfortable chairs had been brought out to a gathering area where the rest of the family and the Deweys waited. Jeremy was still to arrive.

"It was so very kind of Mrs. Waverley to include us this evening. Mother was quite thrilled by the invitation," Charlotte said as they neared her.

She reached out and fingered the lace on Sophia's sleeve. "That's lovely. Is it Irish?" she asked. Then seeing Sophia's confusion she added, "Or Belgian?" She laughed. "Never mind. I don't know the difference, either."

With a wistful expression, Charlotte sighed and then sauntered over to where the Deweys were standing with the Waverleys, swaying her skirts in a graceful rhythm as she walked.

"Such a pretty gown," Aunt Hazel said to Charlotte as she approached. Her smile was genuine, though a touch sad. "I recognize it."

"Yes, Andrew liked the color on me . . ." Charlotte's expression changed, a frown flitted across her face. She glanced toward William and lifted her chin. "Thank you. It is rather flattering. My mother chose the style."

Sophia glanced at Mrs. Dewey, who was wearing a serviceable gown of charcoal gray, with a stark white embellishment of lace at the cuffs and collar. The woman laughed a little too brightly, and said, "No, no. Not a style I would choose. That dress came from London. I believe the modiste there suggested it."

"Perhaps you are right," Charlotte agreed. She glanced over her shoulder to the servants putting the last touches to the table settings as Mrs. Curtis hurried them along. "My mistake."

Not long after, Benton announced Jeremy's arrival. Upon his entrance onto the patio, Jeremy greeted one and all with a general bow. He then strode into the group with his shoulders back and his eyes scanning the company. They stopped when he met Sophia's, and he gave her an extra nod.

His expression was flattering, and Sophia was quite prepared to call the evening a success before it had even started. It was not surprising when Jeremy joined their somewhat select group in the corner.

"How goes the investigation?" Papa asked Jeremy as he sauntered over to join the younger group. It was a genuine question without any hidden meaning; he displayed no criticism or affront at the presence of a Runner in their social gathering.

"Well enough, sir. Though the case seems to reach out in all directions. It's complicated."

"Not surprising." Papa nodded and then proceeded to compare the search for clues to a capricious wind.

Smiling politely, the younger members of the gathering said little, waiting for dinner to be called. When it was, Sophia was pleased to walk beside Jeremy to the table; they could sit next to each other without making any show of doing so. Less fortunately, Uncle Edward was on Sophia's right, and Mrs. Dewey directly across from her.

Mrs. Dewey had most of Uncle Edward's attention, which was to Sophia's taste, and while the older couple discussed land management—*ad nauseam*—Jeremy discussed police procedure and pointed out that observation was one of the investigator's best tools. He said this as he dipped his bread in his wine, meaning to use the olive oil. Good-natured chuckles echoed around the table when he lifted his bread to his mouth, and he gasped at the unexpected taste. When he declared this soggy morsel tasty, Sophia grinned but declined his offer to do the same with her bread.

And so the evening proceeded through five courses and varied conversation. Discussion of the coming fair brought the table back together. With only ten diners and the informal setting, the table became lively, and discussions crossed back and forth across the table. It was deemed excessive to be confined to converse with only those next to you, though it was traditional.

"Same fair as last year." Aunt Hazel looked pleased. "I hope the leather maker will be there again; my soft dove-gray gloves were ever so comfortable. I'd like another pair—in beige, perhaps."

"I'm more interested in the games," Daphne remarked. "Last year there was a turning wheel, and if you could guess where it would stop, you won a prize!" She laughed. "I almost won twice last year."

"Yes, but you had to play twenty times," William said unhelpfully. "To *almost* win!"

Daphne pulled her napkin from her lap and scrunched it into a ball.

"Ah, ah," Aunt Hazel admonished. She wagged her finger at Daphne, who huffed and dropped the cloth back onto her lap.

"What kind of fair is it?" Sophia asked. "A hiring fair? Or a harvest fair?"

"A little of both," William said with confidence. "There will be townspeople there with pitchforks and brooms, looking for work, while others will have brought squash and cauliflower for cooking."

"Still, it is unlikely to be as lively this year as it has been in the past," Charlotte said, spearing her pear in white wine and popping it into her mouth. "Andrew will be on many people's minds; it will temper the jocularity by a significant amount."

Suddenly the table hushed as everyone turned toward Charlotte. She seemed oblivious of the attention, continuing to enjoy her dessert. As the silence lengthened, it became louder until at last Charlotte noticed and looked up.

"What's wrong?" she asked, dropping her gaze to the table. Her hands stilled and she seemed to shrink. "Did I say something . . . oh dear. I did. I am so sorry." She put her hand to her mouth looking upset. "I didn't mean to say that."

"Best keep the conversation away from disagreeable subjects, my dear," Aunt Hazel gently suggested.

Charlotte flushed. "Yes, of course. It was most inconsiderate." She swallowed deeply. "Though, we cannot hide the fact that Andrew was murdered, Mrs. Waverley. It will be on everyone's mind."

The patio echoed with silence—sharp and uncomfortable. It lasted several moments.

"True enough." Sophia looked up, almost surprised that the voice that broke the silence was her own. "But if we all make an effort to avoid the subject, it will be easier on the family."

She glanced at Aunt Hazel and saw that while her aunt's color was now high, she did not look overwrought. However, the same could not be said of Uncle Edward. His complexion was gray and his face unanimated; was he even breathing?

"Excellent advice, Miss Thompson." Charlotte lifted her eyes briefly and then returned her stare to the plate before her. "But I'm concerned that an abundance of decorum might not be in the family's best interest. After all, no one talked about Howard Tuff, and as a result his murder was never solved." Charlotte turned her head in order to look at Sophia sideways. "I would hate for Andrew's murder to go by the wayside."

"Not likely to happen, Charlotte. We have a Runner here to solve the case, remember." Sophia patted Jeremy's arm as if the company needed to be reminded of whom she was referring.

Taking a sip of her lemonade, Sophia watched Charlotte over the edge of her glass, wondering how close the young lady really had been to Andrew. She seemed to be over the most acute sorrow caused by his death, but not entirely ready to put it behind her.

Turning her head to glance at William, Sophia saw that his cheeks were flushed and he wore a sullen expression. He looked ready to make a caustic remark that would ruin the evening entirely.

"Who was Howard Tuff?" Sophia asked quickly, turning to her father.

He shrugged. "I don't know."

Charlotte sighed deeply. "Howard Tuff was the head groundsman here in Allenton Park," she explained in a soft voice. "He disappeared nearly twenty years ago."

"Before you were born," Jeremy interrupted with a casual shoulder lift. "How did you come to know of it?"

"Last year, after Andrew was killed, parishioners started talking about Howard Tuff and his disappearance again. Most folks were certain that Tuff had returned to his life at sea. But some were not so certain, and they wondered if Tuff had suffered the same fate as Andrew. Or rather, Andrew had suffered the same fate as Tuff."

"Twenty years apart? Hardly seems likely," Papa said, frowning. "Were there any similarities?"

"A few," Charlotte answered, her eyes shifting from person to person. "Tuff was seen entering Glendor Wood, likely to meet someone. Andrew was seen doing the same." She dropped the level of her voice, drawing those around the table closer. "But no one knows what happened to Tuff. He was never seen again. And while it was assumed that he was dead"—she sat back, inhaling deeply—"his body was never found."

———•———

Jeremy stared at Charlotte, wondering if she was getting too much pleasure from the effect of her tale on the company, particularly the Waverleys. Her words were clearly hammering at the family—Edward Waverley stared out at the hills with vacant eyes, while Mrs. Waverley found the spoon beside her plate was of great interest.

"This might not be the best time to discuss a murder." Jeremy looked at Sophia for support and was grateful that she understood his expression.

"You're right," she said firmly. "Let's change the subject. Tell me, Charlotte, do you have any favorite shops in London that you would recommend to Daphne for her coming-out?"

Charlotte stared at Sophia as if trying to understand her words. "G. Sutton has a silk shop in Leicester Square that is well worthwhile," she said finally, in a monotone. It was clear that the subject was more of a distraction than a welcome dialogue.

Before Sophia could ply Charlotte for more useless information, Charlotte turned to Jeremy. "When is the best time, Mr. Fraser, to discuss murder?" she asked as if genuinely curious. "I'm surprised by your hesitance. I would think a Runner comfortable with the subject."

"No one is ever comfortable discussing murder, or at least they should not be, Miss Dewey. Besides, it is not a topic for the dinner table." Jeremy sat back in his chair, adopting a casual posture. "If anyone wishes to add to my knowledge of Andrew's murder, please do so after dinner." He attempted a smile, but he knew it had the appearance of a grimace.

The silence up and down the table was resounding. Charlotte nodded as if agreeing with a thought and then turned to her father, Reverend Dewey, sitting to her right. They began a whispered conversation.

The dishes were cleared, and a large silver teapot was placed in front of Mrs. Waverley. Tea was poured, little cakes were nibbled, and the conversation became far more general and far less controversial.

A shallow calm settled over the company. But it was a false serenity, easily destroyed, as they soon learned.

Just as the sun started to dip below the horizon, and the sky turned a riotous combination of red and lilac, a tall footman in livery rushed through the French doors and over to where Mr. Waverley was seated. After a brief hushed conversation, Mr. Waverley stood and gestured toward Jeremy. "Would you come with me, please?"

Puzzled, Jeremy jumped to his feet. He bowed to the company and followed Mr. Waverley back into the manor.

"Is something amiss, Mr. Waverley?" Jeremy asked as soon as they stepped across the threshold and their conversation could no longer be overheard.

"Yes. Your man has taken ill. Apparently it was sudden and severe."

"Stacks? Ill? He was just fine a few hours ago." Jeremy increased his speed, catching up to Mr. Waverley with several long strides.

"Be that as it may, Darren"—Edward Waverley lifted his hand, indicating the footman leading the way—"Darren says Mr. Reyer, the surgeon, has been called, but Stacks—that's his name?"

"Yes," Jeremy said in a toneless voice. His heart raced and he would have run the rest of the way, if he knew where they were going. "Hal Stacks from Smithfield."

"It would seem that this Stacks fellow is not doing well, not at all. He complained of a numbness in his mouth and throat, and then of a fever. He was in the servants' hall with the others when he became ill, gasping for air."

Darren continued to lead them deeper into the maze of Allenton halls, but the corridors were narrower now and not carpeted—no paintings on the plaster walls, and the rooms leading off the corridor were small and abundant. Jeremy knew that they were in the back of the house, nearing the servants' hall. He could hear strident voices up ahead, getting louder.

Jeremy could also hear footsteps, hard heels rapping sharply on the tiles behind them. He whirled around, hoping to see the surgeon rushing with them.

But it was not the surgeon.

"What are you doing?" Jeremy asked in a harsh tone, not hiding his anxiety.

"I wanted to know what was amiss." Sophia glanced at her uncle and then back to Jeremy.

Jeremy frowned. "This is not a game. My man is very ill, Miss Thompson. Go back to the patio."

A scream echoed down the corridor, and they all turned toward it. Jeremy raced past Mr. Waverley and down the hall. Darren was still ahead of him and Sophia was at his side.

They burst into the servants' hall and into a chaotic scene.

Stacks lay atop the long table; his face was gray, his body motionless. On the floor beside him was a foul-smelling bucket. Surrounding him, the staff of Allenton Park wore shocked expressions that had nothing to do with the group bursting through the door.

Cook stood on the far side of the table; she reached over, touching Stacks' neck, and then rested her hand on his shoulder. She shook with the force of her sobs as she nudged his arm, over and over. But Stacks did not protest; his arm flopped lifeless at his side.

There was little doubt that Stacks was either fully unconscious . . . or dead.

———— ✦ ————

Sophia looked over Jeremy's shoulder and gasped. "Mr. Stacks?" she said, trying to push past two maids standing beside the table.

Jeremy grabbed Sophia's arm to prevent her from going closer. "No, Miss Thompson. I will take it from here."

"I'm fine," Sophia protested, feeling anything but fine. Her stomach churned, threatening to cast up her lovely supper. "If I'm to be an investigator, I need to be able to handle seeing a dead body." Her words were spoken in a whisper and Sophia knew horror was written on her face. "He is dead, isn't he?"

The tallest maid, wearing a crisp white apron, glanced at Cook before she nodded tearfully.

"That is a lesson for another day," Jeremy said, shifting so that her view of the table was obscured. He nudged her closer to her uncle.

"But—"

"Another day," Jeremy repeated, visibly upset and distracted.

Then he nodded to Uncle Edward and Sophia was led from the room. Halfway down the corridor, Sophia came out of her stupor and she planted her feet.

"No," she said. "How can I learn anything if I'm shunted away when something untoward happens?"

She tried to duck under her uncle's arm, which was draped around her shoulders, but he held fast. "No, Sophia. Leave it for the Runner to deal with. This is not a show for your entertainment. A man has died. Have some dignity!"

"That is greatly unfair, Uncle. I'm not seeking entertainment. I wish to help."

Startled by the sound of quickly approaching footsteps, Sophia looked up the hallway hoping to see the surgeon racing toward them. But it wasn't the surgeon who neared.

"Sophia does not suffer from a lack of dignity, Edward, but an overabundance of curiosity," Papa said as he neared. "And I will admit to being the one from whom she inherited it. What is going on?"

"Mr. Stacks is dead, Papa. I think he might have been poisoned."

Uncle Edward snorted his derision. "Poisoned, indeed! Your imagination runs wild."

"Mr. Stacks vomited into the bucket by the table, and his clothes were twisted around his body as if he had been convulsing." Forcing her mind back to the scene in the servants' hall, Sophia tried to remember everything that she had seen before being led from the room. "And his pants were soiled." Sophia scowled, the memory of Jeremy's rush to get her out of the room loomed large and she bridled, recalling his dismissive attitude.

Uncle Edward shook his head. "That's still a huge leap of thought into the realm of murder, my girl."

Sophia glanced at her father and was relieved to see that while he was shaking his head as well, Papa's reaction was one of frustration with Uncle Edward's attitude, not agreement. Still, he apparently believed Sophia was better off farther from the scene. "Best we wait until Mr. Fraser is done, Sophia dear. I'm sure he won't be long."

He offered Sophia his arm. "Did you really want to examine the body?" he asked quietly, so that Uncle Edward was not privy to their conversation.

"No, not really . . . But I have to become accustomed to such things eventually."

"Why on earth would you say so?"

"I was not jesting when I told you I was determined to become a Bow Street Officer, Papa."

"Oh dear. I was holding on to the thought that you were teasing."

"I was *not* teasing, as I've said before. And right now, I'm excessively angry with Mr. Fraser."

"Why?" He gave Sophia a puzzled glance. "Do you think *he* killed Mr. Stacks?"

"No, of course not. But Mr. Fraser scooted me out of the room before I had a chance to examine the body. I'll have to rely on him for information now."

"Oh, that's all right then."

"No, it's not! I should be able to make my own inquiries, examine and observe, *on my own*! I'll have to have words with Mr. Fraser about his dismissal of my abilities."

"The fellow has just lost a colleague, my dear. You might want to be gentle with him."

"Oh," Sophia said, instantly regretting her temper. "Yes, quite right. I forgot about that. Mr. Stacks was a kind man . . . Jeremy will miss—I mean, Mr. Fraser will miss him."

"That goes without saying."

"Indeed."

———————

Sophia shifted her chair so that she could see the French doors from where she sat on the patio. Lamps had been set out to help with visibility. She wanted to know the minute Jeremy returned.

It took a fair amount of time, but eventually, as the evening settled around them and the bugs began to hum about in the cooler air, Jeremy stepped out onto the patio once more.

"I apologize for the delay," he said, looking haggard. "Mr. Reyer, the surgeon, only just arrived."

Rather than sit, Jeremy walked over to the short wall that lined the patio and leaned on it for a moment, then straightened and began to pace. "I must be going. I have to write Bow Street and I have to write Stacks' family . . . and . . ." He scratched at his forehead. He turned, scanning those seated nearby until his eyes met Sophia's. "Are you all right?" he asked.

Sophia dredged up a smile from somewhere. "Yes," she said with a nod.

Jeremy turned back to the group. "I must be going," he repeated. Then he paused, emotions of a chaotic nature flitting across his face. "I'll have to walk." He lifted his chin and spoke to the dark sky. "Never driven a large coach before on country lanes in the dark. Wouldn't want an accident. Wouldn't do. No, indeed, I'll walk. Do me good. Fresh air and all that." He dropped his eyes to stare at the tiles beneath his feet and stood still for some time, barely breathing.

"No need, Mr. Fraser," the reverend said, standing and gesturing for his wife and Charlotte to do the same. "We have room in our carriage. We can take you home this evening and you can return tomorrow for your coach."

Lifting his head, Jeremy started at the trio and blinked. "That would be most kind." Then he looked toward the French doors. "Mr. Reyer will see me in the morning to discuss Stacks' . . . situation."

Sophia followed Jeremy and the Deweys to the front door. It was a subdued and melancholy send-off.

CHAPTER ELEVEN

A Pall Across the Estate

Jeremy rose the next morning, read the first paragraph of his letter to Mr. Stacks' parents, and tore it in two. He should not have attempted to write such an important letter when he was beyond exhausted. The letter had been too abrupt. It was impersonal and did not truly convey his deep sorrow and sympathy.

His second attempt was much better. The letter would not be an easy read for the Stacks family, but at least this letter wasn't full of self-recrimination as his first had been.

Questioning the staff of Allenton Park the previous night had led Jeremy to no easy conclusion. Instead, uncertainty was heaped on top of confusion. Had the poisoning been accidental, or had Jeremy's investigation contributed to Stacks' death? Stacks had been sent to ask questions and the inquiries might have pushed the killer into a corner. Did that mean the killer was on Stacks' list, or that the killer feared he or she might be *added* to the list?

It certainly meant that the killer . . . or a killer, at least—had been walking among them the previous evening.

Jeremy scowled, frustrated that someone so twisted could remain undetected. He would have to watch people more closely.

Jeremy was almost certain that Stacks was poisoned. The surgeon had said as much, even going so far as to identify the poison as wolfsbane. A common enough plant found in many ornamental gardens. At first Mr. Reyer had simply identified the poison as plant based: strychnine, wolfsbane, or cyanide. He had narrowed it down to wolfsbane because of the burns in Stacks' mouth.

At first, it was puzzling that Stacks had been poisoned while the rest of the staff were fine. However, with a little digging, Jeremy had discovered that Stacks was the only person to take tea with his meal. The other staff members had had small beer. But as to who had passed that tea to Stacks, no one could agree. It had taken many hands to get it to the end of the table.

They had also found a small flask of brandy in Stacks' pocket—another possible vehicle for the poison. Jeremy had given it to the surgeon for testing. If it or the teacup tested positive for wolfsbane, it would be clear that Stacks' death had been orchestrated.

Why? It was a question that kept bubbling to the forefront of Jeremy's mind. Why kill Stacks? If the murderer intended to hobble the inquiry, why not set his sights on the investigator himself? Why kill the investigator's driver?

Perhaps not thinking as clearly as he would otherwise, it took Jeremy several sleepless hours to acknowledge a gruesome possibility. The murderer thought to remain hidden, to kill without any consequence. The killer knew that more Runners would arrive in force were one of their own found dead, whereas the same could not be said for a Runner's driver. Stacks' death was a safer proposition . . . or so it was thought.

Jeremy clenched his jaw in anger. The killer was wrong. They didn't know that they were facing off against a very determined Runner.

Jeremy would not stop until this twisted piece of rubbish faced justice.

Before going to breakfast, Jeremy folded the new letter with his note to Bow Street, asking for it to be forwarded, and sealed it. He was reluctant to break his fast in the common room as he had been doing, because it had been his habit to eat with Stacks. Jeremy grabbed a roll instead—pointedly refusing tea—and asked the front desk to post his letter. He was about to walk out the door when the innkeeper addressed him.

"Yer coach were brought back to the stable this morning, Mr. Fraser," the large man said, lifting his soiled apron to wipe his hands. "Mr. Stacks' bags were gathered an' placed in the storage room."

Jeremy frowned, displeased that Stacks' belongings had been handled.

"Need the space, ya know," the innkeeper explained upon seeing Jeremy's frown. "Gotta have me rents."

Jeremy nodded and rushed for the door, needing air. He would visit Allenton Park and interview the staff yet again. But in truth, he only wanted to see Sophia. Against all logic, he knew her presence would clear his racing thoughts and offer him a modicum of comfort and calm.

———•———

Sophia was not calm, not in the least. She was itching to investigate, to get to the bottom of Stacks' murder. The likelihood that it would lead to an answer about Andrew's murder, too, seemed high. And so it was that as Daphne slipped into her day dress with Susan's assistance, Sophia paced her cousin's room—having dressed and breakfasted hours earlier.

"You're going to wear out the carpet, Sophia, if you continue to pace. I'll be ready momentarily. Sit, relax. Besides, Mr. Fraser has not yet arrived."

"I'm not certain that Mr. Fraser will remember our plans, Daphne. He was quite disturbed when he left last night."

"Murder is part and parcel of his job, Sophia. He must be used to it to some degree."

"Perhaps, but it is a new post and the victim was someone he worked with, someone he knew personally." Sophia dropped onto Daphne's bed with a thump. "Did you see his face last night? It nearly broke my heart."

Daphne frowned at her reflection in the mirror, straightening a ribbon tied at her elbow. "I agree that he did look upset, but if that were not the case I would think him terribly hard-hearted. But there is no need for you to be upset as well, Sophia. You had nothing to do with the man's death."

"He was a nice man, Daphne, and did not deserve that horrible fate. I can't help but be upset. That's why I need to *do* something. While Mr. Fraser investigates Mr. Stacks' death, you and I should speak to Mr. Dankworth about the knife that killed Andrew. I would see the weapons collector on my own if it would not cause parental distress, but it would, so I won't."

"Besides, I wouldn't let you go off without me," Daphne said with a firm nod of her head.

While Sophia appreciated the company of her cousin, she wondered if Daphne realized that their danger was much higher than they had previously suspected. Someone *in the manor* had killed Hal Stacks, and had done so with an investigator nearby; the culprit was clearly not intimidated by a Runner's presence.

The shooting in the conservatory now had a different complexion as well. How many more victims did the killer have in their sights?

"There, miss. All done." Susan stood back to admire her handiwork; the dress had required a new collar and cuffs. Daphne tugged at her bodice and shook her skirts to straighten them.

"Mr. Fraser might still remember our appointment," Sophia said, already halfway to the door. She was feeling jittery and needed to keep busy. "Shall we see if he's here?"

Daphne caught up to her at the top of the grand staircase.

Below, two women waited by the door. Charlotte had clearly just arrived, as she was undoing her gloves. Mrs. Curtis gestured to the drawing room, but they both looked up as Sophia and Daphne descended the stairs.

"Charlotte, what a surprise." Daphne's tone was more of indifference than surprise. "You've missed the morning meal and Mother has not yet come down. I'm afraid you'll have to wait. Unless . . . Who were you hoping to see, Charlotte? William has gone riding."

"Yes, I saw him leave as my carriage arrived. It's not William I came to see, but your mother. I imagine she's greatly upset and I came to offer Mrs. Waverley the comfort of an ordinary conversation. I thought you and your cousin might be too busy."

"I beg your pardon?" Sophia blinked, nettled by the implied criticism. "There is no lack of company in this house. Besides, Daphne and I are much occupied with catching Andrew's—and now Mr. Stacks'—murderer." She glanced at Mrs. Curtis. The woman, while staring above their heads, exuded utter disinterest.

Charlotte nodded. "William mentioned your wish to be an investigator. It's a rather unusual vocation for a young lady."

Sophia snorted. "That's a bit of an understatement." Sophia turned to the footman standing stiffly by the door. "Has Mr. Fraser arrived, Darren?"

Darren had no opportunity to answer as a rap on the door startled them all.

When the doorman swung the door open, the handsome, but troubled, face of Mr. Jeremy Fraser was revealed.

———•———

Jeremy was well past the Allenton gate when he had finally collected his thoughts, put them to order, and remembered that he had received an invitation to visit Mr. Dankworth at eleven thirty that day. He had spoken to Sophia about it at the dinner before Stacks was . . . before.

Jeremy had been expected to arrive with his carriage and driver at eleven . . . Lawks! What a mess.

With a snort of pent-up frustration, Jeremy realized that he would have to walk back into town and hire a driver. But that meant he was going to be late. Sophia would wonder and perhaps worry, if he did not arrive on time, and Jeremy sincerely hoped this would not put Mr. Dankworth's dander up, refusing to answer questions.

There was nothing for it but to have Benton relay a message about his delay. However, when the door opened to his knock, rather than looking into the grizzled face of the elderly butler, Jeremy met Sophia's gaze over the shoulder of a footman. He stood staring at her in a semi-stupor for a moment, then Jeremy apologized—or at least he intended to, but he was ushered back out the door before he could utter a word.

He tried to apologize again for the lack of a carriage, but again his words were interrupted—this time by the stamping of horse hooves and the jangling of equipage as a smart coach and four fine horses pulled up in front of them.

"Thank you, Mr. Bradley," Sophia said to the driver when he jumped down from his perch and opened the coach door. "Shall we, Mr. Fraser?" She lifted her hand to his.

He could feel the warmth of her person through her gloves as Jeremy handed her, and then Miss Waverley, into the coach. It was all done in a tick and they were almost to the gate before any of them found their tongues.

"I thought it best to arrive in style, Mr. Fraser," Sophia explained. "It's impressive and more likely to encourage a frank discussion. Papa suggested the use of our own carriage and driver. I thought it most opportune and accepted on your behalf. I hope I did not overstep."

"Of course not," Jeremy said, feeling some of his tension sloughing off. "I should have thought of it."

"You're much distracted, Mr. Fraser," Daphne said kindly. "It cannot be helped."

It took little more than ten minutes to wend their way to the home of Mr. Dankworth, including a quick stop at the inn to pick up the knife they needed him to identify. Once at Ramsey Manor, they were immediately ushered into the front entrance and then led to the back of the house and an opulent conservatory.

An elderly gentleman waited underneath a leafy ficus. He was a small, wizened figure, almost lost in his wheeled Bath chair. The contraption looked comfortable enough, with a cushioned seat and back, but somewhat oppressive with a black leather hood, folding coachlike behind his head, and a stiff handle to steer the small wheel by his feet.

"I thought you might not come," Mr. Dankworth said after the introductions. "What with the tragedy last night." Despite his frail form, the gentleman had a robust voice and a twinkle in his watery blue eyes.

"Gracious, news travels fast," Sophia said with surprise.

"Yes, not enough going on to keep everyone busy, my dear. People have to put their noses into other people's business." He smiled, taking away the bite of his words.

Jeremy stood to the side as the young ladies settled themselves on the wrought-iron bench next to Mr. Dankworth's wheeled chair. Looking around, he saw another bench nearby and dragged the heavy piece of furniture over to the group. Before he was seated, the conversation had progressed from weather to the family's health to the church's new pipe organ. When a discussion began on the different conservatory plants under the glass roof, Jeremy grew impatient and interrupted.

"Do you know why we are here, Mr. Dankworth?"

The gentleman startled. He glanced at his knees, then the floor, and then past Jeremy's shoulder. His expression was that of puzzlement.

"Yes . . . I believe so. One of my knives was found in Glendor Wood. Mr. Tilter sent me a note." He laughed; it was a light chuckle but it triggered a fit of coughing that lasted some time. Finally, Mr. Dankworth continued as if nothing had occurred. "Few secrets around here," he said.

Reaching into his satchel, Jeremy pulled out the knife still swathed in cloth and passed it to the old man.

Unwrapping it with the speed of a dawdling snail, Mr.

Dankworth bobbed his head when, at last, the weapon was visible. "Ah yes. I remember this one." He turned the knife over, running his twitching thumb along the carving. "But I sold it quite some time ago. Yes, yes . . . maybe three years or so."

Jeremy fought the urge to react. He leaned forward, listening intently.

"To whom did you sell it?" Sophia asked, the same question on Jeremy's lips. She leaned forward, too, elbows resting on her knees. Even Miss Waverley looked eager.

"Andrew Waverley," Mr. Dankworth said proudly. "Yes, my dear, your cousin. I rarely sell things from my collection, but he was quite enthralled by this knife . . . I think it might have been the figures on the hilt. A kind of primitive art. Said he had a lady friend who liked such things. Nothing like it around here."

He passed the knife and its tangled wrappings back to Jeremy. "Now, now, my dear, why do you look so downcast?" he said to Sophia.

Jeremy glanced her way and was surprised to see that Sophia did look upset.

"I beg your pardon," she said. "I was hoping that this might be a clue, that it would help us understand who killed Andrew . . . But if it was his own knife, it can't be the murder weapon. It's a dead end."

"Not at all, my dear." Mr. Dankworth sat back in his chair, looking relaxed. "Someone could have taken the knife from Andrew and then killed him. Murdered with his own knife. Quite ironic, don't you think?"

"Perhaps you have forgotten that Miss Waverley, here, is—was—Andrew's sister," Sophia said with no inflection in her voice.

Mr. Dankworth frowned, and he glanced in Miss Waverley's

direction. "Yes. Yes, I'm afraid that I did forget." He looked uncomfortable. "I beg your pardon."

"Lady friend?" Jeremy asked, pulling the conversation back to a safer path. "You said that Andrew had a lady friend." He glanced toward Sophia, and saw her take a deep breath.

"Yes, not sure who the young man was quietly meeting, but the town was full of talk. He used to gather his friends . . . You might know the boys. I gave your man, the late Mr. Stacks, the names of a couple."

"You spoke to Stacks?" Jeremy frowned; Stacks had not mentioned Mr. Dankworth when he had given Jeremy the list.

"Oh no. Gracious no." The elderly gentleman looked affronted. "He spoke to my housekeeper . . . and I . . . yes, I told Mrs. Tremor to mention the Rummage boy—son of the squire. He used to go out and about with Mr. Waverley before he went off to Oxford. Mr. Waverley, that is. Todd Rummage would be an unlikely candidate for Oxford."

"How so?" Jeremy asked.

"Well, the boy was always into mischief from what I heard. Even talk of him poaching. It didn't and doesn't bode well for his father. Yes, indeed, young Rummage thinks he is entitled. Wears his father's rank, if you know what I mean. Trouble follows him around like a bloodhound. And . . . and . . . yes, Baxter Temple— he was another one of Andrew's cohorts, the banker's son. Still can't remember the young lady's name. Not sure I ever heard it. Just that Mr. Waverley was out chasing skirts—one in particular."

Jeremy took out his journal and added the information next to the names Stacks had mentioned.

With that, the conversation devolved into more of a social visit than an interview. Daphne asked after Mr. Dankworth's relatives and she offered greetings from her family. Sophia watched, saying little, and Jeremy was itching to leave long before they did.

———————

Sophia took her place in the coach beside Daphne as Jeremy settled across from them. Mr. Bradley had just closed the door and started to climb back up to the driver's bench when Daphne looked out the window and gasped in surprise. She opened the door and leaned out, holding on to the hand strap attached to the side of the coach.

"Mr. Phillips?" she called, staring at a shrub near the rear of the coach. Boots were visible below the thick leaves. She half turned, speaking over her shoulder to her companions. "One of our gardeners," she explained. "Strange that he would be here." She turned back to the open carriage door. "Glen Phillips?" she called again.

The shrub shook, and then was pushed aside to reveal a tall figure with a bushy beard. "Yes, Miss Waverley." He had dirt smudged across his shoulder.

"What are you doing here?"

Mr. Phillips frowned and opened his mouth, but said nothing. He shifted his weight, kicked his boots into the ground, and tried again, this time more successfully. "Had to bring George—that be George Band, the under-gardener here at Ramsey Manor . . . Had to bring George a . . . a rake handle. Yes, a rake handle. His last one broke an' he needed a new one. I'm headin' back to Allenton Park now."

Daphne glanced at her companions. "A rake handle?" she whispered, her tone incredulous. She shook her head and then lifted her chin. "Do we have room for Mr. Phillips up on your perch, Mr. Bradley?"

Sophia could not hear the answer but assumed all was well, as Mr. Phillips joined Mr. Bradley on the driver's bench. Soon they were on the road and climbing the hill to Allenton Park. Other than a casual comment about the gardener's odd behavior, Daphne lapsed into silence, and Sophia appreciated the comfortable lack of conversation. It allowed her to watch Jeremy from the corner of her eye to gauge his mood.

He was disturbed, and certainly didn't look as calm as usual, but he seemed to have weathered the emotional ups and downs of the day. He met her glance with an upturned mouth—not really a smile as it was laced with melancholy, but the attempt was appreciated.

Unfortunately, Jeremy requested that he be left at the gate, leaving her and Daphne to return to the dreary and oppressive atmosphere of the manor alone. Not *alone* alone, but a without-a-handsome-gentleman-for-company alone. It was a shame; Sophia was becoming rather fond of said company.

Mr. Bradley held Sophia's hand overlong when he helped her down the carriage steps. It was a long-understood signal that he wished to speak with her.

"I'll be right in," Sophia told Daphne. Her cousin lifted her hand in a backward wave before slipping through the front door.

Mr. Phillips sauntered off in the direction of the stables and gardening sheds. Sophia said nothing, waiting for the privacy Mr. Bradley clearly wished.

"Yes, Mr. Bradley?" she said eventually, turning toward the Thompson family coachman.

"I were that surprised, Miss Thompson. Mr. Phillips were a bundle of questions from the minute we left Ramsey Manor 'til we were back at the Allenton gate."

Sophia frowned. Mr. Bradley was a calm, mellow sort, and yet here he was complaining about something rather trivial. *Unless* . . . "What were his questions about, Mr. Bradley?"

"They were kinda general, and I would have taken no-nevermind, but that they were all about the same subject."

"And that was?"

"Mr. Fraser, miss. He wanted to know where the Runner were stayin' in town and if there were any other Runners with him or expected in West Ravenwood. He wanted to know if Mr. Fraser had any idea who killed Mr. Stacks or Mr. Waverley. As if Mr. Fraser would share his theories with me!

"Phillips' questions were all about the investigation, Miss Thompson. Made me uncomfortable. I didna ask him why he wanted to know, but I sure didna like the expression on his face. All hard and squinty-eyed. I mean, if Phillips was on the up-an'-up, would he not just ask Mr. Fraser?"

"Mr. Phillips might be one of the many who are uncomfortable around investigators, but thank you, Mr. Bradley. I will let Mr. Fraser know."

The coachman nodded, climbed back up to his perch, and guided the horses around the house to the stables.

As Sophia watched them disappear, she was surprised to see that the gardener had not continued into the stable yard, or even veered off toward the gardening sheds. He stood at the juncture of the two, staring back at her with an expression that was hard and squinty-eyed—just as Mr. Bradley had described.

It was most unnerving.

CHAPTER TWELVE

Tampered Evidence

"Enough!" Sophia said to herself. She was tired of being stared at. There was no call for it, none at all. She was not dressed in a provocative or eccentric manner. This was not a gothic novel. There was no drumroll or other dramatic music to add to the atmosphere, no sense of foreboding whenever she felt unwelcome eyes settle upon her.

There was just a heavily bearded man trying to intimidate her by staring—with menace? Nonsense. She would not be put off so easily. Besides, *why* would the man be trying to intimidate her?

She stared back at Mr. Phillips, mimicking his narrow-eyed expression and then quickly crossed the drive to where he stood.

His stance was a little less confident as she approached, and his eyes lost their anger and instead grew wide with surprise.

"Why are you staring at me, Mr. Phillips?" Sophia asked as she neared his position.

"Didn't know that I was." He dropped his gaze to the ground, staring instead at his boots.

"Well, you most certainly were. And I would like to know why." She frowned at his incongruous brown boots with black toes, shook her head, and continued. "Are you trying to make me nervous? Making a silent threat? It will not work. Or are you merely trying to divine some sort of truth hovering above my head?" Sophia stood with her hands on her hips, looking staunch and authoritative . . . or so she hoped.

"Just looking at the gate, miss," he said, turning his head in that direction. His words were hesitant, his expression anxious. "Surprised . . . yup, surprised to see Mr. Waverley out for a walk. He don't wander about, regular like. Wonder where he's goin'."

Sophia pivoted just in time to see her uncle's capped head disappear down the hill along with the fading tap of his cane. He was heading toward the Allenton Park gate.

"Yes . . . I see. That is rather strange." She turned back upon hearing the scuff and crunch of gravel, only to see that she was now talking to no one. Mr. Phillips had taken the opportunity to rush away.

But rather than follow the gardener, Sophia thought she might follow her uncle. His movements had not been furtive, but Mr. Phillips was right, Uncle Edward usually took the carriage when he went into West Ravenwood. It was a curious happenstance. Yes, indeed, it required the investigation of a novice detective hot on the trail of a . . . well, looking for the trail of . . . yes, the trail of a murderer!

Sophia could finally hear a dramatic drumroll in her head, and she smiled as she rushed after her uncle in a quiet, stealthy sort of way.

Jeremy had not bothered to return to West Ravenwood when he stepped down from the Thompson coach. Time was short and he knew that he would not have made it back in time to meet Mr. Waverley as they had discussed the night before.

Jeremy was done walking gingerly through this investigation; the clock in his head was ticking louder than ever. It was all too clear that the killer was still active and had no compunction about how many lives he took. Jeremy needed to find Andrew and Stacks' murderer before anyone else was added to the killer's inventory.

The Bow Street Runners had taught him that it was best to start at the beginning. That had been his problem; he had investigated willy-nilly. Jeremy needed to begin at the beginning—and quickly, to make up for lost time.

Pacing back and forth in front of the gate while he waited, Jeremy used the time to formulate a theory: The most logical premise involved poachers. Andrew's murderer must have had an accomplice in the house, or the killer was a poacher *and* a member of the staff. That would explain all the incidents in the house.

Jeremy's theory ran as such: Andrew had been meeting someone—a female person for a lascivious purpose?—in the woods, but Andrew had, instead, disrupted a poacher. In fear or anger, the encounter had ended with Andrew being fatally stabbed. Jeremy had to find the person Andrew was waiting for. This person might have seen something or someone suspicious.

Jeremy leaned toward the likelihood of a romantic tryst—with someone not acceptable to his or her family, otherwise there would have been no need to hide the rendezvous. Shirley Chips was on Stacks' list. Was she the type of young woman who would throw good sense to the wind and meet a young man in private? She would have to be found and questioned.

Now, as to Stacks. Did the investigation into Andrew's killing lead to Stacks' murder? Why? Had questioning the people of West Ravenwood been the catalyst? Had the killer felt threatened? Poison, the surgeon had agreed with Jeremy the previous night. It was fast acting and had to have been administered within the hour—therefore, at Allenton Park.

But it had been a cavalier act, brazen and without compunction, for others could have been hurt. If poison had been in the brandy, Stacks might have offered a sip to someone else. Were it in the tea, it could have been commandeered as it made its way down the table. Poisoning Stacks had been a rash act. A careless tactic—yes, the killer couldn't have cared *less* if others had been hurt in the process, and that was assuming Stacks had been the target. It certainly was a puzzler.

"Am I late?"

Jeremy jerked his head up to find Mr. Waverley standing by the open gate watching him pace. He was dressed much more casually than Jeremy had seen before, all in browns with a country cap. "No, sir, not at all. I'm early."

"And thinking hard, it appears." Mr. Waverley gestured to a well-defined path that set out across the lawns toward the woods.

"Yes, but coming to no conclusions—as yet," Jeremy said as he fell into step, feeling frustrated and angry. Frustrated by the lack of progress and angry that Stacks had paid such a high price for being a Bow Street driver. He glanced at the older man and saw that his jaw was clenched and his brow was deeply folded, and moderated his mood. After all, the man had lost his *son* to this monster. "I wish this were not necessary, sir. I know it is difficult."

"It most certainly is," Mr. Waverley snapped and then added in a softer tone, "but if it sees the job done . . . if seeing where Andrew was killed helps, it will be worth it."

"So much time has passed that I can only rely on your memory of the scene, sir," Jeremy explained.

With a curt nod, Mr. Waverley lapsed into silence. Leading the way as the path narrowed, he gestured to his right and then his left. "Glendor Wood proper that way, and there, the trail eventually comes out on West Ravenwood Road."

The woods grew thicker, though it was still easy to see that the forest floor had been groomed. Twigs and collections of leaves were few and far between, and the path was well defined. Finally, they came to a clearing—a quiet glade—and Mr. Waverley guided Jeremy to the edge, near an ancient elm that was gnarled and covered in moss.

"Here," Mr. Waverley said, pointing to a spot off the path near the elm. "His feet were tangled in a rabbit snare. His hands were on the wound in his gut, but the knife was gone and the ground was soaked in blood. The grass by the tree was flattened; looked like he sat for some time waiting. There were multiple footprints all around—by the tree, on the path. All around, but indistinct."

"In which direction did they lead?" Jeremy asked, glancing around the glade to get his bearings. "Were they side by side or facing one another?"

"I said they were indistinct," Mr. Waverley grumbled, then he swallowed visibly. "Besides, the glade was full of people by the time anyone noticed the prints."

"What time of day was Andrew discovered?" a voice asked from behind them.

Startled, the two men flinched and pivoted. Sophia was mere feet behind them.

"I didn't hear you approach," Jeremy admitted. It had been less than an hour since they parted and yet he was pleased to see her . . . actually, no, he wasn't. They were at a murder scene. Not the place for one Sophia Thompson, despite her ambition to be a Bow Street Runner; she should be cutting her teeth with thievery or fraud, not murder . . . if she was going to be part of the police force, that is.

With a lackluster shrug, Sophia acknowledged his comment. "I *was* trying to be quiet."

"You should not be here, Sophia. Go back," her uncle commanded. "Back to the manor."

<hr/>

With a frown and a shake of her head, Sophia stepped closer to the gnarled elm tree, tamping down her irritation as she did. "What time of day?" she asked again, ignoring her uncle's order. "Would Andrew have been squinting into the sun? Could he have been blinded and not seen his assassin coming? Was it a trap?"

"This is not a healthy environment for a young lady, Sophia— even one who has aspirations of being an investigator." And then her uncle slowly shook his head as if in resignation. "I might as well talk to the moon. You are as obstinate as the day is long, Sophia Thompson," Uncle Edward said, clicking his tongue. "I see shades of your father in you."

Sophia half smiled and offered another shrug. "Thank you,

Uncle Edward," she said, ignoring the peevish tone of his unintended compliment. "So, would Andrew have been blinded by the sun?"

Uncle Edward made a sound deep in his throat that was part growl and part groan. "No. Visibility would have been fine—there was no mist or fog that evening and the surgeon believes Andrew was killed in the early evening, twilight. His body was discovered in the morning by Glen Phillips, one of the Allenton gardeners."

"Really?" Jeremy sounded surprised. "Glen Phillips?"

"What of it?" grumped Uncle Edward, leaning casually on his cane.

Sophia swiveled slowly, examining the forested area around them. "A rather strange place for a gardener; his duties would not involve the wooded areas," she said. "Though, it would appear to be a well-kept copse." She pointed to the raked grasses and leafless area surrounding the elm. "It has been groomed, and recently, it appears. Someone looking for something, perhaps?" She glanced up, meeting Jeremy's eyes with a contemplative squint.

"Looking for the knife?" Jeremy turned to Uncle Edward. "Was this you?" he asked, waving his arm in a circle to indicate the whole of the ravine. "Did you tidy up the place?"

The more Sophia stared through the trees, the more it became clear that someone had taken a rake to the long grasses. Leaves were heaped in small piles scattered around the copse.

"Me rake? The very thought! Don't be ridiculous!" Uncle Edward stepped closer to one of the piles of leaves and broken branches, poking at it with his cane. "I searched the path to West Ravenwood first, then the trail east of here, leading back to the manor. The knife was under a stump in a hollow, as if someone had tossed it there. Casually hidden, but effective . . . until I

examined the ground with my *cane* and poked it in every hole."
He frowned at Sophia, likely realizing how driven and obsessive
he sounded. "I wouldn't use a rake," he finished lamely.

"Well, someone did," Sophia said, bending to pick up a brown
and curled leaf.

A sharp pop echoed through the glen.

Something hard knocked Sophia to the ground. She landed
on her back in the pile of detritus with a stone pressed between
her shoulder blades. The fall left her winded, the stone was sharp
and there was a weight on top of her that prevented her from
breathing deeply. It was all vastly uncomfortable.

She squirmed and shoved at the weight, trying to get it off.

"Yes, yes, I'll move in just a minute, Miss Thompson."

"Would like to breathe," she said in gasps of shallow breath.

Jeremy shifted slightly and they were nose to nose.

"Are you hurt?" she asked, observing how blue his eyes were
beneath his deeply furrowed brow. Suddenly, her concern for him
eclipsed her need to breathe. "Are you all right?" she asked again.

Jeremy shifted and slid to Sophia's left side. They continued
to lie prone, staring at each other, listening.

A new sound could be heard echoing across the glade;
branches snapped and feet pounded the ground as someone fled.
The sound of footsteps faded until, at last, there was silence.
Not a true silence, as the trees rustled, birds called, and insects
hummed. There was no way to tell which direction the running
feet had taken—the echoes ricocheted, bouncing everywhere.

"Someone was shooting at us," Jeremy said in a half whisper.
"But I think they're gone now."

Sophia started. "Someone is *what*?! Are you certain? Oh no,
Uncle!"

Sophia pushed against Jeremy, trying to see around his body. "Check on Uncle, Mr. Fraser!" she shouted, ignoring his directive to be quiet.

Jeremy jumped to a stand, then hauled Sophia up from the ground. "Mr. Waverley?" he called, swinging his head from side to side, scanning the bushes and the ground. "What's that?" he asked, tipping his head to listen to an unexpected sound.

Sophia stilled. Out of the relative silence came a moan, some words she did not recognize spoken harshly, and then another moan. She whirled around and looked behind her.

Uncle Edward was lying on his side, with his knees pulled up to his chest. He kept shifting his shoulders and each time he did so, harsh words tumbled out of his mouth. Sophia was fairly certain her uncle was swearing. It was most unusual.

"Uncle! Are you all right?" she asked.

"Well, I'm not having tea!" he snapped, trying to sit up with his arms crossed at his chest.

"Here," she said, offering her hand. "Let me help you up."

Jeremy offered his hand as well.

Uncle Edward laughed. It was a sickly sound without any humor, and he took neither her nor Jeremy's hand; instead, Uncle glared at his right bicep.

Sophia stared at it as well. The dappled sunshine created a pattern on the upper sleeve of Uncle's coat . . . except the shadow on the brown coat was not actually a shadow. When she touched the material, her fingers were coated with a deep red, dripping liquid. Then she noticed the frayed hole. "Oh good Lord, Uncle! You were hit!"

"Yes, it would seem so," he said, and then grit his teeth. "It's a damned shame; this is one of my favorite coats."

Sophia ignored her uncle's attempt to minimize the incident and checked to see that he was not bleeding profusely. She gulped and swallowed, breathing deeply for calm, as she pulled his coat away from the hole in his arm. Jeremy leaned forward to take a look as well.

Sophia sighed in great relief. Uncle had been lucky—very, very lucky. The bullet had only grazed his arm. Painful, but not lethal. For a moment or two, they stared at the weeping wound and then, after realizing that it required some sort of wadding or binding, Sophia lifted her skirt to her knees and yanked on her petticoat.

"Here let me," Jeremy said when the material refused to tear. He reached into his pocket and drew out a folded knife. He drove the small blade into the hem and tore the material from there. The linen ripped in an uneven line, climbing higher than was seemly.

"Careful, young man," Uncle Edward said through a clenched jaw.

Jeremy turned three shades of red, stammered an apology—twice, three times—and offered the dangling end to Sophia to complete the job.

She had soon ripped a length of material free from her petticoat and folded it over the wound. "Just lean on me, Uncle," Sophia said after seeing him sway a touch. She exchanged a glance with Jeremy and then helped Uncle Edward to his feet. He roared out a string of religious words that had nothing to do with asking the Almighty for counsel.

Taking the green sash from the waist of her cream gown, Sophia tied it around the wound and then, supporting his elbow, she tucked his cane under her arm and assisted her uncle back to the path. Jeremy secured Uncle Edward's other arm as they guided him back the way they had come.

"Is all well?" William asked, calling across the distance. He was sitting astride a brown Arabian with a black mane at the edge of the woods. "I heard the blast of a rifle."

"Come quickly, William!" Sophia shouted. "We have to get your father back to the manor straightaway. He's been shot!"

The household was at sixes and sevens for the rest of the day. William remained calm; in the woods, he had helped his father up onto his stallion and then led the horse to the manor at a rapid pace, trotting at his father's side. As soon as they entered the stable yard, William sent one of the grooms for the surgeon.

Aunt Hazel screamed when she saw Uncle Edward being led through the front door. She ordered William to send for the surgeon—which he had already done—and had helped Uncle upstairs to his room. Uncle found this most undignified and complained profusely, but as he could only shout between bouts of pain, Aunt Hazel ignored his protests.

Daphne turned a ghastly color when she saw the blood on the entrance tiles. She rushed to her father's side, but once she saw that he was not at death's door, she distracted him with inane teasing; though her continuing pale complexion caused Sophia some concern. Papa suggested informing Constable Marley, setting him to the task of identifying the shooter, but Sophia pointed out that they already had a Bow Street Runner on the case.

When all was said and done, Uncle Edward was in pain but not fatally injured; the wound incapacitated his left arm but fortunately he was right-handed. Aunt Hazel spent the evening by his side, leaving the large dinner table to seat a mere party of five with Papa acting as host. Jeremy was invited to join them for the meal and they all tried valiantly to *not* discuss the shooting, Stacks' demise, or Andrew's murder.

Within no time, rumors were rampant in West Ravenwood about who was involved in the latest shooting. Gossips doled out blame lavishly. The majority deemed poachers responsible for Uncle Edward's condition, but Sophia wasn't convinced. "Poachers" seemed an easy target—a nebulous and faceless people.

Still, she kept her opinion to herself. There were too many variables to jump to any conclusions.

CHAPTER THIRTEEN

Tumbling Down

Poisons, not rifles, were on Sophia's mind when Betty brought a letter into the drawing room from her mother the next morning. Sophia had entertained a small hope—very small—that her mother might enlighten her about various poisons, their sources, and the symptoms; Mama had often extolled her knowledge of plants and their properties. Though it was more likely that she meant when and how to tie up roses, Sophia had taken a chance that her mother might prove helpful.

While her last letter to Risely Hall had been full of questions, Sophia received a reply amounting to exactly nothing. Mama, instead, complained about Papa's decision to stay in West Ravenwood a little longer. She related anecdotes of Henry's latest escapades with Walter Ellerby and—in what was surely meant to be an amusing account—about a robin redbreast in the twiggy syringa near the garden gate. Really, it was most unhelpful.

Sophia sighed heavily as she glanced toward the window. A

particularly strong gust of wind threw the rain against the glass. It would seem that the weather was conspiring against her, too.

She huffed, in a dejected sort of way.

Continuing her investigation with Jeremy had been her intent for the day, but it was not to be. Jeremy had sent a note blaming the rain for his decision to seek out Andrew's cohorts on his own. Sophia was quite certain it had more to do with the commercial areas of town in which two of Andrew's friends worked—shabby, though not squalid.

Either that or he was trying to be kind, allowing her to spend the day fussing over Uncle Edward. However, Aunt Hazel had thrown herself into the role of fusser-in-charge, and required no assistance from Sophia—or Daphne, for that matter. William had taken himself off somewhere, and Papa was ensconced in the library.

The library. What an excellent place to bide awhile, a place full of information. Books galore about many subjects.

Such as . . . poisons.

Sophia could not, should not, blame the weather, Jeremy, or Uncle Edward for her inactivity; it fell on her own shoulders. Spending the day rehashing events was getting her nowhere. Besides, she needed a distraction—not necessarily from the case, but from her fellow investigator.

Jeremy was often in her thoughts. *Too* often. His expressive face and compelling personality jumped from her memories and into her mind regularly. She stared into the air and tapped her toes, lost in thought—invariably about Jeremy Fraser, Bow Street Runner.

Yes, she definitely needed a distraction.

Sophia carefully folded the letter from her mother, and then tore it in half.

Daphne, lounging on the settee, looked up from her fashion magazine full of the latest styles from London and raised an eyebrow. She flipped a page with a snap—a snap of impatience, it would seem. "Why are you just sitting there?" Daphne asked, her tone peevish.

"I wasn't just sitting; I was think—"

"You should be *investigating*! That's why you came to Allenton—to help discover Andrew's murderer. And now that they've tried to kill Father, too, what are you doing?" She shifted in her chair as if trying to straighten her skirts. "You're staring out the window." A loud harrumph demonstrated just how annoyed Daphne felt.

"Any of us might have been the shooter's target, Daphne. We don't really know. We were huddled close together and rifles are notoriously inaccurate."

Daphne stared at Sophia. "Is that supposed to make me feel better?" Her eyes glistened with unshed tears, and Sophia regretted her words immediately.

"This shooting might have had nothing to do with Andrew's killing," Sophia said, rather lamely.

"Again, how does that help?"

"You're right, it doesn't." Sophia slowly shook her head. "Besides, it would be an odd happenstance to have two murderous persons running through the grounds at the same time."

"Very odd," Daphne muttered, lifting the magazine closer to her nose. "Be that as it may, why are you not trying to find out who *did* shoot at you?"

"No clues were left behind yesterday, and we didn't see the

villain—only heard him—and we're not certain who was the target. With no new information, we're back to solving Mr. Stacks' and Andrew's cases where we might have a chance at success."

"I thought you were going to help. I'm afraid, Sophia," Daphne said, sounding much more aggravated than afraid. "I fear going out of doors; I fear going anywhere. I don't know what to expect. I want to stay in my room behind a locked door and never come out again."

"You would need food and the necessary every once in a while."

Daphne laughed at Sophia's words, as she was meant to, and then her expression grew serious again. "You need to expose this villain, Sophia. He must pay for these lives he has ruined . . . and ended."

Sophia nodded and sighed deeply. "It's not the work of a minute, Daphne. I'm new at this. If villains were easy to catch, investigators would not be necessary. I'm not sleuthing today, as Mr. Fraser is speaking to Andrew's friends this morning."

"That sounds pointless."

Sophia ignored the comment, knowing that it was fear forming her cousin's words, not intellect. But Sophia agreed with one aspect of Daphne's complaint; she should do *something*.

"May I use the library?" Sophia asked, seeing Stacks in her mind—the ghastly color of his skin when he lay on the table. Yes, the library might be able to offer her some information . . . possibly.

Had the library books been cataloged or arranged in any sensible fashion, Sophia would have turned to the large, well-stocked room far sooner. Unfortunately, the collection at Allenton Park was in a haphazard state—none of the Waverleys over the years had shown any inclination toward organizing the many volumes. As a result, fifteenth-century history and the study of stamps sat beside travel logs and descriptions of islands of the South Seas.

"Thought of something?" Daphne asked, returning to her magazine and showing no sign of wishing to move with Sophia to the other room.

"Yes, indeed: poisons. I was hoping to find some information about poisons in the library." She stood, gathering up the ripped paper for disposal. "We assumed that Stacks was killed with wolfsbane, but your gardener says there is none in the flower beds. So, I would like to verify that nothing else could have caused the same effects."

Daphne nodded. "You might want to ask Mrs. Curtis about where the books on poisons might be. She has a knack of finding things. Better than me, at any rate."

"Excellent," Sophia said, opening the door to the hall. "I'll do just that."

———

Jeremy had lied.

It was not the kind of lie that would send him to Hell or have him thrown into a dungeon, never to be seen again. However, it was the kind of lie that might get him into trouble with a pretty young lady staying at Allenton Park. That was even more daunting.

Jeremy had claimed the rain as his rationale for denying Sophia's wish to accompany him in his continuing investigations, which would take him to the seedier side of town and into questionable company. It would be messy and unhealthy—not a good place for a properly brought up young lady.

That was the lie.

Andrew Waverley's friends were part of the middle class, not the criminal class. In truth, visiting them at home or at their places of business would not put Sophia's health at risk directly. But the same could not be said for her overall well-being. Therein lay his objection: The more the killer saw the two of them investigating together, the more likely this twisted individual would make *Sophia* his target, see *her* as a threat.

She could have been shot in Glendor Wood along with her uncle. They had been huddled together, after all; that Sophia had not been hit as well was nothing short of miraculous.

So, Jeremy would do whatever he could to keep her safe—even if that meant spending less time in her company and spouting an occasional lie. She would understand . . . when he explained it to her.

If he explained it to her.

———————

As it turned out, visiting Andrew's friends was a waste of time. They were not in the least helpful. Oh, they made all the right sounds—tsking, and huffing, agreeing and plying Jeremy with questions—but when push came to shove, they offered Jeremy nothing new. No added information at all.

Todd Rummage was a cheeky young man, overly confident and comfortable with his place in the world. His father was the squire of West Ravenwood, and Todd clearly believed that he would follow in his father's footsteps. Rather stout and short with a ski slope nose and a wispy mustache, he spoke with bravado when Jeremy caught him at home. Todd described Andrew as a regular out-and-outer, and his sad recollections of their escapades rang as true—and of little value.

Baxter Temple, the banker's son, added to Jeremy's knowledge of Andrew by describing their pranks. Knocking over haystacks and racing across fields—some planted and others fallow—bathing in the pond, and knocking Joan Bossidy into said pond. Mr. Temple laughed as he described the girl's outrage. Jeremy was unimpressed; his opinion of Baxter Temple and Andrew Waverley plummeted.

Shirley Chips, pretty and petite with thick black hair and quick steps, proved to be the most interesting source of information.

"No, not by then," she said when Jeremy asked if she and Andrew were still considered a couple after his year away at Oxford. "He were interested in several girls." She laughed. "Yes, all at the same time. I could never keep up with the gossip. After a while I stopped caring."

She paused and stared out the window at the rain for a moment. "After a while," she repeated.

They were standing in the back room of the bakery. The heat from the ovens, long since tamped down, dried the damp air wafting through the open door.

"He wasn't likely to settle down anytime soon," she finally continued. "Especially with the likes of me—he needed to find a lady. A lady for Allenton Park. But he were fun. Yes, indeed. We had many a laugh; he was good company and always up for a lark."

Shirley shook her head, pulling her thoughts from her memories. "But if it were jealousy that did him in, you're going to have to talk to Audra. Audra Pratt, the apothecary's daughter. She had Andrew in her sights, but he kept putting her off . . . Or, oh yes, or Charlotte Dewey. Don't know her from Adam, but it were put about that Andrew was trying to look under her skirts. I imagine the reverend took care of that right quick . . . but ya never know."

When Jeremy did finally track Audra down at the haberdashery, she waved him off with little more than a how-do-you-do. She was too busy to bother with the likes of him. And Charlotte was not at the circulating library or the millinery as Mrs. Dewey believed.

All in all, the damp, rainy day proved to be most unproductive. Jeremy returned to the inn to plan his next steps, but found that he was distracted.

Sophia Thompson kept popping into his mind, and he was disinclined to shoo her away.

———————

After having spent the better part of three hours in the library, Sophia closed *The Daily Garden* with a slap.

Her frustration was extreme. She had been through a quarter—no, perhaps an eighth—of the books in the library to no avail. She had found several volumes about roses, the properties of good gardening soil, and the best plants to grow side by side. But she found nothing about poisons.

Sitting in one of the armchairs near the window, Papa frowned over the top of his newspaper. "Is something amiss?" he asked. They had been sitting quietly and companionably for some time without any need of discussion.

"I can't find any books describing poisons."

"I would think that would be a good thing," he said with a reflective expression, and then returned to the article he was reading.

Sophia sauntered over to the window and leaned on the back of her father's chair, staring out the window. "Perhaps I should visit the circulating library."

"Or speak to the gardener. He would be a fount of knowledge."

"Mr. Phillips?"

"No, Mr. Quinn, the head gardener. Very nice man. I'm sure he'll be able to help you."

Sophia continued to stare through the window, but no longer sightlessly lost in thought. No, she was watching a rather odd-looking woman disappear down the path to Glendor Wood.

The woman wore a strange combination of skirts and aprons—plural—on her ample form. A long blue skirt hung to her feet, a shorter pink skirt to her calves. Atop these were two aprons, no longer white, but rather smudged with green and yellow stains. One apron covered her belly, the other covered the woman's backside. She wore a baggy jacket with huge sagging pockets, and a perfectly delightful hat, replete with three long pheasant feathers. It was rather bizarre.

And curious, for Sophia did not recognize the woman at all.

"Who is that?" Sophia asked her father as the feathers, and the woman wearing them, bobbed out of sight.

"Who?" he asked without looking up.

"Never mind. I'll asked Benton," Sophia said, leaving the library and heading to the main entrance.

There, she found Benton staring past the threshold of the front door. Upon hearing her steps, the elderly butler looked over his shoulder and slowly swung it closed. "There you are," he said as if he had been looking for her. "I wondered where you might be."

"I did not know you were looking for me, Benton. I was in the library with Father."

"Not to worry, Miss Thompson. I told her to come back tomorrow."

"Who?" Sophia stared at Benton with a frown creasing her forehead.

"There you are," Mrs. Curtis said, entering the front hall from the direction of the kitchen. Her keys jingled as she moved, and her heels tapped across the tiles until she stood directly in front of Sophia. "You had a visitor. Benton told her to come back tomorrow."

The housekeeper glanced behind Sophia—no doubt at Mr. Benton—and nodded. Seconds later, Benton's footsteps could be heard echoing through the hall, leaving the two women alone.

"Would you be so kind as to instruct her to use the service entrance next time," Mrs. Curtis said waspishly. "It is most unseemly for a person such as Bertha Tumbler to beg entry at the *front* door."

"Who is Bertha Tumbler?" Sophia asked. "And why does she want to see me?"

"I have no idea why she wishes to speak with you, Miss Thompson. It is not for Benton to ask such a question. As to who she is, Bertha Tumbler is a spinster, the blacksmith's sister. She has a cottage and plot of land on the other side of West Ravenwood. She sells plants, seeds, and vegetables to keep food on her table. Rather eccentric and rarely leaves her house. I'm actually surprised to see her out and about; she normally keeps to herself. As to why she asked for you, I expect you'll find out when she returns tomorrow. She said something to Benton about not being willing to talk to a Runner. So, there you have it. Your own little mystery, and it will soon be solved."

There was a sarcastic tone to the housekeeper's explanation that put Sophia's teeth on edge.

"Indeed. Thank you, Mrs. Curtis," Sophia said with a forced smile.

Why would a perfect stranger—and a *strange* stranger, at that—come knocking on the Waverleys' front door asking for Sophia?

A sense of foreboding settled across her shoulders. Something was wrong.

———✦———

The next morning, Sophia worked on her needlework in the drawing room with Daphne, watching the clock as hour after hour ticked by with no visit from Bertha Tumbler. Uncle Edward was showing signs of improvement, sitting in a comfortable chair in his room and complaining about his meals. As a result, Daphne was no longer overwrought with anxiety, and back to planning her Season in London. She seemed to vacillate between abject terror and abject apathy.

The distraction was almost welcome. Almost.

"I quite like this lace," Daphne said, pointing to an illustration in the catalog on her lap.

Sophia could only see that it was white. She nodded with a half smile; it was rather weak, but Daphne didn't notice.

"Mother does as well, I asked her at breakfast. We shall wait, of course. Not order anything as yet. But I'll be ready the moment Mother says we're to go." She smiled at the catalog and flipped the next page.

"That's nice," Sophia said, not paying the least bit of attention.

"If you like I can ask Mother for a length of lace for you as well."

"That's nice."

"We could have a gown made for you at the same time. I'm quite certain Mother would not mind. A day dress or a carriage gown—probably not a ball gown, as you would not have anywhere to wear it."

"That's nice." Sophia was baffled that Daphne could be diverted by such trivia when murder and mayhem met them at every door.

"What's wrong, Sophia?"

She looked up to find her cousin staring at her. "What do you mean?"

She dropped her eyes back to her canvas and saw that it was a tangled mess; it looked nothing like the daisy it was meant to be. With a huff, she secured her needle in the material and tossed the hoop onto the seat beside her. "I keep wondering when Bertha Tumbler is going to arrive and what it is that she has to tell me."

"Or ask of you."

"Yes, or ask. I'm not enjoying the wait; this inactivity is most unsettling. I should be doing something!" Sophia stood and planted her feet in a take-charge manner. "Enough. Where does Bertha Tumbler live? I'll go there rather than wait any longer."

"Should you? By yourself? Horrors. I'd go with you but I promised Father a game of chess," Daphne said, as if glad to have the excuse. "Best not go alone, though. Take Betty. It's not far really, an easy walk to the other side of town. I'm sure Benton or one of the other servants can tell you where the Tumbler house is located."

Sophia found this to be a most estimable idea and set about doing just that. Within a quarter hour, she had her bonnet tied, gloves on, Betty by her side, and directions to the cottage.

It took a little less than twenty minutes to get to the Tumbler place. It was a small cottage set off from the main road by an overabundant garden enclosed by a white fence. It had charm and character and . . . an open door.

Sophia frowned. Her heart began to pound as she stepped through the gate and up the stone-paved walk. The gaping entrance into the cottage was clearly visible as they approached—a gloomy interior rife with shadows.

"Strange," Sophia said in a strangled voice.

Betty offered a reasonable explanation. "A warm day. Likely letting the wind blow through."

Sophia nodded but did not agree, nor did she feel any better.

"Mrs. Tumbler!" she called into the shadows. "Are you here?"

It was dark and dank inside the cottage, smelling of earth and drying plants. It took several moments for her eyes to adjust to the low light cast by the small casement windows. As they did, the table in the center of the room came into focus, the bed in the corner and the unlit fireplace catercorner from the door. Rows of flowers, twigs, and roots hung from brackets on the ceiling, drying.

Betty made a gurgling sound in her throat. It was half gasp and half scream.

Sophia whirled around to see a mound of clothes lying on the floor by the table. An arm stretched out from the mound, cradling a head. Both were soaked in blood, while glassy eyes stared across the room, unblinking.

Bertha Tumbler was dead.

CHAPTER FOURTEEN

The Fitters

For some time, Sophia neither moved nor breathed.

"Is she dead?" she finally asked in a whisper, though it was easy to see that Bertha had, indeed, shuffled off her mortal coil. The blind stare and the amount of blood puddled on the floor told the story even if she could ignore the gaping slit in her throat, clearly the cause of Bertha's demise.

Sophia approached the corpse, slowly and carefully. She apologized to the dead woman even as she reached out to hold her cold wrist. There was no pulse and the woman was not breathing. She was, indeed, dead.

Bertha Tumbler was a stranger, and yet Sophia felt overwhelmed with sadness. She breathed deeply through her mouth, struggling to keep her stomach calm and her nerves steady.

"Get Constable Marley, Detective Fraser, and the surgeon," Sophia told Betty, who was still standing beside the door, shaking like a leaf. A task would distract the poor maid, and hopefully supplant this horrid sight.

"Yes, miss."

Betty was out the door faster than a whip, and Sophia was left alone in the eerie silence. Glancing into the shadows of the room, Sophia squinted, looking for any signs that the murderer was still within. With great relief she saw that nothing moved. There was no large furniture to hide behind and the back door led to a shelf-lined but equally unoccupied storeroom.

Shifting to the other side of the body, Sophia stared at Bertha for some minutes, willing her heart to calm and her shaking hands to still. With the light no longer in her eyes, Sophia could see that Bertha was lying on her side with a sharp knife next to her. As it was spattered with blood and therefore quite possibly the murder weapon, Sophia left it where it lay. She was not an official investigator yet and would not want to be accused of tampering with evidence—a warning that she had read in *Investigating Murder and Mayhem*.

Turning, she noted that the front door lock had not been forced and that the room was tidy—no overturned chairs or broken crockery. The assassin had not pushed his way in, nor had there been a fight. A collection of herbs lay on the table—half had been chopped and placed in small jars. It would seem that Bertha had been preparing bottles when the killer had knocked on the door. Pinching the leaves in one jar and rubbing them together produced the flowery smell of lavender. A shelf of glass jars offered tarragon, chives, sage, and many other herbs. The only label that gave Sophia pause identified the shriveled leaves as monkshood. It was half full.

Wolfsbane had been the instrument of Stacks' death. Monkshood and wolfsbane were one and the same. Sophia eyed it with trepidation, but did not open the jar.

Continuing her search, Sophia returned to the storeroom for a closer look and found three rabbits hanging in the back of the small rough room that had been added, somewhat haphazardly, to the rear of the cottage. On nearby shelves, snares and ropes were a tangled mess. It would seem Bertha Tumbler had not been above poaching a few rabbits for her dinner.

A piece of folded paper had been stuffed into one of the snares. Sophia pulled it free, but replaced it when she saw that it was a personal letter.

A half hour or so passed before Sophia heard footsteps coming up the walk. Constable Marley was the first to rush through the door, Mr. Reyer hard on his heels. Both were panting, and when Jeremy arrived in much the same state, the cottage was suddenly full of the noises of three gentlemen trying to catch their breath.

As such, Sophia's sigh of relief was not audible—being alone with a corpse had not been a comfortable situation. She did her best to hide her anxiety, dismay, and roiling stomach—disappointed that she had reacted adversely to the violent death. The gentlemen did not have to clench their fists or avert their eyes.

Naturally, the surgeon focused on Bertha, announcing the obvious—that she had died from a loss of blood.

Constable Marley wandered the room, clumsily shifting chairs and blankets, even looking in the kettle, of all places, and in the fireplace. Then he watched Jeremy as the Runner examined the different herb bottles on the shelf, paced out the room, and wrote notes in his journal.

"Why are you here?" the constable asked finally. His words were clipped, his expression angry as he glared at Jeremy. "This has nothing to do with Andrew Waverley; you are out of place and interfering with an investigation. The parish will not pay you for this work."

Jeremy stared at the constable for a moment with a clenched jaw. "Nothing to do with Andrew? That remains to be seen. However, you cannot say the same thing about Stacks' murder. There are several poisons on these shelves, including monkshood."

"Bertha came to Allenton Park to speak to me yesterday, Constable Marley," Sophia said, jumping to Jeremy's defense. "I don't know why, but it stands to reason that whatever her purpose, it had something to do with Andrew or Stacks. The whole town knows that I'm helping with the investigation. The rash of violent deaths have to be connected. It would be foolhardy to think otherwise."

Constable Marley bristled at the word "foolhardy" and made a sweeping gesture with his arms. "Matters not. You are in the way. Out you go, both of you. Reyer and I have work to do."

And then, as if wishing to appear benevolent, he added, "I will let you know as soon as we have solved this case."

———•———

"I would like to go back, miss," Betty said as they marched up the hill to Allenton Park. "Back to Risely Hall."

They had just parted company with a very disgruntled Mr. Fraser, who had chuntered most of the way back through the town. Still, he had pulled himself out of his temper long enough to bow elegantly to both Sophia and Betty as they said goodbye. And now Betty had quickened her pace as they neared Allenton Park and forced Sophia into a brisk walk—nearly a trot.

She frowned, glancing at the girl. More than a little disheveled, Betty's dress was smeared with dirt, and blood edged the hem of her skirt. But more concerning was the fearful look on the maid's face.

"Please, miss. I'll take a stage. There'll be no need to inconvenience anyone. I would just rather not be at a place that has a murderer running around, killing willy-nilly."

"Not willy-nilly, Betty," Sophia said, despite knowing that her words were not in the least helpful. "There is a purpose behind these killings; they all tie together in some way. I just haven't figured out how as yet. But I will. It's only a matter of time."

Sophia tried to instill her words with confidence and reassurance, but even she could hear the skeptical tone. "I know you're upset; it's not surprising. I would suggest that you either rest the remainder of the day, or throw yourself into some labor-intense work so that you don't have a chance to dwell on it. Put what you've seen today out of your mind, if you can. If you still wish to go back to Welford Mills in a couple of days, I'll make the arrangements."

Sophia had no idea how she would do so, but she would cross that bridge when she came to it.

There was a carriage waiting by the open front door as they approached Allenton. It was not overly large, and with only two horses and no driver, it was clear that the passengers had not come any great distance. The diminutive figure of Marty Sneed, the new boot boy, held the horses in place, yawning with boredom.

Skipping around the vehicle, barely giving it a glance, Betty almost crossed the threshold into Allenton ahead of Sophia, but Benton stopped her with a look that could have curdled cream. When Sophia nodded for Betty to go ahead, the girl lifted her cheeks in an attempted smile. Her complexion was mottled white and red, her hair hung in bedraggled clumps from where she'd been pulling at it, and her expression was that of a traumatized young woman. In short, she looked rather ghastly, and Sophia felt terrible about having dragged the poor girl through such an afternoon.

Sophia knew by the heat on her cheeks that her color was high as well, but her hands no longer trembled and her steps were sure as ever. She had weathered a terrible storm and kept a level head. There was hope that she would find her footing as a Bow Street Investigator, after all.

"Miss Dewey and the reverend are in the drawing room, Miss Thompson," Benton said, still holding the door. "With Mr. and Mrs. Waverley."

Sophia looked back at Benton with surprise. "Uncle is downstairs?"

"Yes, miss. Insisted on it. Wouldn't stand for any more molly-coddling." Benton allowed the corner of his mouth to curl up, and Sophia was fairly certain that the words originated from Uncle Edward.

"Indeed, no mollycoddling," Sophia said with a straight face.

While not enamored with the idea of spending time with the Deweys, Sophia thought that she might check to see that her aunt and uncle did not require a distraction. Placing her bonnet and gloves on one of the front hall chairs, she made her way to the drawing room and tapped on the door before entering.

The large room was not crowded, as neither Daphne nor William had joined their parents to play host to Reverend Dewey and his daughter. At the far end by the wide French doors, Aunt Hazel stood behind Uncle Edward's chair, while Charlotte and her father sat across from them on the velvet settee. Coats and bonnets had not been left with Benton, indicating it was not going to be a long visit.

They all looked up and watched Sophia as she crossed the floor to join them. She was greeted with enthusiasm. Aunt Hazel was particularly effusive.

"*There* she is. I told you, Charlotte, that you had no need to be concerned." Aunt Hazel stepped away from Uncle Edward's wingback chair and turned to Sophia, taking both her hands in her own. "Just out and about wandering the garden, as I surmised."

Aunt Hazel squeezed Sophia's fingers before dropping her hands and bobbed her eyebrows as if trying to relay a message.

Flummoxed, Sophia merely nodded—it was the safest response.

"Oh, I am so pleased to see that you're well, Miss Thompson. The gossipmongers can be so cruel." Charlotte rose and stepped closer. She wore a soft pink carriage gown with a ruffled neckline and pleated skirts. Charlotte's father, standing near the mantel, wore the usual attire of a clergyman, as drab and dreary as his expression. He greeted Sophia with a formal nod, dipping his mop of unruly gray hair.

After acknowledging the greetings, Sophia turned back to Charlotte. "Gossip . . . about me?" She had a feeling that this conversation was not going to go well.

"Oh dear, you didn't know," Charlotte said with a worried frown. "I'm so terribly sorry to be the harbinger of such uncomfortable news." She glanced at her father as if needing reassurance. "They say—*they* being the gossips—that Bertha Tumbler was murdered and that you were there. A witness."

Sophia ignored Aunt Hazel's look of warning and turned to address Charlotte. "Gossip is rarely right and this is a case in point. I arrived at Bertha Tumbler's cottage well after the incident. I most definitely was *not* present when she was murdered. What a cruel suggestion."

Charlotte's eyes widened. "Oh, I'm so glad," she said with obvious relief. "I was quite horrified on your behalf. I did not mean to suggest that there was something improper in your behavior, not at all. I thought that you might have seen something important and raced after the killer. I can see you doing something like that. There's a heroic flair to your character."

Sophia snorted, thinking about her pounding heart as she glanced around Bertha's cottage, praying the killer had taken his leave. "Nothing heroic about happening upon a murder scene," she said, deciding an abridged version of the day's events might satisfy everyone's curiosity—one without drama and unpleasant details.

"The rumor mill was wrong but not by much. I discovered Bertha Tumbler's body when I went to call. I had Betty run for the constable." She neglected to mention Jeremy's presence, as it might not sit well with her uncle. He was not pleased with the Runner investigating anything other than Andrew's murder. He, like many others, did not believe the incidents were connected.

Aunt Hazel looked troubled. "So, it's true then. Bertha Tumbler *was* murdered." She paused for a moment, her eyes focused inward. "Is there any chance it was an accident?"

Sophia shook her head, trying not to think of Bertha's slit throat. "I'm afraid not."

"Time to change the topic," Aunt Hazel suggested, likely seeing Sophia's suddenly nauseated expression. She slid behind Uncle Edward's chair once more. "The country fair, perhaps. Are you going to have a booth for the church at the next fair, Reverend?"

As the conversation veered away from the sensational to the banal, Charlotte crossed the room and secured Sophia's attention with a touch on her arm. They sauntered to the windows as Sophia pointed out the buds of the asters; purples and pinks preparing to bloom in profusion.

Seated on the window seat, Sophia could see into the room and watch for any signs of distress in her kin. Sophia thought that all was well, for a few minutes. A very few minutes, as she soon learned.

"Sophia, I'm scared," Charlotte said, wide-eyed. "This *flood* of unexplained deaths in West Ravenwood. West Ravenwood of all places! And now, an ordinary woman slain in her kitchen. There's no telling who'll be next. There's no rhyme or reason. Are we all in danger, or just those in league with the Waverleys?"

Sophia snorted a laugh as if Charlotte were making a joke. In league, indeed. It sounded like the Waverleys were a satanic cult or a criminal gang, not a family of the upper crust.

"No, indeed. Not everyone is in danger. If I were to hazard a guess, which is all we can do at this stage, I would say that there *is* a rhyme and reason; we just have not figured it out yet. And I believe the family association is significant."

And then . . . Sophia tried to remember if she had ever specifically mentioned that Bertha had been killed in her *kitchen*. Though she supposed the town gossips could have spread that rumor; it was not hard to guess, as a cottage was usually more kitchen than anything else . . .

"Really?" Charlotte replied. "Andrew thinks that it's all nonsense, that the murders have nothing to do with us . . . you . . . the family. Other than his brother's killing, of course."

Sophia frowned at Charlotte, wondering if she realized her mistake. "You said Andrew . . . do you mean William? That William calls it nonsense? And when you speak of the *family*, are you referring to the Waverleys?"

"Did I say Andrew? I meant William, of course. I'm so glad that he wasn't here to hear my slip. He would have been terribly hurt."

"Do you still think of Andrew?" Sophia asked gently, trying to understand how close the pair had been before her cousin's death. Perhaps not a sociably acceptable question, but Sophia could hardly ignore the opportunity.

"No, not anymore. I had become close to Andrew, without a doubt. I thought of him with great affection before he died. But he was devious in his attentions—hid them from his family . . . and others. William, on the other hand, has a quieter charm than Andrew, an easier manner." She giggled girlishly. "I did not realize how different the brothers were or how much more suited William was to the role of his father's heir until after Andrew's death. It was Mrs. Curtis who pointed out William's stellar qualities."

"Mrs. Curtis?"

"Yes, the family was so terribly distraught about the murder that I visited regularly to offer what comfort I could. It was a difficult time, as you can imagine." She smiled wistfully and breathed out slowly in a sad sigh. "Difficult for us all. I was devastated. My mother did not understand how I felt—she had not seen how close Andrew and I had become. But Mrs. Curtis had. One day, as I was taking my leave, I sat in one of the seats of the entrance hall, exhausted from all the emotions . . . and Mrs. Curtis sat in the chair next to me. She asked if she could do anything to help. We talked for hours and she helped me find perspective, helped me stay strong. I used that strength to aid Mrs. Waverley and William in their hour of need."

"That's amazing," Sophia said, ignoring the drama of her words. "And William? How does he fit into all this?"

Charlotte tittered a laugh, soft and musical. "Mrs. Curtis talked about how much William was like Andrew, but a gentler version. She encouraged me to look deeper. And the more I got to know William, the more I realized that our personalities were more suited to each other. I saw that Mrs. Curtis was right: Andrew was *not* my match, William is. And unlike Andrew, William does not want to look higher for a wife. He sees no gap in our social positions."

"Well, that does explain a few things," Sophia said, more comfortable with Charlotte than she had been thus far. "I've seen you and Mrs. Curtis chatting quite amiably several times. As to William . . . well, I can understand the attraction there."

"Not unlike you and Mr. Fraser."

"I beg your pardon?"

Charlotte leaned forward, putting her hand lightly on Sophia's arm. "I've noticed the way he looks at you and . . . I've noticed you looking back."

"Nonsense," Sophia said, but with no heat. "He thinks of me as a colleague, nothing else. Certainly not in a romantic sense, which is what I assume you're getting at."

"There is nothing that says Mr. Fraser cannot be both a colleague and an admirer."

Sophia frowned. "It would get in the way."

She didn't like the way her heart accelerated at Charlotte's suggestion, nor the sudden vision of Jeremy's intense stare and the way it made her feel invincible.

"In. The. Way," she repeated, more to establish the thought in her mind than to convince Charlotte.

CHAPTER FIFTEEN

An Arresting Development

As Sophia waved the Dewey carriage away, her eyes lifted to an approaching figure. Someone was hastening up the drive. She recognized his bearing and his brisk manner of walking immediately.

Jeremy bowed and doffed his hat as the carriage passed on its way to the gate, and Sophia watched Charlotte's arm stretch out of the window with a casual wave.

Rushing across the flat stones, Sophia met Jeremy at the first step. He was rather frazzled, and paid no heed to social niceties. He did not ask after the family, her health, or comment about the weather or compliment her looks. It was clearly a time of urgency.

"They found a note," he said without preamble. "From Mr. Tumbler to his sister. He tells all—accuses his sister of poisoning Stacks and blames her for forcing him to take justice into his hands."

Sophia stared at Jeremy, trying to understand. "That makes

no sense," she said eventually. She continued to stare as his anxious expression cleared, replaced by a grin . . . a grin?

"I quite agree, no sense at all," he said. "What killer would warn his victim? Mr. Tumbler would not *warn* Bertha that he was going to kill her—"

"And to put it in writing would be foolhardy in the extreme. Anyone could get ahold of the note and use it as evidence against him."

"Anyone—such as a daft constable."

"Exactly, such as Constable Marley. Besides, if Bertha had received such a letter, she would have sought protection or gone into hiding. Even if she thought her brother to be full of bluster, she would not have gone about her day as usual, chopping herbs. She would not have let him in the door, either, if he threatened her. Nothing was disturbed in her cottage. He wasn't there!"

"We don't know that as a certainty."

"If someone threatened you, would you let them into your house?"

"No, of course not."

"Exactly."

"And the wording . . ." Jeremy reached into his jacket and pulled out his journal. "I had to write it down." He lifted his eyes to hers. "Marley would not let me have the letter to study. I copied it in its entirety: *Dear Bertha, sister of mine,*" he read aloud. "*I don't know why you killed Mr. Stacks but you ought not to have done so. He were a good person just doing his job. He did not know it were you who killed Mr. Andrew Waverley. Stacks had not figured it out yet. I can't have you going about killing people as you see fit. You have forced me to be the hand of justice.*

Your brother, Harvey Tumbler."

Sophia snickered as Jeremy got to the end of the note, then she clamped a hand over her mouth. "I apologize, that was insensitive . . . But really? *Your brother, Harvey Tumbler?*" Sophia erupted into a giggle. "First name and last name *and* relationship? Who talks like that to a sister? It's almost as ridiculous as addressing the letter to *sister of mine.*"

"It is a fraud, of course. A fake note. And it cleverly lays the blame of both Andrew's and Stacks' murders on Bertha. Who is now dead and cannot defend herself," Jeremy said, glancing behind her at the manor. He nodded, acknowledging whoever was standing at the door. "We are under scrutiny, Miss Thompson. Shall we go for a stroll?"

He offered her his elbow and led her toward the side garden at a relaxed pace.

They sauntered with shoulders back, taking light steps and remaining silent for some minutes as they tried to exude a sense of fellowship and comradery—not the aura of sleuthing partners. Following the path, they wove between the flower beds, and finally feeling comfortable, they continued their conversation.

"Where was the letter found?" Sophia asked, still watching the path ahead. It was likely the letter that Sophia had found and then returned without reading.

"In the shed attached to Bertha's cottage—a storeroom of sorts. It was tucked under a snare."

Oh dear, it was *that* letter. She would have to learn to ignore decorum and manners, plunge ahead and get all the answers . . . even if it meant engaging in some discourteous behavior such as reading someone's letter. "Under a poacher's snare?"

"Likely, but we cannot be certain."

"You like to deal in certainties, Mr. Fraser?"

"Yes, most times. Don't you?"

"Actually, now that you ask, I do as well. So, let me say this: I'm *certain* that Bertha, having received a threatening note from her brother, would not have folded it and placed it with her traps. In a pocket, perhaps, or tossed it in the trash. But she would not have stepped into her storeroom and tucked it neatly behind a snare."

"You could *certainly* be right," Jeremy said with a smile in his voice.

She did not look at him directly, as there was a distinct possibility that he might see how much she was enjoying their conversation and his company . . . and it was an inappropriate time to make such a discovery. "So, this note was meant to sidetrack the investigators," she observed.

"Exactly as it has done with Constable Marley."

Sophia glanced skyward, knowing that Jeremy would not lead her into a shrub as they walked. She considered the many possibilities of the note. "It was rather foolish, wasn't it?"

"To leave the note? Indeed."

"Mr. Fraser?" Sophia asked as she watched the wheeling starlings. "Would a blacksmith use the words 'hand of justice'?"

"That, my dear Miss Thompson, is not the question."

"It's not?"

"No, I think we should find out if Harvey Tumbler, blacksmith of West Ravenwood, can even write at all."

Sophia jerked her head up. "Yes, of course," she agreed. "And if by an odd happenstance he *can* write—for that would have required schooling of some sort—we should get a sample of said handwriting and compare it to the note. Better still, we could dictate the letter to him while he writes it down. We could compare the two directly." Then with a toss of her head, Sophia huffed. "It will be hard to do without the note in hand . . . to compare them, I mean."

Jeremy nodded, but he did not look downcast. "If need be, I can go to the justice and ask that he intervene with Constable Marley." He pointed to his chest. "I'll soon be a Bow Street Runner, you know."

Sophia laughed, feeling very pleased with her career choice and Jeremy's company. One day *she* would say the same thing, and her words would be instilled with just as much pride.

———

The next morning, Jeremy rose at his customary time, performed his customary ablutions, and dressed in his customary suit of grays. However, when he stepped down onto the floor of the common room of the inn, it was oddly full. Every table, every seat, and every corner of the room was occupied. And the patrons did not look happy—at least not with Jeremy. A murmur began the moment Jeremy entered the room, and it grew louder as he searched for a place to sit, but there was no empty seat to be found.

"Up!" Mr. Pettigrew, the innkeeper of the Unicorn and Crown, shouted. "You're not helping matters." He pointed at a scruffy young man with a long nose and arched back, and then glanced at Jeremy, jerking his head toward the now empty chair.

Jeremy sat and was about to order his breakfast when a laden plate was plopped on the table in front of him with a resounding thud. Jeremy frowned at the greasy sausages and fried tomatoes, egg yolk spilling over the entire plate.

"I didn't order yet."

"You won't find him. These here blokes are going to make sure ya don't." Mr. Pettigrew waved his arms about and then put his hands on his hips. He stood akimbo and loomed over the table.

"Find who?" Jeremy asked, confused by the hostility and the warning.

"Mr. Tumbler, of course."

Jeremy lifted his knife, stared at the messy plate, and put it down again. The room was suddenly quiet—the heavy silence of anticipation—as they waited for him to speak.

"Why would I be looking for Mr. Tumbler?"

"We know you're going to arrest Mr. Tumbler for his sister's murder, just as we know he didn't do it."

"I beg your pardon," Jeremy said, clearing his throat in order to speak louder—pushing his words into the ears of everyone in the room. "But I have no plans to arrest anyone. I'm still investigating. And if Mr. Tumbler didn't kill his sister, he should step forward and say so."

A few whispers drifted through the air, but Jeremy could tell that he was not going to win them over anytime soon. His youth and inexperience were fighting against him. "Why, Mr. Pettigrew, do you believe I'm going to arrest Mr. Tumbler?"

"It's all through town. Ask anyone."

Jeremy pushed back in his chair, no longer interested in eating. "Really? All through town?"

While there was never any doubt that gossip spread at lightning speed, an imminent arrest should not have been part of it. Bertha Tumbler's death was one thing; who the police suspected was quite another. Someone had been talking a little too easily.

Someone who should have known better.

Jeremy stood and marched to the door, joined by a dozen

or so townsmen. They jostled one another as they crossed the threshold ahead of him and then stood waiting on the street until Jeremy stepped out.

"I'm going to The Pins and Needles," he said to the nearest man. The name of the haberdashery rippled through the crowd.

Stepping past them, Jeremy gained the high street well ahead of the group. His long strides continued to increase the distance until he arrived at the haberdashery with the others trailing some fifty feet behind. It allowed Jeremy to burst through the door with the authority of a Bow Street Runner and not that of an unruly crowd.

"Mr. Fraser," a voice greeted him with surprise and pleasure. "I thought I might see you today."

It wasn't Constable Marley, but a young lady who invariably lifted his spirits. Sophia Thompson tipped her head in a small bow and drew him to the back of the store. "Constable Marley has yet to come in," she said in a soft near whisper, her breath caressing his cheek. "I assume you're here to convince him that arresting Mr. Tumbler is a mistake—my same purpose."

"Indeed, that would be a grave mistake. Though the damage might already have been done, Miss Thompson. Mr. Tumbler has been warned and gone into hiding. Speaking of which—" Jeremy frowned. He looked down the aisle past Sophia and then toward the office. While they were not alone in the store, it was clear that Sophia had no companion. "Where is your maid, Miss Thompson?"

"Betty?" she asked and then continued at his nod. "The poor girl was terribly distraught yesterday. One can hardly blame her really; Bertha Tumbler's body was a ghastly sight and it was a shock to the system. But she is feeling better today—says that keeping busy helps. But . . . well, she wasn't inclined to accompany me this morning, and I didn't want to delay."

"It is not safe or seemly to wander about on your own, Miss Thompson. Had you requested it of me, I could have come to Allenton Park to act as escort."

"That is very kind of you, Mr. Fraser," Sophia said with a shrug. "But I thought it imperative to speak to Constable Marley, convince him to *not* arrest Mr. Tumbler, but merely speak with him. I might have known that you would have thought the same and had the situation under control." She smiled and nodded, agreeing with herself. "I also thought this might be an opportunity to ask Mr. Tumbler questions about his sister. If he knew any of her customers—particularly to whom she sold the wolfsbane."

"My thoughts exactly, Miss Thompson. And if she had a ledger of any sort—pardon?"

"Not likely. Possession of a ledger would have required mathematical skills as well as the ability to write. The letter in her storeroom was left by the killer; we still don't know if Bertha could read or write . . . and now we can't ask Mr. Tumbler."

"She did label her plants; that must tell us something."

"True enough," Sophia agreed.

"Hello, hello," Constable Marley said. He had come in quietly behind them and tapped Jeremy on the shoulder, causing the Runner to spin around in surprise. "What are you doing here, Detective Fraser?" the constable asked, sporting an uncharacteristic grin. "Did you hear that I've solved the case? Have you come to congratulate me?"

"No, indeed not. Congratulations are not in order as yet," Jeremy said, trying not to sound disagreeable.

Sophia followed the constable into his small office. Jeremy stood at the door.

"Everyone is talking about Mr. Tumbler, Constable. The whole town is talking," she said. Disapproval frosted her words.

Oblivious, the constable laughed. "Yes, I might have been a tad talkative on my way home yesterday. I was so pleased to have solved the case. Mentioned it to Mrs. Collins in the bank and Mr. Learner when I passed the church. Oh, and then Ella at the bakery and . . . It's not to be wondered at; this case has been hanging over me for near on a year since Andrew Waverley was killed. Can hardly blame me for being excited."

He laughed again, not realizing that his jovial demeanor was extremely insensitive. Instead, he dropped down onto the chair behind his desk and leaned back, relaxed and cocksure.

"That was ill-advised, Constable Marley," Jeremy said, clipping his words with anger. "As well as indiscreet. You won't find him now, he's gone to ground."

"Proves his guilt then, doesn't it? Wouldn't run if he were innocent."

"He wouldn't be the first."

"Speakin' from your years of experience, are you?" Marley sputtered his lips, mocking.

"It's not surprising that he's gone into hiding," Jeremy said. "Tumbler likely doesn't trust the system. One could hardly blame him; the record is rather spotty."

"The record? Bow Street making mistakes, now, are they?"

"I was speaking of all law enforcement," Jeremy said with his chin lifted. "Training has become a requirement in London but in the counties—well . . ." Jeremy's voice trailed off as he waited for Marley to jump in and admit to his lack of training. But the constable remained silent, a mulish expression on his face.

"Aren't we lucky," Marley said eventually, "to have one of those *distinguished* and *educated* Bow Street gents in our midst." His expression was not at all pleased. "What makes you think Tumbler is not at his forge? I've yet to pay him a visit."

Jeremy flashed a frown and then glanced at Sophia.

"I'm afraid your exuberance and enthusiasm about an imminent arrest has flown through town, Mr. Marley," Sophia said. "You ought not to have been so cavalier with your conversations. Even Allenton Park was all atwitter with gossip of Tumbler and why he's disappeared."

"*Constable* Marley, Miss Thompson. *Constable.* Not Mister—"

"I was met by a crowd at the inn," Jeremy said, interrupting Marley's snit. "And they followed me here."

"Oh, so that's why I have a gathering of persons in front of my store." He leaned toward a saleslady standing by the door. "Mrs. Nesbitt, would you kindly ask the men on the street to make way for my customers? Better still, send them back to the pub."

There was no reply from Mrs. Nesbitt, but the floor tapped with the sound of heels and the front door squeaked as it opened.

Jeremy leaned on the doorjamb and crossed his arms over his chest. "They don't believe Mr. Tumbler to be guilty and will not allow you to arrest him."

"What they believe is irrelevant, Mr. Fraser. I *am* going to arrest Mr. Tumbler. The note that we found at his sister's place is clear evidence that he did her in."

"But the letter was planted by the killer," Sophia said, her voice full of indignation. "Or rather," she added with less force. "It *seems* likely the letter was planted by the killer."

Constable Marley chuckled, clearly not convinced. "Now why would the killer do that?"

"To divert the investigation," Sophia insisted. "Lead us in the wrong direction. Force the arrest of an innocent man. There are many possibilities."

"Yup, an' the best bein' that he done her in."

"But that doesn't make sense!"

"Desperate to be right, are you, Miss Thompson? You wouldn't be listening to this here fella, taking your lessons from *him*, now would you? Mr. Newly Minted Detective has a lot to learn."

"Not as much as you think, Constable." Jeremy straightened, now blocking the doorway. "I know enough not to talk about an upcoming arrest to all and sundry. You've encouraged Tumbler to go into hiding and he won't be interested in answering any questions even if you do track him down."

"Perhaps, but I'll run him to ground, don't you worry. I know how to do my job. And you can run back to London. Tell the Bow Street Runners that you were outwitted by a town constable." He laughed again, but there was nothing jovial about the sound. It was mocking and full of contempt.

Jeremy gestured to Sophia, moving out of the way to allow her to pass. "I'm not returning to London until the job is complete— until the murderer is found and incarcerated," he said over his shoulder. "It is most unfortunate that your incompetence has lengthened the process. But not to worry: I will, indeed, speak to the Bow Street Runners about the West Ravenwood constable. But you will not be pleased with the description."

CHAPTER SIXTEEN

A Deep, Dark Abyss

"Right there," Mrs. Curtis said, waving her hand in such a way that it took in three shelves.

"Where?" Sophia asked, feeling stupid and frustrated.

She had made a point of asking Mrs. Curtis about a book on poisons two days earlier, only to have her request dismissed with a casual gesture toward the library. It had taken several more petitions before the housekeeper realized that Sophia needed Mrs. Curtis to show her exactly where the books were located. With a snort of impatience, Mrs. Curtis had dropped the flowers into the vase that she had been arranging on the dining room table and marched through the door and down the hall.

Once in the library, Mrs. Curtis had stepped to the right of the fireplace and waved toward the shelves. Upon Sophia's question, Mrs. Curtis reached over to the middle shelf and took down two books. She dropped them in Sophia's outstretched arms and walked back out the door without another word.

Two books! Sophia pivoted looking at the overflowing shelves that covered the walls of the entire room. *Two!* Among hundreds. It was no wonder she could not find them.

"Thank you," Sophia called as she dropped onto the settee.

One book was of no use; it was elementary in its approach to poisons. It offered the Latin names of various plants and described reactions as mild, medium, and severe, giving no symptoms or antidotes. With no illustration of the flower or the seeds, the book was all but useless. Sophia tossed it onto the cushion beside her.

The second book, however, was exactly what Sophia was looking for.

She found monkshood in the index where it was referred to as wolfsbane, leopard's-bane, mousebane, women's bane, devil's helmet, and queen of poisons. Better still, the article about monkshood was boxed in a bright red border with a skull and crossbones in the corner. There was no doubting its lethal nature.

The illustration showed the monkshood to be a lovely ethereal plant with blue or purple flowers. The leaves looked similar to the shriveled greenery in Bertha's jar, and the notation about poison indicated that it was lethal. It affected the heart and the nerves in minutes to even hours after swallowing. The symptoms included numbness, nausea, and abdominal pain.

Sophia sat back, staring into space above the book. She nodded to herself. This sounded very much like the description of Stacks' last minutes. This information would be of great use to Jeremy. She was just thinking she would send him a note when a soft knock on the door produced one of the housemaids, who informed her it was time to dress for dinner.

With a glance at the clock on the mantel and a huff of impatience, Sophia assured the girl that she would do so. Sophia knew

Betty would be waiting—having recovered, for the most part, from the ordeal of Bertha Tumbler's death.

Lifting the book to the light before closing it, Sophia noticed an imprint in the margin. It appeared as if someone had written something next to the article about monkshood and then used a rubber eraser to delete it. Shaking the book produced several pieces of rubbed paper in the crease, verifying Sophia's suspicion. She ran her finger lightly across the indented words, wondering how to bring them back.

Another quick glance at the time encouraged her to close the book for now and bring it up to her room while she dressed. After dinner she would devise a manner to read what had been written and then erased.

With any luck, it would state by whom, and how, Stacks had been poisoned. It was highly unlikely, but Sophia hoped that there had been enough difficulties with this case for their allotment of luck to be overflowing.

It was a faint hope.

———•———

"You were quiet at dinner," Daphne said as they strolled the upper hallway to their bedrooms. Ahead, Daphne sashayed, swinging her skirt from side to side, practicing a flirty manner. Then she stopped, turned, and fixed Sophia with a piercing gaze. "Have you made a discovery or heard from Mr. Fraser?"

Sophia frowned, trying to decide if she could share her concerns about the margin writing with her cousin. If the words erased in the poison book were of an incriminating nature, that could only mean that the killer had been in Allenton Park—in the library, to be exact.

How had this monster found the book when it took Sophia several days and the assistance of a grudgingly helpful housekeeper? It was alarming to again think that, even if for a short duration, they had shared space with a murderer.

"No, nothing to report," Sophia said, trying to sound official. Her first order of business was to decipher the indents on the book. No need to worry anyone until she knew what it said. "I was thinking of making a time line. Would you happen to have a pencil that I could borrow?"

"Of course." Daphne skipped to her bedroom door and disappeared for a moment. She returned quickly with a stub of a pencil—it barely resembled its original form.

Sophia stared at it, willing her amusement not to show. "Ah. Excellent, thank you." She took the tiny piece of unfinished wood and said good night.

Pulling the book from under her mattress, Sophia carried it to the small table next to the window. As twilight was long gone, Sophia lit her lamp, opened her window for cooler air, and then sat, pencil in hand.

Holding it on its side, Sophia lightly scraped the graphite stick across the indents. She worked slowly and methodically, smiling every time the pencil caught and produced another letter.

The light had entirely gone from the sky when Sophia completed her task. And while the lamp revealed that there was a mark to read, it was too shadowed to see what it said.

Taking the book to the window to make use of the last glimmer of light, Sophia turned it this way and that, trying to catch a glimpse of what had been revealed. To no avail; it was far too dark.

Sophia lowered the book and stared out the window. The

trees just beyond the lawn waved in the breeze, and she breathed in the freshness of the night air. A small light flitted across her field of vision and drew her attention. Sophia watched as it bobbed through the copse; it looked as if someone were carrying a lamp on a trek through the woods.

Sophia leaned out the window for a better view and listened. Other than the occasional snap of a branch, the woods remained still—except for the bouncing light, of course. Why was someone wandering through the park in the dark?

Had she been at home in Welford Mills, Sophia would have gone after that light—or, rather, whomever was carrying it. She would have knocked on her brother's door, coerced Henry to join her, and raced outside into the shrubbery. But to grab Daphne for the same purpose would be irresponsible, and to go by herself was worse: reckless and dangerous. She would have to wait.

Turning with a heartfelt sigh, Sophia admitted to herself, if only for a moment, that it would have been a perfect excuse to rouse Jeremy in the middle of the night and go off on an adventure. But Jeremy was in West Ravenwood, Sophia was at Allenton Park, and this was not a game.

As soon as the sun came up, she would be off.

Jeremy sat at a table in the main room of the Unicorn and Crown, using the lamplight to scribble out a letter. He had neglected his correspondence to Bow Street for some days. Sir Elderberry would be ready to string him up by his toes if he didn't report soon. But how could he send an update when there was nothing to say?

Still, he was his father's son. Jeremy waxed on about the upcoming fair—it would give him the chance to observe large numbers of people all at once—and he extolled the virtues of having a partner to advance the case. But Jeremy found that thinking about Sophia was a distraction, not a help, and after spending the better part of an hour trying, unsuccessfully, to *not* think about Sophia, he made out a quick list of clues he was following and sealed the letter. That would have to do.

He pushed the letter to the middle of the table, planning his next move. The villain needed to be caught before anyone else died.

Jeremy could not allow his inexperience to be a boon for the murderer; the very thought was horrifying.

———

Sophia slept surprisingly well and awoke just as the sun was rising. She dressed in one of her wool gowns, pulled on a pair of sturdy boots, and threw a warm shawl over her shoulders—mornings were beginning to offer a slight chill to the start of the day. She retrieved the poison book that now lived beneath her mattress.

At the window, Sophia took a deep breath and flipped it open to the marked page. She stared at the pencil squiggles in the margin, frowning and squinting. They made no sense. She continued to stare until the letters blurred . . . and still, nothing. It was profoundly disappointing.

As a last effort, Sophia turned the book sideways and then upside down. Immediately, the poor handwriting coalesced.

Mix with distilled water and boil for two hours—It was a recipe with a warning: *nausea, vomiting, diarrhea—death in two to six hours.*

Sophia sat with a thump on the edge of her bed, staring at the book. Her greatest concern had been realized. The murderer *had* been in the house. It was horrifying; they could have been murdered in their beds, the whole family. Alarming but . . . fortuitous at the same time, for it provided another avenue to investigate. She must remember to tell Jeremy about the recipe when she saw him.

With a heavy sigh, Sophia placed the book on her bedside table and slipped down the stairs. Despite the hush on the family floor, the main floor was humming with busyness.

Sophia tiptoed past a footman carrying wood to the kitchen, a housemaid sweeping the main hall carpet, and another dusting the knickknacks of the drawing room. As there was no sign of Benton or Mrs. Curtis, little Marty ran to open the front door for her.

Sophia stepped out into a clear morning with a blush-tinged sky. A webbed dew threaded across the lawn and a thick mist smoked the distance.

Chasing away all thoughts of nastiness, the tranquil atmosphere of the quiet, calm morning filled Sophia with resolve and purpose. She was determined to find the path that was used last night, and find some clue as to the reason it was being used in the dead of night.

Had her exploration required her to go off the Waverley property, Sophia might—*might*—have asked Daphne or William or the head gardener . . . or Jeremy . . . to go with her. But as it didn't, she felt quite comfortable plunging ahead.

And so with a wave to Mr. Quinn, who was digging under the rhododendrons by the fence, Sophia marched into the woods. The light was halved as soon as she was under the canopy of the trees, but visibility was still good. She wended around several trees, searching the dappled patches for a path that was well defined, as she would suppose a woods trek at night would be difficult otherwise. But there was no path. With a frown, Sophia scanned through the trees, looking for an opening.

As she progressed further and further into the woods, Sophia lost sight of the manor—which was hard to do, as it was not a small building, but the bushes were thick and plentiful. And still she found no path, trail, or track. Just as she was about to admit defeat, she spied a clearing with trampled grass. The trampled grass led to a subtle trail; imprinted here and there were the markings of a boot.

Placing her boot next to one of the footprints, Sophia was surprised to see that it was similar in size to her own. Fortunately, the tread was different; she had not walked in circles and just discovered her own print.

Moving slowly so as not to lose the trail, Sophia hunkered on her heels, moving the grass gently out of the way. She was hoping to discover a piece of cloth that might have snagged on one of the shrubs or a letter dropped, unobserved, from a pocket. Actually, a large sign giving her the name of the villain, why said person was acting in a villainous manner, and where this disreputable person was going would have been even better.

But it was not to be. Sophia continued to step methodically and search for . . . well, she was not sure what oddity she searched for, but she would know it when she found it.

A breeze fluttered through the trees, rattling the leaves and carrying the chirps and trills of the chiffchaff and the common whitethroat through the air. The growing warmth and sweet smell of honeysuckle brought her a feeling of peace. It was hard to imagine a hostile person skulking through these lovely woods.

And as she walked, logic poked its unwelcome nose into her

business. It was possible that the light-bearer of last night had no sinister intent or any connection to her investigations. One of the gardeners on his way home, perhaps. Or . . . yes, this was more reasonable . . . a poacher checking his traps. She would have to present this possibility to Jeremy—

A branch snapped.

Sophia whirled around, holding her breath as her heart threatened to pound out of her chest. She stared into the woods behind her and then slowly turned to the left and then the right.

Nothing.

Sophia breathed again, beginning with a long but quiet draw of air. She continued to stare for some time, not moving, not creating any sound.

And still the chiffchaff warbled.

With a slight giggle, Sophia acknowledged her overreaction. "Just a woods sound," she said, not entirely sure what that meant, other than it was supposed to be reassuring. She turned back to the path, but again scanned through the dappled sunlight before continuing.

Sophia was surprised to notice an odd sort of object in the shadows—unidentifiable from where she stood. Curiosity pulled her closer until she could make out the lumpy and matted thatch of crisscrossed branches and twigs lying on the ground, half tipped into a ditch. Looking more carefully, Sophia could see that it was a long ditch—too straight edged to be natural, and too overgrown to be recent. The blanket-like thatch had fallen into the ditch and exposed a trench of mud.

But it was not just mud. As Sophia shifted her stance, a glint of white flashed and caught her attention.

Curious. It seemed rather strange. It was stark white—a color seldom seen in the wild unless it was a flower. Perhaps it was a piece of cloth, blown into the woods by the gusty summer breezes . . . a letter. Yes, an incriminating letter. Perhaps, a confession—

Sophia shook her head. She was getting carried away. The white object was likely nothing of interest and the chance that it had something to do with any of the murders was slim, slim, slim.

Still, it required a look-see. Orderly investigation demanded it!

Climbing over a fallen tree to the edge of the trench, Sophia looked down into the hole. It was much too deep to simply stretch her arm out to reach the white object. However, the thatch was woven tightly together, almost ladderlike, certainly man-made. Was it an animal trap? If so, it was from eons ago—the leaves were dry and brittle. Built and then forgotten?

Glancing at her gown, Sophia contemplated the messy process of retrieving the mysterious object. Her boots were already caked with mud. Threads hung from her shawl where the twigs had caught, her skirt was streaked with dirt, and the elbow of her dress was ripped. In fact, on closer inspection, she saw that her sleeve must have snagged on a branch; a square of material was missing.

"Bother, most inconvenient," she muttered to herself. "Betty will not be best pleased to make that repair."

Sophia huffed in frustration, glad that her mother was not here to comment—or more likely, criticize.

Throwing caution to the wind, she hunkered down, brushing the grass and leaves aside, clearing an area to kneel. After having done so, she leaned forward and caught the thatched branches. They had been woven together years earlier, if one could go by the moss hanging down in slippery ropes into the hollow below. The carpet-like cover had been draped over the trench and was still secured on one side, making the possibility of this being an animal trap even stronger.

Sophia tugged and pulled at the woven cover, using all her strength, but it did not give way.

"Excellent," she said to . . . the hole. She dropped the loose end of the thatch into the trench. Now, she could use it like a ladder; she could climb down and get that white object. The thing might be of no importance, but if it was and she left it behind, she would never forgive herself.

Besides, it was odd, and she was curious.

Maneuvering her leg over the side proved to be awkward and near impossible until she hiked her skirts up to her thighs. She glanced around her and listened for a moment, but there was no one about to see her scandalous abuse of her wardrobe.

The dirt edging the trench crumbled as she slowly lowered herself, stick over stick, toward the bottom. She was thoroughly muddied by the time she had gone eight or so feet. Looking down, Sophia could no longer see that glint of white and prayed that she was not ruining her dress for nothing. She could not see the bottom, either.

Shifting, she leaned out a little farther and was rewarded with the sight of a stone—gray and rounded—only five or six feet below her. And with that thought she straightened and stepped down one more "rung."

There was a loud snap; the branch broke and her other foot slipped. With a jerk that stung her palms, Sophia lost her hand-hold and dropped, grabbing at the sticks and branches above her head on her way down. Her hands managed to seize a thicker branch and she jerked to a stop.

Sophia dangled from her arms, her feet hanging uselessly in the air. The gripped branch above her head sagged, and Sophia's heart started to pound in fear. This thatch was her lifeline—the only way back up—and that was, now, the only direction she wanted to go. She no longer cared about white or gray objects. The forest could keep its secrets, she just wanted *out*.

Wheeling her feet in front of her, Sophia tried to find another foothold, but each time she thought one secured, it broke or her foot slipped. She no longer cared that there was a mysterious man-made trench in the middle of the woods. It was ages old and the purpose long gone.

She should not have tried to climb down. She should not have come into the woods alone. She should have told someone—*anyone*—where she was going . . . because if she fell she would not be able to get back up.

Foolhardy and stupid . . . yes, just plain stup—

The branch snapped and Sophia plummeted to the bottom of the trench.

———•———

Jeremy arrived at Allenton Park at the positively indecent time of eleven in the morning. He had a duty to update Mr. Waverley about Marley's failure to locate Mr. Tumbler. It was exactly as Jeremy had expected; the town had closed ranks and would not give the constable the whereabouts of the blacksmith.

He was not, however, expecting a gathering of men on the front lawn of the manor. Had he not spotted Mr. Waverley at the center, waving his arms about in a very dramatic fashion, Jeremy would have simply bypassed the group and proceeded to the front door.

As he approached the cluster of five or six men, Jeremy noticed that they were all dressed in brown tweeds, the sort more often worn by landed gentry. It was unusually warm attire for the summer months; tweeds were most often used during hunting season in the fall. While the men were not carrying rifles, they still looked very much like a hunting party.

While not seeming to be aware of his presence, the gathering shifted and allowed Jeremy to step to the center. Before he could ask what they were about, Mr. Waverley turned and addressed Jeremy abruptly.

"How are your tracking skills, Fraser?" Mr. Waverley asked.

Jeremy almost laughed, until a second glance at the gentleman's face showed that he was in earnest. "Fairly good, sir."

"I don't mean running around the back streets of London after a thief."

"No, sir, you mean tracking someone or something through the woods. I was raised in the country, hunted every fall." He didn't think now was a wise time to mention that his skills were honed on following deer, not people. "What are we going after?"

"Sophia."

"Miss Thompson?" Jeremy asked, his voice unusually strained. His heart began to pound, drumming in his ears. "What happened?"

"She's disappeared. Been gone more than four hours. Was last seen going into the woods right there." Mr. Waverley half turned, pointing to the trampled grass at the edge of the forested part of the park. "Warren insists that she would not miss breakfast and yet she has. The family is certain that something is terribly wrong. Warren was going to go out after her, but that would be foolish; he's as likely to get lost as his daughter has done. I've sent William for Constable Marley, but the man is taking his time in getting here. So I'm sending out these fine gentlemen"—he glanced at the men around him—"to track her. Find her. She might have twisted her ankle or become lost." His expression grew horrified, his conjecture implausible. "Attacked by a wild beast, or kidnapped by marauding . . . kidnappers. Any number of things that might have occurred."

Jeremy blinked, staring at the men more closely. There was something belligerent about their smug expressions. Self-satisfaction?

And then Jeremy realized what had happened, who these men were.

Mr. Waverley had had to call in the best trackers, the best hunters; the men that knew these woods inside out and backward.

Mr. Waverley had had no choice but to call in poachers. The very men that he hounded and forced the authorities to charge with crimes of theft were the very men that he had turned to for help.

No wonder they looked rather pleased with themselves. The situation was rather ironic.

CHAPTER SEVENTEEN

Them Bones Will Rise Again

Fidgety with concern, Jeremy shifted his weight from foot to foot: anxious to get going, anxious to start the search, anxious to find Sophia. Where was she? Was she all right? What trouble was she facing? She was quite adept at getting herself into trouble, after all . . .

He prayed that she had simply lost track of time. It was an unlikely scenario, but it was a far better image than the horrors that had started running through his mind.

"Has anyone instituted a search of the house?" he asked. It was more of a formality, knowing full well that it would have been the Waverleys' first course of action.

"Of course!" Mr. Waverley clicked his tongue and shook his head. "You go with these men. Help find the trail."

It wasn't a request; it was an order. Grateful to be actively searching, Jeremy nodded and took a half step toward the folded grass.

"No need to send him, too, Mr. Waverley. The Runner will just get in the way," sneered one of the men dressed in tweed.

His manner was churlish, though Jeremy was not surprised in the least. Poachers and detectives made odd collaborators; it made about as much sense as pairing a hen with a fox.

Undaunted, Jeremy marched ahead of the others and hunkered by the forest's edge, staring at the path that lay out before them. Sophia's skirts had folded the grass in the direction she had headed, and a few boot prints marked the mud. The trail wove around the trees and shrubs, but it was clearly visible for the first twenty-five feet or so.

As the hunters discussed at length the meaning of a particular snapped branch, Jeremy grew frustrated and pushed onward, determined to find Sophia sooner rather than later. He left the men behind staring at the ground.

Speed *and* efficiency were needed, not one or the other. Jeremy squinted into the shaded forest, looking—and finding—where Sophia's skirts had continued past. He rushed forward, stopping just as the trail petered out. Dropping back onto his haunches, he slowly scanned the horizon.

A fluttering piece of material caught his eye. Around one plant and then another, Jeremy wended his way along Sophia's trail, leading right to the waving swatch of material.

Pulling it off the branch where it had been snagged, Jeremy stared at the small square of light blue wool for a moment, trying to determine if it was indeed Sophia's. He was still puzzling when a horrendous sound filled the air and echoed through the forest.

It was a loud and long scream. The shrill sound filled Jeremy's ears and left him swallowing hard and breathing deeply to remain calm. There was no doubting the fear, no doubting the panic, no doubting the distress of the person issuing that dreadful noise.

And worse still, there was no doubting that it was Sophia.

Sophia clamped her hands across her mouth, stifling her scream. She stared at the smooth sphere in abject shock.

She had landed on the bottom of the trench with a jarring thud. The distance of her fall had not been great, so while she did not suffer any broken bones, scrapes, cuts, and bruises were aplenty. Her gown was also muddy beyond repair and her boots were scratched and positively caked. Dragging herself to her feet, Sophia found that while her situation was not immediately dire, it was disastrous.

The covering that Sophia had been using as a ladder was broken and hung useless two feet above her reach. After jumping at it until her muscles refused to jump again, Sophia only managed to pull free a collection of twigs and branches that now littered the floor of the trench.

A short rest lengthened into an hour or two as she tried to regain her strength and ignore her hunger. She was filled with regrets more than ever and even mentally counted them off on her fingers.

Regret one: Going into the woods without telling anyone where she was headed.

Regret two: Going into the woods without having breakfast.

Regret three: Going into the woods and not following a trail in which someone might happen upon her.

Regret four: Going into the woods in a gown; she should have borrowed a pair of William's trousers—although as regrets go this was fairly minor.

Regret five: Going into the woods assuming that she knew what she was doing.

Regret six: Going into the woods, finding a trench and trying to climb into it.

Regret seven: Going into the woods and allowing a white object to compel a foolhardy attempt to climb into said trench . . . oh, did that count? It was a little like regret number six.

Try regret seven again: Going into the woods—

Wait. What *was* that white object? Yes, what was it that had first caught her eye?

Sophia stood, realizing that the bottom of the trench was brighter than before. The sun had shifted, climbing higher in the sky. It illuminated the trench, allowing her to see that it truly was dismal: mud, mud, and more mud. But over there . . . there was the white object, gleaming in the sun.

Using a small stone and her fingers, Sophia dug around the object, shaking the mud from her fingers as she worked. It was bulbous at one end, tapered in the middle, and was rounded at the other end. It took a fair amount of work—Sophia's fingers were stiff from all the cuts and scrapes, and cold from the mud. It would seem that the summer temperatures had yet to find their way down here.

At last, Sophia freed the object and lifted it into the air. She shook the mud away in great globs, ignoring the splatters on her skirts, and saw that the white object was the tip of a bone. A large, reddish-gray bone stained by the mud.

It hadn't belonged to a rabbit or bird. Not the right shape for a deer, either. With alarm she realized . . . she was holding a human bone.

Sophia dropped it immediately, shuddering.

A terrible thought came to mind, and she scanned the floor for the smooth gray object that had also caught her attention before. She found it in the shadows. Ignoring another shudder, Sophia dug around the gray sphere with another stone—a larger stone, meaning less contact with the mysterious object. It popped free fairly quickly with a suctioned squelch that was more than a little disconcerting.

Sophia turned it over slowly and sucked in a ragged breath.

A skull.

She grabbed her shawl, pushing it against her mouth as her stomach turned over. Looking around, she saw bits of gray and white sticking out from the ground.

Bones . . . everywhere.

This wasn't a trench. It was a grave.

Sophia didn't drop the skull, but rather placed it carefully back on the mound of mud from which she had dug it. She patted the thing with a modicum of respect, expressed her regrets for the loss of life, and then quickly moved to the other side of the trench. Well away from the poor soul's remains. Someone had taken a walk in the woods and never come back. They had fallen in this hole and never gotten out. Lonely and starving, with no water, it would not have been a pleasant death.

Try as she might, Sophia could not put the fate of the victim out of her mind. It was an appalling death, and one she would share if she did not get out of the trench. Sophia shivered—not from cold but fear.

She, too, could turn into a moldering skeleton. She would starve to death just like that person had done. Her family would always wonder why she had run away. Left them, never to return. They wouldn't know that she lay in this muddy trench clawing at the dirt in countless attempts to free herself.

She called out until her throat ached, only to hear the cheerful twitters of the birds going about their business, oblivious to the agonies of one Sophia Thompson and her unfulfilled dreams of being a detective. She knew her efforts were wasted; the screams, shouts, and yells would not make it over the lip of the pit. She was well and truly trapped with little hope of rescue.

Thoughts of Jeremy followed and her melancholy deepened. She had hoped for more time with the handsome Mr. Fraser. She had even harbored a tiny hope that he found her appealing, but unless she found a way out of this trap her life was over.

She admitted she was being a little melodramatic, perhaps. But she was cold, wet, filthy, and contemplating a grizzly death . . . who wouldn't be a trifle gloomy and grappling with deep emotions under similar circumstances?

Sophia allowed one tear to dribble down her cheek—but just one. As soon as it had fallen, she straightened her shoulders, grabbed a hunk of hair that had come free from her updo, and tucked it behind her ears.

"No," she said aloud. "I won't die here."

Spotting a thicker branch overhead, Sophia made that her target. If she could reach it, she could walk up the wall, for here there were just enough rocks to offer support.

Tucking her skirts up over her waistband, Sophia then squatted, ready to leap higher and farther than before. She dismissed her previous tries as weak and lackluster. This time she would make it. She would grab the thatched cover, pull herself up over the lip of the trench, and trot on back to the manor where everyone would be amazed by her adventure.

And with that thought, she poured strength and determination into her leap, missed the branch, and landed back on the trench floor in a jarring crash.

Jumping to her feet, ignoring the cuts on her palms and pain in her knees, Sophia screamed in frustration and anger at freedom just twelve feet away.

Twelve impossible feet.

Jeremy stopped. He raised his hand, directing the men who were following behind to stop as well. All sound but that of the scream ceased. It ricocheted across the forest floor, bouncing from tree to tree, making it near impossible to pinpoint its direction.

Jeremy was certain the sound came from Sophia. And yet, other than assuring him that Sophia was nearby, the scream meant that she was hurt, or in pain, or upset, or all the above. Though, truth be told, there was a touch of temper to the sound. Vexation and exasperation—yes, that would be acceptable; far better than a scream of injury.

Returning his gaze to the path of broken grass and occasional boot prints, Jeremy continued to press on.

Pulling her shawl tighter around her neck, Sophia fingered the material and thought a lifesaving thought.

"Finally, a useful idea," she said, glancing at the skeleton. "You could have tried it with your jacket." She tipped her head, frowning at the ground surrounding the skeleton. "If you had a jacket, that is . . . never mind. Hindsight and all that."

She shook her head at the foolishness of talking to someone long since dead. "I'll just give it a try, shall I?" she added as a final remark.

Taking off her shawl, she held it up, stretched from arm to

arm. The shawl was long, perhaps as much as six feet. She wound it around, twisting and twisting, shortening it somewhat but not worryingly short. It was now almost rope-like. "Perfect."

Standing underneath the thatched cover, Sophia squinted at branches above her head, looking for one strong enough to hold her weight. When she saw a branch that she thought just right, she balled up one end of the scarf, and leaped, throwing the scarf at the same time. The scarf covered half the required distance, stopped midair, unwound, and fluttered to the ground in a pretty cascade of color. Three more tries with ever increasing leaps proved the method faulty—it would not sail high enough to get over the branch before unraveling.

Looking around, Sophia puzzled out her dilemma. There was precious little on the trench floor besides leaves, spindly twigs, bones, and rocks.

"Leaves, twigs, bones, and rocks," she repeated, listing them again for the benefit of . . . no one. "Leaves, twigs, bones, and *rocks*. Yes, rocks!"

Sophia danced across the trench floor, grabbed up an odd-shaped rock with some heft, and tied one scarf end around it, leaving the other end free and dangling. This time the problem was mastering the direction of the throw, for with the rock attached, the scarf could go much higher. Knowing that freedom was near at hand, Sophia threw the scarf over and over. She knew it would eventually be caught at the right height and in the right spot. It simply required patience and tenacity, and so she continued, over and over.

And over.

Just as Sophia's enthusiasm had almost entirely vanished, the shawl caught in the Y of a branch thick enough to hold her weight. The untied end of the scarf drifted to hang within arm's reach.

"Yes!" Sophia hooted with great enthusiasm, creating an echo above her. And then, carefully and diligently, she grabbed the scarf and twisted it to secure her hands. She lifted her feet to the trench wall, walking her hands up the scarf as she walked her feet up the wall.

Just as she reached the spot where the rock was secured, a tremendous crack split the air and Sophia dropped.

With lightning reflexes, she reached into the thatch blindly, grabbing for anything, anything at all.

She clamped onto a thick branch and held fast. The branch sagged with her weight, but it did not break.

Sophia dragged in a ragged breath and continued to climb.

———◦—◦———

Jeremy heard something moving up ahead. The crash and snap of the bracken was unmistakable for anything other than a large creature headed this way, and with speed. He stood up from where he had been examining a boot print and glanced behind him.

A considerable distance separated Jeremy from the other hunters; they were not spurred on by any strong personal feelings for Sophia Thompson. Jeremy was all speed, all rush, all hurry.

"Look sharp!" he shouted. "Stop dragging your feet!"

He had to know that Sophia was safe; it was all he could think about.

And so distracted, Jeremy was looking the wrong way when he was nearly knocked over by a figure rushing through the woods.

It slammed against him and squeaked in surprise. Lifting his arms to secure her, Jeremy's grasp slipped on the muddy mess.

"Oh, Jeremy!" Sophia said, grabbing him about the middle and giving him a squeeze, smearing the muck deeper into his waistcoat. "I am so glad to see you." She stepped back at arm's length, and regarded him with some intensity.

Jeremy stared back. Sophia was covered from her head to the bottom of her skirt in mud, grass, and dried leaves. Dark hanks of curly hair hung in stringy lengths across her shoulders, while beautiful brown eyes stared out from an oval face almost entirely covered in mud. Still, it was, indeed, the face he recognized.

"Sophia," he breathed with relief, and then quickly corrected himself. "I mean, Miss Thompson."

She nodded, grinning broadly. "Good afternoon. Fancy meeting you here." Mud dripped from her chin as she performed a ceremonious curtsy.

Ignoring her foolishness, Jeremy frowned. "What happened?"

"I'm so glad you found me," she said, jumping to the end rather than the beginning of her adventure. "I've had a bit of a rough morning." She looked skyward, through the treetops. "It *is* still morning, isn't it?"

"Yes, indeed. Though, just barely."

"Oh good. I'd hoped that I hadn't been knocked unconscious and missed a few hours." She paused. "I *am* rather hungry."

"You did skip breakfast."

"I did indeed."

"Come," he said. "Let's get you home . . . and cleaned up."

He hooked his elbow with hers, not caring about the dirt. He was inordinately relieved—Sophia was safe and sound. It was hard to see under all that mud, but it would *seem* that she was sound. The sun could continue to shine and his heart could slow its pace—all was right with the world.

"Cleaned up?" She laughed. "You don't like me in brown?" And then her face changed; the mischievous smile disappeared and she suddenly looked upset. "I found a body, Jeremy—I mean, Mr. Fraser—at the bottom of a ditch. It's been there for a long time, I believe, as it is now only bones." She shuddered and then looked up, pulling their parade to a halt. "Come, I will show you."

She yanked her arm free, pivoted, and headed back the way they had come.

CHAPTER EIGHTEEN

Fair Weather

"Please, Daphne, stop laughing. I feel most uncomfortable."

Sophia stood in the front entrance of Allenton Park, dropping clumps of dried mud onto the lovely black and white marble tiles. The grandfather clock in the corner announced that the hour was now two—and she was positively starved.

She would have returned sooner had she not been possessed by a strange sense of comradery toward her trench companion; it kept her with Jeremy and the huntsmen as they organized the retrieval of the skeleton. When shovels and blankets were brought in, Sophia succumbed to Jeremy's persuasion and accompanied him back to the manor.

The family greeting was effusive and flattering, particularly that of her father, who held her hands and sighed very deeply. Unfortunately, he also asked, "Why? Why did you go into the woods on your own?"

Sophia had just finished answering the same question from Jeremy and, as a result, her answer was far more succinct than it had been moments earlier. "I saw a strange light in the woods last night . . . and sensibly decided to wait until this morning to find out what it was." She paused, hoping—in vain—for some sort of recognition of her exemplary restraint.

"And did you?" Papa asked. After seeing her confused expression, he added, "Did you find out about the mysterious light?"

Sophia laughed and glanced at Jeremy. He lifted his eyebrows in a *see I told you* look, which precipitated a frown. Sophia turned back to her father with a shrug.

"Actually, I was distracted by a white object, and then I fell into a rather deep hole." She stepped back, spreading her skirts to show that it was ingrained with dirt. "I'm the instrument of my own disaster. Had I not been so curious, I would not have been in such a perilous situation." She glanced at her cousin, hoping for some moral support.

"We were very glad to hear of your survival," Daphne said, making a valiant attempt at nonchalance. Though her tone made it amply clear that her words were an understatement.

Sophia's survival had been announced some hours earlier, when shovels and more helping hands had been sought and she missed the "party," as William described it. A loud, joyful, and spontaneous celebration that apparently involved Daphne skipping from room to room and Aunt Hazel singing the "Hallelujah Chorus."

The family had come rushing into the front entrance upon her arrival, and now she stood before them all in her glory. Glory meaning . . . covered in mud.

Sophia knew that she was a disaster, but had not realized to what degree until a laughing Daphne had guided her to the ornate framed mirror at the back of the hall.

The creature staring at her in the mirror was almost unrecognizable, and Sophia thanked the heavens, once again, that her mother had not come to West Ravenwood.

"I might consider a wash," Sophia said airily, turning to see that the mud streaked down her side, across the back of her skirt, and collected at her hem. "And what is this, a hole in my sleeve? The gown is in total ruin," she huffed in disgust. Not one of her favorites but it had been practical and demure—exactly the image she wanted to project as a Bow Street Runner. Now she would have to get another.

Shifting her gaze back to the mirror, Sophia's eyes met those of Jeremy's in the reflection. She was puzzled by his expression. There seemed to be admiration in his eyes, despite her thoroughly mucky condition, and his smile was gentle; it turned her insides into melted butter. She wanted to turn and wrap her arms around him. Feel the thrum of his heart against her cheek and perhaps even . . . even place her lips on his—

"I can lend you one of my gowns," Daphne offered.

Sophia shook her head, pulling her thoughts from Jeremy and his lips. "Thank you, but no. There is no need."

She left the group chatting companionably in the entry as she headed to her bedroom. Though Sophia could feel Jeremy's eyes on her as he watched her climb the stairs, she did not turn until she was halfway to the first floor. When she did glance over her shoulder, Jeremy offered her an elegant and well-executed bow.

Plodding up the remainder of the stairs, Sophia decided that there might be side benefits to becoming a Bow Street Detective . . . such as spending time in the company of a Bow Street Officer by the name of Jeremy Fraser.

—•—

Mr. Reyer paid a visit to Allenton Park the next morning not long after Jeremy had joined Sophia and the family in the drawing room. Wearing a thoroughly rumpled jacket, the surgeon appeared wrinkled and tired, as if he had been up all night. Constable Marley was at his side, and they both looked decidedly uncomfortable.

"Perhaps a private interview would be best, Mr. Waverley," the constable suggested, looking around the room at all its occupants. The whole family was present, including Papa—even William had joined them. Sophia sat with Daphne on the settee, needlework in hand.

"No, no need," Uncle Edward said, waving toward Aunt Hazel. "They'll want to know everything you say anyway, so they might as well have it from the horse's mouth."

Constable Marley did not look pleased by the association to a horse, mouth, or otherwise. Still, he shrugged. "As you wish." He turned to the surgeon. "Go ahead," he said with a flick of his hand. "Let's get the medical stuff over with first."

"Indeed." Mr. Reyer patted his coat pockets and pulled out a small but thick notebook, though he barely looked at it, and began to speak as if delivering a lecture. "I'm happy to say that most of the skeleton was found. I put it together in my cold room last night."

He yawned as if to demonstrate how time-consuming the process had been. "A few fingers were missing, but for the most part the body was intact. Unfortunately, it became abundantly clear how the man died. There was a deep groove along the collarbone, one such as a knife blade would make. It was exactly where an artery is located. The man would have bled out very quickly. Another murder victim, I'm afraid, though from many years ago . . . perhaps as much as fifteen or twenty years."

The room was silent for a moment; the only sound was that of family members shifting uncomfortably in their seats. Sophia looked from person to person, gauging their reaction to see if anyone was in great distress and in need of reassurance. Fortunately, Constable Marley allowed the news to settle before stepping forward to continue.

"So, the first question is who this person might be." He held out a chain and medallion. "This was found next to the body, along with several tin buttons. The medallion is, in fact, a coin from the Dutch East Indies with a hole drilled through it to accommodate the chain. There are no inhabitants of the East Indies in West Ravenwood, and there never have been, so I was told.

"However, there were several sailors who ventured to the other side of the world from here. One man, in particular, was recalled for speaking about the islands in the South Seas with enough nostalgia that he might wear such a thing as a keepsake. Few remember him, as he sailed away almost twenty years ago—"

"Sailed away?" Jeremy asked, startling the deeply engrossed listeners.

"Yes, he left after telling everyone he was going off to some place called Bali. Though, he never actually said goodbye. That were almost twenty years ago. He'd been talking about going out to sea again and it were assumed that he had done so. No one I spoke with recalls hearing anything from him after that."

"This is starting to sound familiar." Uncle Edward was sitting forward in his chair, his eyes focused on the constable. "Are you talking about Howard Tuff? He worked here as an under-gardener for two summers . . . a few years—"

"Yes, a few years after we were married," Aunt Hazel chimed in. "That was over twenty years ago. There was quite a fuss when he disappeared; he didn't say goodbye to anyone . . . not even Mrs. Curtis. Being a housemaid, we called her Pearl at that time. Yes, I remember Tuff and Pearl were quite sweet on each other. Perhaps we should ask Mrs. Curtis if she ever heard from him . . ."

Aunt Hazel's voice trailed off as she glanced around the room. "Though a little more privacy would be kinder."

Daphne nodded and stood. "Shall we check on the new litter of pups, William?"

Her brother rose immediately, straightening down his waistcoat as if he meant business. "Yes, indeed. I might pick one out for Charlotte. She needs a companion, don't you think?" It was a rhetorical question and as such received no reply as they stepped into the hall.

"Come, Warren. Let us find Mrs. Curtis." Aunt Hazel gave Uncle Edward a significant look—which Sophia did not understand—and then turned back to Constable Marley. "I'll send Mrs. Curtis in to talk with you."

Constable Marley nodded with approval as the party's numbers dwindled, standing straighter, chest thrown out, preparing to exert his authority. He glared at Sophia when she did not leave with the others. He harrumphed—loudly—and suggested that this might not be a meeting in which Sophia would wish to participate.

"I will listen but not interfere, Mr. Marley," Sophia said with such finality that no one else offered an objection. Jeremy frowned slightly, but nodded.

Uncle Edward stood, paced in front of the unlit fireplace, and chuntered to himself. "Tuff disappeared. Took his belongings with him. The skeleton can't be Tuff—someone would have noticed, missed him. They would have sent for the authorities. No, it can't be Tuff."

The knock, when it came, caused a flurry of furtive glances. Sophia held her breath and watched Jeremy do the same.

Jeremy was not surprised when Constable Marley tried to take control of the interview. The constable stepped forward, greeted the housekeeper, and then—without an explanation—passed her the medallion dangling from its chain.

Mrs. Curtis stood straight and proud. She glanced at the object in her hand, started in surprise and looked again. The hard lines of her face disappeared as she held the coin gently cupped in her hands. "Where did you find this?" she asked in a near whisper.

Jeremy watched with discomfort as Constable Marley spoke in a churlish manner to the housekeeper, announcing that *he* would be the one to ask the questions. Many people did not believe the working classes deserved delicate handling or kindness, even in such circumstances.

While Jeremy was not surprised by the constable's approach, he was quite taken aback by Mr. Waverley. Mrs. Curtis had been in the Allenton household for decades, and yet Mr. Waverley did not step in, did not try to tone down the derisive attitude of Constable Marley. Jeremy was incensed and near to causing a fuss on the woman's behalf.

"When did you last hear from Howard Tuff?" Marley asked brusquely.

Jeremy stood and took up a position by the fireplace. "I'm

afraid the medallion was discovered in the bottom of a ditch, Mrs. Curtis," he said, glaring at Marley before returning his attention to the housekeeper. "Miss Thompson's *accident* yesterday involved a trench, as you know. The trench was, in fact, an old trap—a large one in a secluded area. The kind used for deer some twenty or so years ago. It could not have been an area much visited, or the trap would have been discovered long ago. It was likely built by poachers."

"Hunters," Mrs. Curtis corrected. "They were hunters then . . . only poachers since the enclosures." Her voice was strong again—ready to fight, ready to argue.

"I stand corrected," Jeremy said, slowly walking between Marley and Mrs. Curtis, establishing that the interview was now in his hands. He could not leave it to Marley; the man was inept and would get no answers by browbeating the housekeeper.

"But Howard left twenty years ago," she said, and then touched the medallion on her palm. "He always wore this—how did it get in a ditch?"

Jeremy chewed at the inside of his cheek, and then breathed deeply through his nose. "There was a body with it, Mrs. Curtis. The bones were weathered, as if they had been there a very long time."

He paused for a moment to let the information sink in. He did not want to press the point too quickly. "Could you tell us when Tuff left West Ravenwood and if you've heard from him since?"

Mrs. Curtis glanced around the room, looking at each of the occupants in turn. When her eyes lit on Sophia, the housekeeper nodded. It was a slight movement, likely unintended. Wrapping her arms around her waist, she continued to meet Sophia's eyes.

"I thought we were to be married, but Howard started talking about going back to sea. I was nearing the end of my thirties and despite our differences, I thought we were well suited." The older woman pulled a handkerchief from under her sleeve and dabbed at her eyes. "I don't know why he had wanderlust. It was unexpected. For him and me. Suddenly, all he talked about was the color of the Pacific Ocean, islands covered in palm trees, and mangoes growing by the dozens. Wanted me to see it with him."

She snorted. "As if I could . . . really! Me, traipsing around the world, as if that were a normal life. A satisfying life?" She glanced back at Sophia, likely expecting some sort of agreement, and then shook her head. "Said if I wouldn't come, he would go without me, and then one day . . . he was gone and I never heard from him again. A letter explaining why he left so abruptly would have been kind—but he never contacted me again. I thought of him sitting on a tropical island somewhere with a parcel of children at his knee, getting fat and useless. And now you're saying that he never left England?" She looked over at the gentlemen. "Why was he in a ditch?"

"It would seem that he were killed, Mrs. Curtis. Murdered. There be signs of a knifing, and no belongings in the rubble." Constable Marley shifted his weight, rocking side to side. "Now, we need the reason why he was killed. Did he have an argument with anyone at Allenton or West Ravenwood? Could he have been robbed? Did he usually travel with a quantity of coin?"

"No, no, and no," Mrs. Curtis said. "No argument, and nothing for robbers. We were dirt poor, but we were going to be happy. Or so I thought."

With a nod of finality, Mrs. Curtis dismissed the subject of Howard Tuff. "That was twenty years ago. Times have changed.

People have changed. Now, if you'll excuse me, I have to see Cook about Mrs. Waverley's apple pie."

And with that, Mrs. Curtis marched to the door, looking nothing like the fractured and heart-heavy woman of moments earlier.

"We need to be certain, Mr. Waverley. While it is logical to assume that the body is that of Howard Tuff, tin buttons and a medallion don't make it a certainty."

Jeremy was advocating for further investigation of the ditch after the departure of Mr. Reyer and Constable Marley, who criticized the idea as pointless.

"We also have to look around and try to understand why there were lights shining through the woods in the middle of the night," Jeremy continued. "I believe the lights were meant to be a lure, to bring Miss Thompson into the woods late at night. Though why is up for debate. I've spoken to Benton and learned that there are no other occupied bedrooms with windows facing in this direction. The glow of her bedroom lamp would have shown her to still be up. I can only wonder how long the villain stood in the woods trying to encourage a late-night stroll."

"This is not your case, Mr. Fraser," Uncle Edward replied. "You're here to investigate the death of my son, not that of Howard Tuff. I'll write to the justice of Thersby and ask after the Tuffs. Marley believes too much time has passed to make it possible to solve this particular case, and I don't disagree. But it must be attempted. As to why, I don't believe that Sophia was targeted at all. The poachers were likely hunting, and Sophia just happened to see their lamps."

"But no one poaches the east woods, especially at night, Uncle," Sophia said. "I asked Mr. Quinn. Old traps were known to litter the grounds—something that was not mentioned to me before this—" She glared at her uncle with accusation in her eyes. "A decade or two ago, some were found and filled in or dismantled. But it was known generally that there were more and the area was dangerous."

Uncle Edward chuckled. "I fostered that belief; it kept them away."

"With good reason, apparently," Sophia said rather heatedly, not best pleased with her uncle's attitude.

"The source of the lights needs to be investigated," Jeremy said, sounding official and determined.

"No. You need to go about your own business. About the business of solving my son's murder—and that of Mr. Stacks and Bertha Tumbler."

"Quite right, Uncle," Sophia said, placing her hand on Jeremy's arm. She tugged him into a walk, ignored his halfhearted protest, and marched him to the front hall.

"You won't win that argument," she said, without turning toward him. "Uncle is focused on Andrew, and you need to show that you are, too."

"But—" Jeremy began.

"We'll get Aunt Hazel to take care of it."

"What am I to take care of?" Aunt Hazel asked as she and Daphne walked into the front hall from the opposite direction. They had changed and were dressed finer than was traditional for late morning, in gowns embellished with lace, pleats, and in Daphne's case, bows.

"A more thorough search of the trench," Sophia replied

quickly, before Jeremy could complain that Uncle Edward frowned on the idea.

"Oh. I'm ahead of you. I've already sent two gardeners to complete the job. They'll shift through the rest of the muck and get it done before the fair this afternoon."

"Excell—" Sophia started to say but was cut off.

"You must get ready, cousin," Daphne said, although there was no excitement in her expression, only anxiety. "For the fair."

"Fair?" Jeremy asked, tipping his head as if seeing Daphne from a different angle would supply the answer. "Already? I thought it was next week . . . But I have been much occupied."

Daphne scowled. "Indeed, you have. Time has slipped away on you. The fair was always scheduled to start today. The excitement—for some—is extreme. Town has been talking about it for days." She waved her hand toward the door, in the general direction of West Ravenwood. "It's a country fair that we host in the north field—it is supposed to start this afternoon and run for two days. All the Waverleys and Thompsons have to participate. Father will give a speech, the mayor will make announcements, and the townsfolk will sell their wares. Booths with games . . . lots of senseless frivolity." She harrumphed. "I can't think of a worse time for such foolishness."

"Nonsense, the distraction will be just what everyone needs," Aunt Hazel said, crossing the hall and walking toward the drawing room. "Besides, the farmers still need to sell their crops, tradesmen need to be hired, and children need to get into mischief."

And with that declaration, Aunt Hazel entered the drawing room, joining Uncle Edward and Sophia's father.

"A few months ago, I thought the fair such a grand scheme, but not any longer," Daphne said, turning to face Sophia. "I would prefer to hide for the next two days. There will be too many people, too many chances for some nefarious deed—"

"But your parents are the hosts, and you're expected to put in an appearance." Sophia could not imagine her cousin being anything but enthusiastic about an occasion in which she could flirt and be flattered.

"I've secured a new driver for my coach," Jeremy said. "You might feel less vulnerable in a carriage than walking or on horseback, even though the distance is not great."

"There is no need—" Sophia began.

"I know we're expected to be there . . . but do you think it is safe?" Daphne asked Jeremy directly, this time. "Aren't you concerned?"

Jeremy glanced at Sophia, but she couldn't read his expression before he turned back and answered her cousin. "I think that the murderer is very clever and overly confident. Attending the fair will show that we will not be intimidated—that we are united and coming for them. It is the murderer who must be afraid."

Sophia lifted her hand to rub at her forehead. She knew Jeremy's words were nothing but bravado.

CHAPTER NINETEEN

It Takes Two

Leaving the young ladies to their preparations, Jeremy took a couple of hours to wander about town, casually asking after anyone who knew Howard Tuff. The sense of being unwelcome had not disappeared, and he was greeted with more dark looks than smiles. Still, it was not the unfriendly attitudes that forced him to rethink his approach, but the genuine surprise at his question. It would seem that Howard Tuff had walked out of everyone's lives and minds twenty years earlier, never to return.

The streets of West Ravenwood were far busier than Jeremy had seen them thus far. Wagons and drays trundled by carrying various wares, including pigs and goats, up to Allenton Park's north field. Signs announcing the best cheese, the smoothest butter, or the softest gloves were tucked under the arms of various drivers, ready to be positioned by the booths to draw customers in. A few people passed carrying a broom or pitchfork or some instrument of labor to illustrate that they were looking for work.

A young boy flicked his whip to keep a small herd of cattle walking up the road. It was active and there was an air of anticipation . . . and some familiar faces.

"Miss Dewey, Reverend," Jeremy said, nodding as they passed. Charlotte was seated with her father on the bench of a wagon that carried a prebuilt booth. Beside it leaned a sign, still to be attached, announcing that the church was collecting funds for the new school. Reverend Dewey flicked the reins, encouraging his horses to step lively, but there was nowhere to go—the road was congested up ahead. Still, the gesture was enough to inform Jeremy that a conversation was not desired.

———

Sophia was dressed in her finery and back downstairs before luncheon was called. She had watched from her bedroom window as the long line of traffic wended past the Allenton gate and up the path to the north field.

The transformation had been amazing. Flags strung across the entrance, seating benches built next to an open arena-like space, a temporary paddock housing horses and ponies, and a street of booths sprung up like weeds. People and goods abounded; the cheerless atmosphere caused by the murders and distrust disappeared, erased by smiles and slaps on the back, fresh baked goods, and slippery pigs. Sophia could see it all quite clearly from the vantage point of her bedroom.

She had skipped down the stairs, ready to share her impressions of the festivities. But it was commonplace to the Waverleys, having participated countless times before, and she was greeted with apathy rather than excitement. And in one case, apprehension.

"Would you mind sticking close by?" Daphne asked, taking Sophia's arm and leading her into the dining room. "When we're at the fair? I won't be as nervous with you by my side."

Sophia chuckled until she realized that Daphne was not funning. "Yes, of course. But I believe Mr. Fraser is correct. We'll be safe; there are too many eyes at an event such as this. No one will take a chance to harm us or the family with so many watching."

"You *would* say that."

"I beg your pardon?"

"You *would* say that Mr. Fraser is right. If Mr. Fraser said that the sun was the moon, you would agree."

"I most definitely would not!" Sophia dropped with little grace onto the chair that the footman was holding out for her. Daphne could be so annoying at times. "I rarely agree with Mr. Fraser. We are *seldom* in accord."

It was a redundant added comment, but Sophia was too indignant to be grammatically correct . . . mostly because she thought Daphne might be right.

Not that she thought Jeremy right all the time, but that she would give him the benefit of the doubt. That sort of instinctive trust made no sense, but she did seem to be confused when they were together and he looked at her in *that* way. It filled her with the oddest sensation, the oddest, extremely pleasant sensation that started at the top of her head and carried on to the tip of her toes. It brought with it a desire to throw herself in his arms—

"Sophia! Sophia! Do you want some fish or not?"

Sophia started. A serving platter of trout had appeared next to her. She shook her head and took some ham instead.

———•———

"Are you well?" Sophia asked Daphne as Jeremy handed them down to the fairgrounds. Her cousin had been quiet for more than fifteen minutes—most unusual. Sophia smiled her thanks to Jeremy and tried not to blush when his fingers left hers. Even with gloves, she had felt the heat of his skin and the shiver it brought with it.

"Yes, yes, I'm fine. I'm just worried." Daphne looked up at her cousin. "Aren't you?"

Sophia nearly shook her head but realized that any well brought up young lady would find this situation daunting, not exciting; it shouldn't fill her with energy, but it did.

Her excitement was surely brought on by the possibility of learning more about the mysterious deaths, picking up more clues. It had nothing to do with Jeremy.

Sophia stared at a tuft of grass flattened by her shoe and changed her mind, disagreeing with herself. Actually, her enthusiasm had everything to do with Jeremy and the way her breath disappeared when he looked at her.

Glancing up and beyond the family circle, Sophia met the stares of many fairgoers. Quick furtive glances kept turning their way. Children stopped and pointed until being dragged away, and smiles became frowns when heads turned in their direction. The townsfolk of West Ravenwood were very aware of their presence—which was not to be wondered at, as they were on Waverley property. Sophia smiled and waved at several people she knew, only to be ignored.

"As soon as the case is solved, everything will go back to normal," Jeremy said, offering first Daphne and then Sophia his elbows. He led them down the makeshift lane to the arena and podium where most were gathering for the opening ceremonies.

After having gone no more than twenty or thirty feet, Daphne squeaked, drawing Sophia's instant attention. However, all was well: Daphne was not in distress but, in fact, grinning—almost in a foolish manner. With a jerk of her head, Daphne indicated a small gathering of young men standing next to the gate into the arena.

"Dylan Crewe," she said softly, turning a bright shade of red.

Though the gathering by the gate was comprised of half a dozen young men, only one had blond hair and blue eyes and a cute dimple on his cheek. Sophia picked out Dylan Crewe immediately if for no reason other than his focused attention on Daphne. It would seem that the attraction was mutual between them, and Sophia gave her cousin a toothy smile of approval. It would be interesting to see if Mr. Crewe followed Daphne to London for her Season.

Continuing past the young men, they found Uncle Edward already in a deep conversation with the butcher. Father and Aunt Hazel sat on one of the lower benches; Jeremy guided Sophia and Daphne to join them. Charlotte and William shifted to make room for the girls, leaving Jeremy to stand at the end. The couple shared an intimate look that took Sophia by surprise. Had their relationship progressed to a secret engagement?

Sophia slid closer to Aunt Hazel to allow them a modicum of privacy, but Charlotte touched her arm and drew her back.

"You look none the worse for wear."

Sophia frowned, confused by the comment. "Worse for what wear?"

Charlotte laughed lightly, running her hand down her cream and soft green skirts. "The wear and tear of your ordeal yesterday. The trench, an' all that." She blinked as if she were now the one confused. "I'd heard that you were covered in mud from head to toe."

Sophia leaned forward to glare at William.

"Wasn't me," he protested, holding his hands up as a shield.

Charlotte giggled. "No, no," she said. "Not William. I was discussing your *adventure* with Mrs. Curtis. The staff was all atwitter about the incident." Silence met her comment. Charlotte glanced around at the frowning faces and dropped her voice to a semi-whisper. "The description of your condition was surely exaggerated. Mrs. Curtis said that you were covered in filth, hair every which way, clothes ripped—"

"Do you often engage in gossip with our staff?" Daphne asked from over Sophia's shoulder.

"Oh no, no, no." Charlotte shook her head with vehemence, sending her red curls bouncing. "We were sharing news, not gossip . . . although, I suppose it could be mistaken for such." She glanced toward William, looking contrite. "I would never belittle anyone in the family. And I was only talking to Mrs. Curtis."

Sophia clenched her jaw for a moment before speaking. "By *the family*, you mean *the Waverleys*." This was not the first time that Charlotte had distanced herself from the people that had raised her and given her everything—except, perhaps, her golden red hair.

"I don't mean the Deweys, of course." And then with a wide-eyed look of innocence, Charlotte Dewey shrugged. "I think very highly of them, Mother and the reverend, but . . . they are not my real parents. I'm sure you know that I was adopted."

"Were you, indeed?" Sophia was not going to admit that she already knew. She made a show of looking at the crowds around them, catching Jeremy's eye while doing so. "Perhaps this is not the time or place for such a conversation."

Jeremy could not hear their words, but he frowned—likely seeing her tense posture—and started toward her. Sophia shook her head and watched him return to his place, though still watching.

"Oh. Oh yes, you're quite right. Not the time or place." Charlotte paused, frowned again, and chose another subject—equally unsuitable. "You should not let finding the body upset you, Sophia." She patted Sophia's hand. "It might be anyone. Even if it is Mr. Tuff, I've heard he was not a good person. So do not allow yourself to be upset."

The group gasped as one.

"Charlotte, how can you say that?" William asked sharply. "You didn't know the man and he has nothing to do with you. Above all, you should know not to speak ill of the dead."

Charlotte drew in a ragged breath. She nodded and then stared at her toes. "You're right, William. I apologize. I should not have said anything. I was trying to ease Sophia's concerns, not criticize Mr. Tuff."

Participating in the fair was a tiresome business after all. Following the opening ceremony, Sophia was expected to chitchat with all and sundry. At length, she discussed the weather, the price of bread, and the charming character of each snot-nosed child running about the field, screaming like a banshee. Sophia thought that she might scream, as well.

She was more than ready to return to the manor; the fair had not been nearly as entertaining as she had expected. She did not wish to join the crowd in guessing the weight of Mr. Baley's pig or the age of Mrs. McBean's white duck. Even fruit tarts, while looking delicious, didn't entice her.

Several times Sophia looked to Jeremy for relief, but saw that he was jawing with various craftsmen; she could expect no rescue from him.

Sophia had just been talking to the milliner, commenting on the cooler evenings in yet another scintillating conversation about the weather when the woman smiled weakly and backed away.

"His family is well placed, even if he has decided to become a Bow Street Runner," Charlotte said, coming up beside her. William was not at her side for a change.

"You mean Jere—Mr. Fraser?" Sophia asked, not looking in Charlotte's direction.

"Of course. I can tell you're sweet on him."

Sophia laughed, a little too heartily. "I wouldn't say that I'm sweet on him. I admire Mr. Fraser and hope to learn the ways of investigation from him, but that would be all."

Even as Sophia spoke, she knew the words to be a lie. Well, not a lie, exactly—just not the entire truth. She *did* hope to learn how to be a detective with Jeremy's direction, but the thrill of being near him did not stem from their shared profession.

"If you say so." Charlotte shifted her stance, stamping the dust from her boots. "But I'm not the only one to notice how you keep looking at each other."

"Charlotte, you shouldn't gossip. As I've said before, gossip is rarely right," Sophia said heatedly. "Mr. Fraser and I are trying to find a murderer. Attending a fair will *not* help us toward that goal. If we do look at each other on a regular basis, it is in commiseration. We would both rather be investigating!"

The words "doth protest too much" suddenly came to Sophia's mind, and she snapped her mouth shut.

Daphne, likely hearing the strident tone of their conversation, meandered over to where Sophia and Charlotte were standing, staring at the riders ringing the paddock.

"Have you heard?" she asked, twirling her parasol. It was a lacy thing doing little to protect her porcelain complexion. "The gardeners found a couple of rings in the trench. Mrs. Curtis identified them as belonging to Howard Tuff." She looked past Charlotte toward Sophia. "The mysterious body is no longer mysterious. It is Howard Tuff, after all."

"Oh," Sophia said with great eloquence.

She swallowed several times in succession and then glanced around looking for Jeremy. He was on the other side of the field, standing beside the innkeeper of the Unicorn and Crown. Their eyes met and instantly his brows rose and then folded together. He nodded his farewell and hurried across the field to her.

Had Jeremy been one to care what others thought, he might have left the north field of Allenton Park after the first dark look—certainly after the second or third. But by the time he was deflecting his tenth glower, Jeremy was blasé about the animosity. It was, after all, a hazard of the policing trade. And so it was that Jeremy felt the hostility blowing toward him like a cold gust of wind as he walked around the fairgrounds. It was merely something to ignore.

A few of the townspeople deigned to speak with him, though the majority preferred to watch from the shadows. While most knew Jeremy was investigating Andrew Waverley's murder, more than a few were still suspicious, thinking that he had been called in to catch poachers.

They resented anyone insisting on obedience to the new enclosure law; it made Jeremy a pariah. He was caught in the middle of that age-old battle between the estate owners and those that worked their land. Being the son of a baron did not help; that very fact alone seemed to put him on the other side of the divide.

Jeremy stood his ground, but was thoroughly out of sorts. He marched across the field, ready to have words with whomever had upset Sophia, because he could see that she was upset. Her complexion had gone white, her expression troubled, and her stance was stiff.

Yet, when he joined the two young ladies, Sophia simply smiled; her expression changed to that of calm, and his annoyance drained away. Perhaps he overreacted.

"Is all well?" he asked when near enough to do so without yelling.

"Certainly." Sophia glanced at Charlotte.

The reverend's daughter stared back, one of her brows almost raised to her hairline. "We were discussing Howard Tuff," Charlotte said, fiddling with the ornate sapphire ring on her finger.

"Ah yes, I bumped into Constable Marley a few minutes ago." Jeremy frowned. "Poor man. Such a sad way for Mr. Tuff to die, and with no one to know where he was for twenty years. It must be very hard on his family."

They all nodded and fell into a silence that was almost immediately interrupted.

The disruptive sound was a murmur at first, then became a buzz of voices. Then the possessors of those voices could be seen walking speedily across the field, and snatches of words drifted across the fairgrounds: *Bow Street. Time. Investigate.*

A group of several townsmen followed three men who were headed directly toward Constable Marley. Jeremy stared; the men were not strangers to him, but the last time Jeremy had seen this trio was in the London Bow Street office.

Botterill trailed behind the other two, as if unsure of his role. He was wearing the layered cape coat of a coach driver; he had a considerable girth and a large curled mustache. Collingwood was long and lanky; he wore a cap pulled over his eyes, shots of black hair poking out in a helter-skelter fashion from under the brim. He tried to match the pace of the man beside him by taking long unnatural strides that tripped him up more often than not. And lastly, a man wearing a top hat better suited to a night at the opera, a black coat, and charcoal waistcoat led the procession.

The man sporting the top hat was not one of Jeremy's favorite people—quite the opposite. Inspector Jefferies, darling of Sir Elderberry of the Bow Street Runners, approached Constable Marley with a broad insincere smile spread across his square jaw.

"Ah, there you are, Constable." The man held out his hand to Marley. "Edgar Jefferies, Principal Officer of Bow Street in London at your service. I've come to solve Andrew Waverley's murder. Yes, indeed," he said proudly, even hooking his thumbs into his waistcoat and rolling back and forward on his toes. His voice boomed out across the fairgrounds, as it was undoubtedly meant to do. "Going to find the killer and bring him to justice. No more dillydallying. It's taking too long, much too long."

The insult, said with a friendly chuckle, was a stab with a jagged knife—painful and unnecessarily cruel.

Jeremy stepped forward, wanting a private conversation, but Jefferies' next words brought him to a halt.

"What's that? Jeremy Fraser? Hardly worth your time." The big man chuckled again, showing his teeth.

Jefferies had been one of Jeremy's harshest critics ever since he had stepped across the Bow Street office threshold in London. There had been no doubting Jefferies' feelings toward the new recruit. The man's sudden appearance was not a kindness, not help. This was a takeover. Uncalled for but, clearly, Sir Elderberry had despaired that Jeremy would ever solve the case.

Jeremy's stomach dropped with humiliation.

"Oh no, thought you might need an investigator who knows what he's about," Jefferies continued. "Mr. Fraser will be heading back to London by the end of the week."

CHAPTER TWENTY

Wild Goose Chase

Sophia was quite determined that Jeremy Fraser was not about to go back to London with his tail tucked between his legs. She would not allow it! Besides, it was much too soon; the lack of progress on Andrew's case was not Jeremy's fault and . . . and . . .

Well, she was not ready to say goodbye to Jeremy. His company was exhilarating—her heart pounded in a most thrilling manner when he leaned closer, met her gaze with a penetrating stare of his own, or touched her arm. Her steps were lighter, laughing was easier, and all felt right with the world when Jeremy was near.

She had never felt such a strong affinity to anyone before. It was a wonderful and most energizing novelty.

But that had *nothing* to do with her resolve to keep him in West Ravenwood. Gracious, no. Although aware that she was allowing her emotions to rule over all else, Sophia thought her faith in Jeremy's abilities well founded. She had seen him at work. She would *not* agree to him being sent back in disgrace. Never.

As a consequence, she spent a restless night devising all kinds of strategies to distract Botterill, Collingwood, and Jefferies. She made a few inquiries of the staff the next morning and sent a note to Jeremy about her findings. Then after concocting many convoluted, illogical stratagems to distract the superfluous detectives, Sophia waited for the Bow Street Runners to arrive en masse to speak with her uncle.

Jeremy was the first to arrive. He entered the manor by himself; no other Runners dogged his heels. But after speaking with Jeremy, it became apparent that they would not be receiving a visit from the other investigators at any point that day. Jeremy had devised his own plan, he explained; it was a far simpler plan than any she had concocted.

"I sent Jefferies and his companions to Thersby." He smiled with the recollection. "It only required a feigned interest in the whereabouts of the Tuffs.

"I hurried through my breakfast, making a great show of urgency. 'I'm off to Thersby,' I said as I passed their table. 'Want to speak to the Tuffs.' Then I threw on my coat, pulled on my gloves, and looked prepared to rush out. They jumped up and ran for the door just as I expected." He chuckled and then continued. "'No need for you to go,' Botterill shouted over his shoulder; then Jefferies called for their horses as they ran into the yard." Jeremy pursed his lips, fighting his amusement. "They will soon learn that the Tuffs no longer live in Thersby, but not before wasting the day to travel there and back. It gives us the freedom to investigate unencumbered." Jeremy gestured toward the front door.

"Well done, Mr. Fraser," Papa said, coming up behind Jeremy and Sophia in the entrance hall.

Whirling around at the sound of his voice, Sophia saw that

her father's eyes were alive with mischief. He nodded with approval. "A journey to Thersby should keep them away most of the day. The good people there are likely as uncomfortable with Bow Street Investigators as they are here." He laughed. "Oh dear, it will not go well."

Sophia glanced at Jeremy with a grin. When they locked eyes, Sophia found it suddenly difficult to look away. She quite liked staring at him and the feeling of her heart beating to quick time.

"I'm almost certain it won't," she said. She swallowed and watched Jeremy do the same. Giving her head a shake, Sophia turned back to her father.

"Going for a drive?" Papa asked, looking out the wide window beside the front door. Little Marty, visible to everyone, waited patiently outside with the reins of Jeremy's hired horses in his hand. "Perhaps you should take Mr. Bradley and our family carriage, Sophia," Papa said. "You would not be crowded in a larger carriage. That one is rather . . . cramped."

And then he frowned, another thought only just occurring to him. "Without Betty, though? Is that seemly?"

Sophia flushed. She had been anticipating Jeremy's company with great enthusiasm; surely Papa wouldn't deny her the pleasure.

"Thank you, Papa, but all is arranged. We'll stay to the country lanes." She hated the pleading note that had crept into her voice. "Few will see us. We won't be gone long . . . And if we stay in the carriage, no one—"

"Sophia, not to worry, my dear. I was just asking, not forbidding. I trust Mr. Fraser here. I know of his family and they have an exemplary reputation. I'm certain he will take good care of you." Papa shifted his gaze. "You *will* take good care of my daughter, won't you, Mr. Fraser?"

"That I will, sir," Jeremy said, straightening his shoulders. "However, I should warn you that we will be getting out of the carriage."

Papa looked nonplussed. "Oh?"

"Yes," Sophia interjected. "You see, I have discovered where Harvey Tumbler is hiding. Or at least, where I believe him to be hiding." Sophia nodded enthusiastically. "It wasn't that hard. I asked the stable boy if he knew the dead herbalist's family." She grinned. "He did . . . but not Bertha or Harvey. He knows the Tumbler cousins—everyone is related in these little places. We're going up to see Mr. and Mrs. Hummel on Savor Road, first cousins of the Tumblers on their mother's side. There's a good chance that they'll know where he is."

"You're in your glory, Sophia," Papa said with no small hint of pride.

"I do like puzzling things out, Papa. And if doing so should help solve Andrew's murder and bring peace to our family, how could I not continue to investigate?"

Papa glanced at Jeremy, but his expression did not change; Sophia was certain that her father, while not overly pleased, understood. He turned as if to leave them and then pivoted back. "Could Daphne not go with you?" he asked.

Sophia snorted a laugh. "No," she said. "There's not enough room in the carriage; we would be squeezed together in a very inappropriate way."

Sophia felt the rush of blood to her cheeks and she was very aware of Jeremy at her side. "Besides, she is at the fair today, helping

Aunt Hazel and Charlotte at the church booth. It's the last day of fun and frivolity. Collections for the education of the poor are going well."

"Excellent, good to hear." Papa nodded. He lifted the book in his hand, staring at it as if unsure where it had come from. "Yes, well . . . I'll be in the library. If you should have need of me. And Sophia?"

"Yes, Papa?"

"We need to discuss our journey home soon."

Sophia gulped, giving Jeremy a furtive glance. "The journey home will be soon, or the discussion?"

"Both. Your mother—"

"Yes, I . . . I understand."

Sophia followed Jeremy out the door. She glanced sorrowfully over her shoulder and saw that her father had not moved, watching them depart with a brooding expression.

———◦—◦———

Sophia tried to remain silent—a poised, contained silence with an air of preoccupation. It was a manner she imagined a proper detective needed to cultivate.

The silence lasted three, perhaps four, minutes.

As soon as the small carriage slipped out of the Allenton gates and turned up the hill away from West Ravenwood, Sophia turned to Jeremy. "It sounds as if our time to investigate is soon to be limited," she said and then shook her head. "Nonexistent, really. Neither you nor I can investigate if we're not here in West Ravenwood. We're out of time. We must solve this quickly."

"We were not exactly dillydallying before, Miss Thompson."

"You might call me Sophia. In fact, I think it is a requirement."

"I beg your pardon?"

"I believe we know each other well enough to use first names. I think of you as Jeremy in my head, so . . . let's make it official." A blush rose up her cheeks, ruining her attempt at casual friendliness. "Though not when we're among others, of course. Much more might be read into it . . ."

Ever the gentleman, Jeremy ignored her embarrassment. "Excellent idea, Miss Sophia. Please call me George."

"George?"

"Teasing, just teasing." Jeremy chuckled, a low welcome sound. "Please, call me Jeremy."

"There, now that we are over that hurdle, we—"

"We have many more to conquer." Jeremy's brows puckered across his forehead, and he flicked the reins, encouraging the horses into a trot.

"Yes, indeed. I've been thinking about the lists." She turned back to face the road, which narrowed as it continued up the hill and past a collection of small cottages. Escaped—or escaping—chickens scattered as the carriage rolled by.

"What lists?" Jeremy asked.

"Oh yes. I might not have mentioned them before. I was making a list of everyone at Allenton Park—family and staff—as well as all those I could think of in the town itself. I stared and stared at the names, jotted notes—I was well occupied by this worthless venture for days. But I have since come to a realization."

"That until we know why, we will never know who."

"Exactly. It was one of my first conclusions, but it got away from me. I really do need to get a journal and keep it with me at all times." Sophia laid her hand on Jeremy's arm and then quickly removed it. "Until you—and I—arrived and began to investigate, nothing unpleasant had happened since Andrew's death."

"That is not entirely true. Didn't you say that Daphne was subject to poisoning by chocolate?"

"Yes, yes, I did, but I had forgotten to factor it in as part of the whole. It felt like a separate event, but you're right; it is another piece of the mosaic. So, I'll amend my statement: There were no more *murders* until we arrived."

She squinted into the distance—not seeing the fields and rolling hills but her list sitting on her desk in her bedroom. "Since then, Hal Stacks was poisoned, shots were fired at Uncle Edward—"

"And you in the conservatory."

"Yes, right! And then Bertha Tumbler was killed. If Andrew's murder was the beginning, the others could have been attempts to hide incriminating evidence. Stacks was in the process of asking around town about people, gathering names for you. And Bertha wanted to speak with me about something. She sold various herbs, including poisons. I'm guessing she sold the one that killed Mr. Stacks to the killer."

Jeremy turned the horses at the crossroad. Off in the distance, the music and laughing crowds from the fair could be heard echoing across the hills.

"So, you think that Andrew's death was the catalyst, and everything else has been to hide the murderer's tracks."

"Except Daphne and Uncle Edward . . . that doesn't fit." Sophia huffed. Abandoning her perfect ladylike posture, she slumped back on the seat of the carriage. "Oh bother, this is so confusing. Are all cases like this?"

Jeremy lifted one side of his mouth in a lopsided smile. "No, indeed not. This is far more complicated than I've dealt with before. Though to be honest, while it is my *third* case, it is only my *first* murder."

He directed the horse into the yard of a small cottage. "I believe we're here. According to my directions, this should be the home of the Hummels."

Sophia sat back up and glanced around. It was a neat, though small, white stucco cottage with a thatched roof and a large barn. Chickens wandered aimlessly around the yard, stalked by a large calico cat. A muddy pen off to the side housed several fatted pigs, and a well-tended garden grew on the other side of the barn. Open windows allowed air and sound into the cottage and would have informed the occupants of their arrival, and yet no one came out to greet them.

"We are not welcome," Jeremy said, jumping down from the carriage. He wrapped the reins around a pole by the garden gate specifically for the purpose of tethering horses and then offered Sophia a hand down.

Once she'd joined him on the ground, he turned toward the cottage. "Hello? Hello!"

The head of a woman, gray haired and overly thin, appeared at the window next to the door. "What do you want?"

"Hello, Missus. I'm Jeremy Fraser, Investigating Officer of Bow Street. I'm looking for Harvey Tumbler. Would he happen to be here?"

"Be off with you. We know who you be and we know Harvey's not done it."

"Not done what?" Sophia asked, assuming a look of puzzlement.

"Whatever you come to arrest him for."

Jeremy laughed lightly and shook his head. "No, no, Missus. Be reassured. I would have brought other officers with me, had I been meaning to arrest Mr. Tumbler. I just came to talk."

"Harvey did not kill his sister," the woman said. "Ask anyone. We know he's innocent and we won't let you take him."

Sweeping his arm toward the small carriage, Jeremy looked incredulous. "We can't take him anywhere, Missus." He glanced at Sophia with this statement and now she understood why he had intentionally brought the limited two-seater carriage.

"I just came to talk," he repeated.

"Don't care! He's safe where he is and there he'll stay."

"Please, Mrs. Hummel, let us speak with him," Sophia said. She attempted to suffuse her voice with authority and a touch of humility—a difficult combination—but she thought she had pulled it off until the woman spoke again.

"Get off my property."

"Mrs. Hummel, while the town might know Mr. Tumbler did not kill his sister, until the true murderer is caught, the authorities will still have their suspicions." Sophia did not name the inept constable but Mrs. Hummel would understand of whom she spoke. "Mr. Tumbler will have to stay hidden forever!" A trifle dramatic, but in essence true. "How can a blacksmith run his business that way? If he helps us find the killer, he helps himself."

"Off. My. Property!" the woman bellowed.

Her shout startled the horses. Sophia and Jeremy grabbed the reins, pulling their heads down. They stroked the horses' necks and murmured calmingly until they no longer pawed the ground, nickering in distress.

"No use in staying," Sophia said softly. "Mrs. Hummel is not going to cooperate."

"Nay, but I might," said a voice behind them. "I'm Harvey Tumbler."

Sophia and Jeremy whirled around to see a large, swarthy man standing in the doorway. Shadows across his face hid his expression. "Depends on what you have to say."

"Ask," Jeremy corrected. "We've little to say, more questions to ask."

"Better get started then. I ain't standing here fer long," Harvey Tumbler said. His voice was a deep bass, almost a growl.

Sophia glanced at Jeremy, and in unison they stepped a few feet closer to the cottage. They saw Harvey Tumbler straighten and lean back, and they halted. The message was clear: "That was close enough."

Sophia opened her mouth to speak but hesitated—after all, this man had just lost his sister and was hiding out in fear that the law was going to arrest him for the crime. Harrowing times for the poor man.

"Ask yer questions." Harvey Tumbler rocked back and forth on his feet.

"Yes, well . . . our deepest condolences, Mr. Tumbler," Sophia began solemnly.

Mr. Tumbler stared at her with his mouth turned down. "An' I accept them. Bertha were a bit odd, there was no doubt of that, and we weren't close—no one would say so, not even her. Still, we was family an' she didn't deserve to die like that." He dropped his eyes to the ground. "No, didn't deserve it. Never hurt no one. It's not right!"

"Absolutely, Mr. Tumbler," Jeremy agreed. "Not right in the least!" He huffed a deep sigh before continuing. "There is a possibility . . . that she sold monkshood to ease joint pain, not knowing that it would be used as a lethal poison."

"Did she say anything to you about it?" Sophia asked, taking up the thread of questioning. "Anything at all about selling the poison, or even to whom she sold it?" She tried to contain the desperation in her voice, but she could hear it painting her words. "Or who was the target?"

"Mentioned the poison. No names. Kept her mouth shut, that one." The man stepped back into the shadows and started to swing the door closed.

"Can you make your letters, Mr. Tumbler?" Jeremy asked quickly.

The door slowed. "What?"

"Can you write?"

"O' course I can. Though not as anyone can read—bit of a scrawl. What's that got ta do with Bertha?"

"There was a letter in her larder from you," he explained.

Mr. Tumbler snorted. "Not from me. Haven't put pencil to paper in years."

Jeremy exchanged a glance with Sophia.

"Did you see her on the day she died?" Jeremy asked.

"Yup. Early that morning. I dropped by with a . . . a bit a meat for 'er table."

"Did you see any of her customers while you were there?" Sophia asked.

"Saw a woman leave. I didna pay attention, an' I didna recognize the woman; she were covered in a great cloak and 'ad her hood up. Bertha called her 'lady of death.'"

———◆———

Driving back down the road, Sophia and Jeremy were silent for some minutes.

"We didn't learn anything of value," Sophia finally said, ending her sentence with a huff.

Jeremy frowned and flicked the reins. "Actually, I think we learned a great deal."

"Oh?"

"Bertha's last client was a woman. That is significant. Half the population just dropped off the suspicion list. We also know that the act of poisoning would have needed someone accommodating in the manor's staff to help—a stranger could not have wandered the halls of Allenton, dropping poison into tea. Not without being noticed."

"Yes, you're right. It was not a wasted visit or time. Perhaps I was just wishing, hoping, for more." Sophia shook her head, looking skyward. "I keep expecting the solution to jump out at us. Sooner than later would be nice—time is of the essence."

"We also learned—I did, at least—that I quite like having someone with me during an investigation, someone with a different perspective. Your questions are different from those I would pose. If we thought in a like manner, it would be redundant."

Sophia's heart beat a little faster and she smiled, though it was weak. "You think I'm contributing?"

"You are indeed. Oh. What is this now?"

Jeremy guided the horses to the side of the road. Sophia lifted her head, looking past the brim of her bonnet and over the horses' heads.

Charlotte Dewey, dressed in ruffles and pink, strode purposely down the road toward them, a basket in her hand swinging as she walked. She paused every few feet to look into the bushes beside her. At one point, Charlotte looked over her shoulder. After each pause, she continued on with more speed, until she was nearly running toward them.

"Good day, Sophia, Mr. Fraser," Charlotte said, a tad winded. She approached Jeremy's side, leaning on the side rail. "How opportune. I hope you can help me." Her voice warbled, and she seemed apprehensive.

"Is something wrong, Miss Dewey?" Jeremy asked, sounding concerned.

Sophia wanted to smack his arm to bring him to his senses. Charlotte was breathless—too much so for a wander down a country lane, even at a quick-footed pace. It was clearly all an act, bent on securing his sympathies. And it seemed to be working.

"I'm delivering a ham." Charlotte gestured needlessly to a chunk of meat in her basket. "To the Priddys." She pointed to a spot behind them. "Up the next road."

Sophia frowned and shook her head. "There is no other road up there, Charlotte. We're coming from that direction." She smoothed her skirt across her knees for want of something else to do. "Just the Hummel place at the top of Savor Road."

Charlotte lifted her chin. "The path is there, on the other side of that boulder. I've been on it before. The road, I mean, not the boulder . . ." She laughed weakly. "It's hidden by the grasses. They're tall at this time of year. Anyway, I'm to deliver the ham. Mrs. Priddy won it at the fair but had a parcel of children with her, and I offered to bring it up after I finished my time at the charity booth.

"So, here I am. And . . . I keep hearing noises in the bushes. There are no creatures in the woods—at least, none that I have spotted so far. And yet, I hear noises. Rustling, as if someone is moving around in the shrubbery behind me but trying to stay concealed." She took a deep breath and shuddered dramatically. "Could I get a ride with you to the Priddy farm? It wouldn't take you more than ten minutes out of your way."

Jeremy glanced at Sophia, and they both looked down at the tiny space between them.

"Apologies, Miss Dewey," Jeremy said. "We have no room for a third person. However, I could lead the horses, and then the three of us could walk to the Priddys together."

Sophia shifted in her seat, swiveling her legs to the end of the bench. Before Jeremy could protest, she jumped down.

"Or," she said, "you take Charlotte and I'll walk back to Allenton. The distance is not great." Sophia gestured Charlotte toward the empty seat.

"Oh no, Sophia, I couldn't do that," Charlotte said . . . even as she rushed round the back of the carriage. She leaped up without being aided and made herself comfortable on the newly vacated bench. Tucking her arm around Jeremy's elbow, she bestowed on him a surprisingly flirtatious smile. She didn't even glance in Sophia's direction. "I think Miss Thompson's solution quite superior."

Sophia chuckled, secretly pleased with the way Jeremy studiously stared straight ahead. He clearly didn't appreciate the exchange of passengers; it erased any shadow of jealousy that might have sprung up from the cozy picture of Charlotte clinging to Jeremy's arm.

"Poor Mrs. Priddy would be quite overwhelmed should a party of three arrive to deliver her one ham," Sophia remarked lightly.

Charlotte leaned toward Sophia, still holding Jeremy's arm. "There's someone in the woods, someone sneaking around. I keep hearing noises."

"So you said." Sophia shrugged in an attempt to appear nonchalant when, in fact, she was beginning to wonder if Charlotte really was afraid. "We could all return to Allenton and I'll have a footman deliver the ham."

"No, no." Charlotte flapped her free hand toward Sophia. "Mrs. Priddy needs her ham. She has eight children, you know."

"I didn't. I don't know the Priddys at all." Sophia stepped away from the carriage and looked past Charlotte to Jeremy. "I'll see you back at Allenton," she said.

"You don't need to walk. Here, take the carriage," he said to Sophia, ignoring Charlotte's squawk of protest. He started to shift, but Charlotte clung to him, preventing him from getting down.

His face grew red, though with discomfort or anger, Sophia was not sure which. He looked down at Charlotte and spoke in a clipped tone. "If you would unhand me, Miss Dewey, I would give the carriage to Miss Thompson, and the two of you ladies could deliver the ham. I'll walk back to the main road. And I'll ensure there are no murderous villains in the shrubbery as I go."

"Oh no, Mr. Fraser. Please, I feel so much safer when you are near. And you, too, Sophia. Come, you can sit on my lap."

Sophia laughed, caught Jeremy's puzzled glance, and turned it into a cough. "Thank you, Charlotte, but I would rather walk back to Allenton. I assure you, there is no one in the woods."

CHAPTER TWENTY-ONE

Grave Concern

Sophia watched the carriage as a reluctant Jeremy turned the horses to trot back up the road.

Once alone, she leaned her ear toward the side of the road and listened: birdsongs—lovely, and not the least mysterious or intimidating . . . a rustle of wind . . . the buzz of insects. Nothing untoward, no sound of stealth. Charlotte was being overly sensitive.

Sophia snorted in derision.

And yet, with no conversation to distract her, Sophia's uneasiness began to build with every step that increased the distance between her and Jeremy. The situation was now critical; if she and Jeremy didn't solve these murders soon, he would be forced back to London and she to Welford Mills, both having failed. How would anyone be convinced that she would make a career as a Bow Street Runner after having such a dismal start?

Not only would her hopes and dreams be in ruins, but she would also no longer have Jeremy's company. They had so much in common and shared the same ideals; to find such like company seemed near impossible. Would they have found each other only to be torn apart?

No, it would not be. She would not allow it.

Organizing the thoughts in her head, Sophia started down the list of clues and suspects, beginning with Andrew's death and ending with Bertha's. Certainties were practically nonexistent.

Except one.

The murderer had no remorse—no limits and no boundaries. The mix of lost souls, the murder victims, were from all walks of life and social classes, no age similarities or personality types between them.

What Sophia needed was the *purpose*—what the murderer hoped to accomplish. What tied them all together in a neat bow in the murderer's mind?

Wiping a drop of perspiration from the nape of her neck, Sophia undid the ribbon below her chin and pulled off her bonnet. Now she could feel the sun directly on her head and allow the warmth to soak into her, hopefully encouraging the development of ideas. Rocks crunched under her boots and the thatched roof of a cottage up ahead peeked through the branches and leaves.

Sophia began to hum; it was a contemplative, tuneless hum that had nothing to do with music. Perhaps a different linear direction would reveal an inconsistency.

First, the herbalist's murderer was a woman—or someone dressed as a woman. A local, not a random stranger off the street killing on a whim. The person was likely associated with the Waverleys, as all the murders were associated with Allenton Park. "Accidents" in the manor itself—toys left in dangerous places, chocolates poisoned, shots fired through the conservatory window—all suggested a knowledge of the persons in and about Allenton. The book of poisons and the recipe she'd found had been in the manor library. And where did the poachers come into the picture, with their snares around Andrew's feet and in Bertha's larder?

It had to have been someone at Allenton.

Deep in concentration, Sophia heard a rustle in the bushes beside her. She stopped mid-thought and slowly turned her head.

Three pairs of eyes stared back.

Sophia stood still—very, very still—and breathed deeply. Her heart started to race and yet, she still did not move. She didn't want to startle the staring persons; she would never catch them if they decided to run.

Charlotte had been right; she *had* been followed, and the owners of those three sets of eyes were now following Sophia.

They had been stealthy, but not stealthy enough. Sophia had heard the snap of branches and the crackle of dried leaves; she had seen the shadows change shape and followed the thump of footsteps mere yards from where she stood.

She should have been nervous or even scared; wisdom dictated that a young woman by herself on a deserted road should be in want of security—but she wasn't scared. She was going to be a Bow Street Detective; she would have to be resilient, strong-minded, and not easily unnerved. Perhaps it was experience, little enough though it might be, that told her stealth wasn't necessarily a sign of villainy, merely of secrecy. Also, this trio was clearly not skilled in furtive, quiet movements. A good sign.

"Well?" Sophia said to the shrub. "What do you want?" She waited as the eyes blinked and grew wide in surprise. "You're not very well hidden. I know you're there."

The shrub remained silent and still.

"Fine." Sophia dropped into a squat, grabbed a handful of pebbles off the road, and stood again. She pitched a small rock with moderate force into the bushes, then another with more force.

She heard a soft grunt. "I have more where those came from. Step out at once or I'll pitch them all at you!" To show that she meant what she said, Sophia raised her arm to toss another rock.

"All right, all right. Don't throw any more, they sting like the devil," a male voice said.

"Serves you right for following a poor defenseless young lady around," she retorted.

The bush shook as it disgorged three figures. They were swathed in long cloaks, browns and green to blend in with the vegetation, and they clutched their hoods, trying to pull them over their faces.

"Didn't feel defenseless to me," one of the men muttered under his breath.

"Just checking on you, miss," one of the men said in a falsely high voice. "Making sure you be fine."

Sophia looked down at his boots sticking out from under the cloak; they were brown with black toes. It took her only a moment to recall the last time she had seen those rather odd boots.

"That's very kind of you, Mr. Phillips. But staying hidden and trying to avoid detection does not fill me with confidence in your benevolence."

"I'm not Mr. Phillips," the man said, his voice even higher than before.

"I recognize your boots, Mr. Phillips. Come, gentlemen, you must be hot. Take your cloaks off and then you can tell me what this is all about."

Sophia dropped her rocks back to the ground and dusted off her hands. Slowly the men started to tug at their cloaks.

"Just trying to understand what was going on, Miss Thompson," Glen Phillips said as he dropped his cloak to the ground; his face was red and sweat dripped down his cheeks.

"What do you mean?" Sophia watched the other men as they flung off the heavy material of their disguises. She did not recognize the other two.

"We wanted to make sure you were safe," Phillips explained. "There's lots of nasty things going on hereabouts and we didna want you gettin' yourself into any kinda trouble."

"And we didn't want to be blamed for it if ya did," a tall bearded man with protruding ears said. "Best we know what's goin' on so as we can defend ourselves."

"That's a rather weak excuse for frightening a young lady walking down a road minding her own business." Sophia leaned forward toward the two unknowns. "And who might you be?"

"Brent Hayter, miss."

"Leonard Priddy," the last man said softly, as if not really wishing to be identified.

With a nod of her head Sophia indicated for Hayter go on.

"You haven't been minding your own business, miss. You been investigating. We all know that, and now the town is full of Runners. It's just a matter a time before they come after the woodsmen an' say we was the ones what did Mr. Andrew in."

Sophia shook her head. Woodsmen? No, indeed. They were poachers. And with that realization, Sophia's confidence evaporated. She had always had a sneaking suspicion that the local poachers were involved in these dire deeds, and now they were following her. She pursed her lips, lifted her chin, and glared with disapproval.

Clearly unaware that he should have been intimidated, Phillips continued. "We been keeping an eye on the family since Mr. Stacks were killed. We knew the wind of blame were headin' in our direction. And now more Runners have been called in. Whatcha do that for? They's just going to muddy the waters."

"I did not call them in, and neither did Mr. Fraser. Bow Street, in their infinite wisdom, decided that extra help was needed. Also, Andrew was found with snares wrapped around his feet," Sophia said with a shrug. "Thinking that poachers might have been involved is not a stretch of the imagination."

"An accident—"

"Hardly, Mr. Hayter. Andrew was stabbed."

"Missed his footing, stabbed his-self."

"A knife was not found with him," Sophia said. "What did he do, pitch the weapon into the woods as he lay dying? That's not in the least logical."

"Hunters wouldna done him in. Waverley were one of us." Hayter scuffed his feet and looked up at Sophia from under his deep brows. "He knew where the traps were."

This gave Sophia pause. "One of you? Andrew?"

"Waverley was always up for a lark," Phillips explained. "An' that included hunting. He'd meet us in the clearing whenever we had a full moon."

"Andrew was a poach—a woodsman?"

Her cousin had been wild and flouted authority, but would he have gone so far as to befriend the local hoodlums? Did he have so little to do and so little sense of responsibility?

"Andrew Waverley weren't a poacher, miss," Phillips replied. "This be his family land—he could hunt to his content."

"Yes, he could. But you could not," Sophia said. "Not legally, anyway."

"It were a caper to him, miss," Hayter chimed in, "an' he gave us what he caught or shot—helped feed our families. No harm to no one. So, like I said, Waverley, he knew where the traps were. He wouldna stepped in one unless . . ."

"Unless he were chased into it," Priddy finished. He stared at Sophia with squinted eyes and a sour line to his mouth. "You want answers? Ya shoulda been talking to Waverley's friends. To us."

"But I didn't know about you, did I? I didn't know that Andrew had found mates in . . ."

Sophia stopped before she said anything that the men might find insulting. These men were not of the same social class as Andrew and would rarely bump into one another, or so Sophia had assumed. She should not have presumed that Andrew's friends only ran in the same elevated circle. Lesson learned.

Sophia groaned inwardly, hiding her frustration with a smile. "I believe Mr. Fraser, the Bow Street Detective, spoke to some of Andrew's friends," she said, hoping Jeremy had not been as select in his interviews as she had.

"Just the toffs." Priddy waved his hand dismissively.

Phillips turned on Priddy. "Baxter's not a toff! His family's farmed for decades—"

Sophia interrupted what appeared to be an old argument. "Principal Officer Fraser is quite determined to find Andrew's killer, and you need not worry; there will be no false blame. You can feel comfortable talking to him. He'll want to speak with everyone."

"He'll take us in fer poaching," Hayter protested.

"No, he will not," Sophia snapped. Still, she knew their fears were valid. Had they been dealing with Constable Marley, matters would have been quite different. But it was Jeremy they were talking about—an honorable, trustworthy young gentleman. "He just took Miss Charlotte up to the Priddy place to deliver a prize ham." She half turned, facing the upper road. "Your family home?" Sophia asked over her shoulder, and when no answer was forthcoming, she turned to look at the young man who had introduced himself as Leonard Priddy.

Priddy's brow folded tightly over his pointed nose, and he scratched at his head. "Don't remember anything about a ham."

"A different branch of the Priddy family, perhaps?" Sophia asked. Her heartbeat started to accelerate and she swallowed with difficulty, despite being certain that there was nothing worthy of alarm in the young man's words. She was jumping at shadows.

"No other Priddys 'round here. Besides, we live 'cross town." He pointed down the hill toward West Ravenwood and the collection of buildings in the distance. "No one up there." He used his head to nod in the direction. "Just the Hummels an' the old church."

"Old church?"

"St. Michael's—been a ruin for an age," Priddy said. "Not much left, just the arches and the bell tower. There's a path up there, near the big boulder. Hard to see from here, it's almost grown over."

"Boulder?" she squeaked. "No other cottage? No path? Are you certain?"

"Yes, indeed, miss," Hayter replied. All three men were visibly confused now. "Everyone knows the bell tower; great spot to watch for deer or to grab a kiss from your girl."

Hayter turned a bright red with this declaration and looked vastly uncomfortable. But Sophia barely heard him. She brought her hand up to her mouth, suddenly feeling sick. Fear gripped her insides, and bile crawled up her throat. She stared up the hill to where the carriage had been stopped moments—no, a quarter hour ago.

"What is it, miss?" Phillips asked, coming to her side.

"Why did Charlotte insist that they go up the hill to the Priddy house . . . if there is no house and nowhere to deliver a ham?" she asked, thinking aloud.

Phillips would have no idea what she was talking about. Sophia glanced at him. Then she straightened, lifted her skirt to knee height, and started running as fast as she could.

If Sophia believed the men, which she did, then there was no doubt that Charlotte had lied. It had been a planned distraction. A decoy.

Charlotte knew the area; she had lived in West Ravenwood nearly all her life. She knew that there was no other house at the top of the road—just the Hummels, who were related to the Tumblers. It had been a logical hiding place for Mr. Tumbler. And it was just as logical that Jeremy and Sophia would look for Tumbler there. It would be a simple matter for Charlotte to *bump* into them as they came down the hill.

And Charlotte's gamble had paid off; with most of the town at the fair, few would see her on the deserted road. She had pretended to be scared; she had lured, or tried to lure, both Jeremy and Sophia to the church.

To what end?

Was Charlotte their murderer? Had she killed Andrew—her lover—and then Stacks and Bertha?

Was she now going to kill Jeremy?

Sophia nearly tripped, awkward in her distress. She could hear the men behind her running to catch up.

"There's trouble ahead," she shouted over her shoulder. "I may need your help!"

One of the men kept calling her name as if she were a runaway puppy. She did not have time to stop; no time to explain further. She needed to get to Jeremy. He was in grave danger, she could feel it in her bones.

Sophia hurried up the road, breathless as much from fear as exertion, and then rounded the boulder. There the grass had grown tall but had recently been crushed and bent—as might happen when ridden over by a carriage.

She wanted to see the carriage—Jeremy's rented carriage—returning. It should be coming back down by now, with a frustrated but hale and hearty Bow Street Runner at the reins. He would be annoyed about the wild goose chase. Charlotte would be flustered because she had failed . . . but what was she trying to do? Compromise Jeremy? No, Charlotte was interested in William. She wanted to be a mistress of a grand estate . . . like Allenton.

Then why? If Charlotte was the murderer, why would Jeremy be on her list? Had he discovered something that incriminated her in Andrew's murder?

Try as she might to villainize Charlotte, Sophia could not see the young woman stabbing Andrew or Bertha or feeding Stacks a poison. No, it didn't make sense. None at all.

A sound broke through her thoughts. It was a rumble and snap—not close by but not distant, either.

Sophia scanned the hill and listened again. The lea was broad and seemed deserted. No other sound reached her, certainly nothing loud enough to be heard over her own heavy breathing and the footfalls of the men behind her.

Finally, the top of the bell tower came into view. As she crested the hill, the sizable meadow was dominated by the large ruin of a gothic church. Abandoned for centuries, the front door was gone. Crumbled walls exposed the arched backbone down the length of the nave, and the stairs leading up the tower were visible even from the far side of the meadow where Sophia stood. What had once been an area set aside for carriages of parishioners was now dotted with undergrowth—bushes, shrubs, weeds— and a carriage.

Sophia blinked. She came to an abrupt halt and squinted across the distance. She could not see Jeremy. Where was he?

A figure moved closer to the carriage, a figure in soft pink. Charlotte.

Picking up her skirts once more, Sophia ran. Her boots pounded the path—grasses tried to trip her up, but Sophia plowed through them all. She was focused and determined. She would chase Charlotte. She would get answers.

Even as she watched, Sophia saw Charlotte step into Jeremy's carriage; she flicked the whip, and the horses started off in a casual trot. The nerve!

Sophia wanted to call out, wanted to scream for answers, but she knew better. She would bide her time. The only way out of this meadow was the path on which she stood.

With a twist, Sophia pivoted. The three men were running in tandem behind her.

"Spread. Out. Hide," Sophia panted, putting her hands on her waist. She bent, briefly, trying to catch her breath. "Don't let her get away," she puffed, pointing to the carriage that was approaching.

They must have felt her urgency, as they immediately separated and spread out across the path and then hunkered into the grass, hidden among the weeds and bracken.

Turning back to face Charlotte, Sophia watched as the vehicle grew closer. Hooves pounded the ground in a quick rhythm, drawing ever closer. Sophia wondered if she could grab the bridle as the carriage passed. It was dangerous, but Sophia was desperate.

She had to find Jeremy.

CHAPTER TWENTY-TWO

Catch Me!

Jeremy flicked the reins to encourage the horses into a quick trot. He wanted to get this detour over with as soon as possible. He didn't like leaving Sophia on the side of the road; it felt wrong, despite her reassurances. He would rush to the Priddy house and hurry back. With luck, he would return to Sophia before she was even halfway down the hill.

Trying to hide his anger, Jeremy stared at the road ahead. He was frustrated, irritated, and generally annoyed with Charlotte. She had manipulated Sophia out of the carriage with deft maneuvering, and the last thing he wanted was private time with the reverend's daughter.

As they approached the turnoff to the Priddy property, Jeremy slowed the horses and then brought them to a stop just after the boulder. "This can't be right, Miss Dewey. The road is overgrown. No one has been down here in a dog's age."

"It does look rather deserted. Perhaps there's another way in, a secondary drive or path . . . but this is where Mrs. Priddy said to turn. She made a point of mentioning that rock." Charlotte pointed to the boulder. "I should think she would know how to get to her own house."

"I think you've been sent on a wild goose chase, Miss Dewey. But . . . I suppose we can go a little further to verify."

"Oh, thank you. I would hate to have to explain to Mrs. Priddy that we did not continue down her road because of its deplorable condition. It would be insulting."

With careful steering, Jeremy kept the carriage on the road and plowed through the long tufts of grass. He undertook a comfortable pace past the boulder, and they crested the hill safe and sound, but what met their eyes was not the Priddy house. Indeed, it was not a house at all.

A stone church, aged by centuries, stood in a dilapidated state at the far end of the clearing. There were no intact windows or doors or, for that matter, a roof. Ivy hung from arched rafters, vines fingered into the cracked stones and the ground was strewn with mortared rocks. The bell tower that rose high above the arched entrance was all that remained in reasonable repair. Stairs leading up were visible through the opening due to the lack of doors.

Frowning, Jeremy stood on the foot rail as the horses continued to plod forward. He twisted left and then right, scanning the edge of the forest, looking for any hint of a cottage or dwelling other than the church.

"Oh dear." Charlotte, likely vexed, snorted. She waved toward the church. "Behind perhaps?"

Shaking his head, Jeremy sat back down and guided the horses to the church. He pulled them up near a tall collection of fallen masonry, a temporary stand-in for a hitching pole. "The road is worse here; pocked with holes and parts of the church have tumbled into the grass. I'll have to check the rest on foot. Stay here, I'll look—"

Charlotte slid off her seat before Jeremy had finished his sentence. "The church is so pretty. I might want to sketch it one day. I'll just take a quick peek inside, I'll only be a moment."

"If you wish, Miss Dewey. However, it would be more productive if you helped with the search first—"

"I'll be right there," she said, and with great enthusiasm rushed toward the church, leaving Jeremy sputtering with frustration, and the ham abandoned on the carriage floor.

If it were not for his obligations as a gentleman, Jeremy would have turned the carriage around and started back down the hill right then and there. He wanted to get back to Sophia. He was almost certain that she would not have encountered a murderer on the way back to West Ravenwood, but there was just enough of a doubt that he was anxious to return to her side. She could take care of herself—she was rather adept at it, in fact—but she was also adept at getting *into* trouble.

A squeal from inside the church drew Jeremy out of his thoughts. Charlotte was behaving like a child—they were preforming an act of charity, not taking a jaunt. Frivolity was unseemly.

With another huff of frustration, Jeremy wended his way around several scraggly bushes, ignoring the happy chortles echoing through the nave of the church.

"Mr. Fraser, you must see this!" Charlotte called from within. "There is an engraved stone on one of the walls. Come tell me what it says. I think it is in Latin. You know Latin, don't you, Mr. Fraser? All well-educated young gentlemen know Latin."

As Jeremy had already walked around to the other end of the church, he stuck his head through one of the nearest windows rather than go around to the door. Overlooking the apse, Jeremy glared at Charlotte's back. She stood in what used to be the center aisle of the church; her soft pink gown contrasted sharply with the cold gray tones of the stone pillars and half walls.

"I'm not in a Latin reading mood, Miss Dewey," Jeremy said, watching her jump and whirl around in surprise. When her eyes met his, she smiled—an insipid display that was most unappealing. "We need to find the Priddy place before we do anything else."

"I can see through all the windows." She gestured toward the gaping holes in the walls. "But I have yet to see a cottage. However, there is a better vantage point, which can offer us a view in all directions: the tower. Yes, come check out the view from the tower. I'm sure with the two of us looking, we'll be able to spot the Priddy cottage in no time."

Giving the meadow one last glance, hoping—to no avail—for the magical appearance of the Priddy cottage, Jeremy stepped through the window. It took little effort, as the sills had rotted and the stone below them crumbled. It was now no more than a two-foot barrier.

"I don't think a higher view will make a nonexistent cottage suddenly appear," Jeremy said dryly. "We're in the wrong place, Miss Dewey. Your directions were off. Let's go back down to West Ravenwood, pick up Miss Thompson, and ask after the Priddys. Besides," he started to say when he heard Charlotte's footsteps hasten to the front of the church.

"Besides," he repeated louder, calling after her. "The supports to the tower might have crumbled. Best—Miss Dewey, don't go up yet, wait!"

Jeremy dashed across the stone floor to the front entrance hall just in time to see Charlotte's skirts disappear around the corner on the first landing of the bell tower. With a quick glance at the stone columns beneath the stairs, Jeremy shook his head and took a deep, calming breath. He no longer needed to rush; the supports were well preserved, and though the pillars showed signs of age, they were not about to collapse. He followed Charlotte into the tower.

The staircase was wide, the treads worn down in the middle from countless footfalls. At each of the three landings, windows were placed high on the wall. Unfortunately, the windows were small, and while they offered light, they didn't provide any view.

The stairs led to a roofless, crenulated enclosure of considerable size, and as Jeremy stepped out into the open, he saw a figure seated opposite and nearly tripped.

Across from the stairs, Charlotte Dewey rested on a stone bench that was clearly feeling the effects of the weather and age. The deteriorating wall behind it showed signs of decay, missing several large chunks of mortar.

"Careful, Miss Dewey, the wall is crumbling," he said, lifting his hand in warning.

Turning toward him, Charlotte lifted her chin. "I'm hardly a child, Mr. Fraser. I know what is safe and what isn't." She turned back to the notched wall, leaning out in what Jeremy considered a foolhardy fashion.

"Besides, you would catch me, wouldn't you, Mr. Fraser? Oh dear, oh dear, I'm going to fall!" she said, flailing her arm in a dramatic but unconvincing manner.

Slowly, Jeremy stepped closer. "You're smarter than that, Miss Dewey. You would not take such a chance."

Charlotte turned back toward him. "How do you know? We're virtually strangers."

And then she smiled. It was a most unappealing grimace and gave Jeremy pause. Something was not right.

Charlotte's eyes were focused on something behind him, and her churlish expression had disappeared. In its place was a look of triumph—a gloating sort of smirk.

"What is this about?" Jeremy asked. His heart pounded out an accelerated rhythm even as he stilled, listening to the stealthy footfalls behind him. "Is this a prank? Do the Priddys even live in West Ravenwood?"

Without waiting for an answer, Jeremy whirled around, arms raised in a defensive position.

He didn't know what to expect, but Mrs. Curtis would not have been his first—or tenth—guess.

As he turned, the housekeeper swung a wide plank at his head. But it was heavy, and missed when Jeremy jerked back; the board smashed painfully into his shoulder instead and pushed him to the ground.

Mrs. Curtis stepped closer and swung the plank again at his head. Jeremy rolled onto his back, but rather than deflecting the blow, he grabbed the board and ripped it out of her hands. He tossed it to the side with a great heave and watched as it sailed over the crenelated wall and clattered to the earth below.

Mrs. Curtis' look of surprise was priceless—surpassed only by that of Charlotte, who stood opposite the housekeeper. Mrs. Curtis recovered first, pulling out a sizable knife that had been hidden in the folds of her black skirts. Holding it in a white-knuckle grip, Mrs. Curtis lifted the weapon and brandished it at Jeremy.

Still on the ground, Jeremy watched the slow hypnotic movement of the knife until it came to a menacing halt.

The housekeeper glared at Jeremy as she spoke. "Where is Miss Thompson, Charlotte?"

Surprised by the familiar address, Jeremy swiveled his head toward Charlotte.

"I tried to get her to come, didn't I, Mr. Fraser?" Charlotte circled around Jeremy to where Mrs. Curtis stood blocking the stairs—the stairs down to freedom and safety. "But she would not be convinced. We left her on the road just before the boulder."

"Did she see you? Did Miss Thompson see you, Charlotte?" Mrs. Curtis asked, still staring at Jeremy. "Ah, ah, Mr. Fraser, stop. I can see what you're doing. Stay right where you are." She straightened her arm—the one holding the knife.

Jeremy took a sharp, silent breath and leaned back, ignoring the pain in his shoulder. He looked at Mrs. Curtis with new understanding as the clues fell into place.

Someone in the house. Yes, who better than one of the guiding forces of the domestic staff? The housekeeper could go anywhere unquestioned—to the attic for a toy, into the kitchen with poisons, to the library to find a book. Grabbing a rifle from the gun cabinet might have required some implausible story if she had been caught . . . but she hadn't been. Yes, Mrs. Curtis was perfectly placed to mete out her murderous mission.

But *why*? Why would she do such a thing? And where did Charlotte figure in this whole mess?

He stared at the knife, somewhat unnerved. His training had not covered the threat of physical violence.

"A knife? Really?" Jeremy snorted. He tried a derisive laugh, swallowing against the tightness in his throat. Mrs. Curtis was in lunging range, and she held the knife with well-practiced ease. "I thought a rifle was your weapon of choice."

Mrs. Curtis lifted the corners of her mouth in a slow, calculated smile. "As you know, rifles can be woefully inaccurate. Especially shooting through glass."

"And unwieldy, at times."

"Exactly," the woman said calmly. "I've learned to rely on a good sharp knife. Gets the job done every time."

Jeremy nodded. "Good to know." He shifted his balance. "I'm getting up now, Mrs. Curtis. The stones are eating into my hands and it's rather painful."

He didn't wait for a reply, using his movement to stealthily grab a stone from the ground and hide it in his palm. The two women stood between him and the stairs, and he wondered if he could barrel past them to escape. He glanced at his forearm, assessing the number of layers of material that would protect him from the blade of Mrs. Curtis' knife.

Again, Mrs. Curtis spoke to Charlotte without looking away from Jeremy. "Did Sophia see you leave with Mr. Fraser, Charlotte?"

"Of course Sophia saw me. I tried to get her up here as well, but she didn't want to be squished in the carriage." Charlotte turned to Jeremy with a sour look. "Why did you have to hire such a small vehicle?" She shook her head and frowned. "Sophia said she would walk to Allenton Park. She hasn't had time to get back to the main road yet, she—"

"Go, now! Stop her from getting any further."

"No!" Jeremy said with more emotion than he intended. He took a calming breath. "You don't need to fetch Sophia. She doesn't know that you were involved in any of this, Mrs. Curtis.

And we did not suspect Charlotte. Nothing has changed. Sophia doesn't know anything. Let her be."

"Why then did you send for the other detectives—your reinforcements—if not to make an arrest?" Mrs. Curtis demanded.

Jeremy squinted at the woman, trying to assess her temper. He kept his tone passive, watching the finely honed edge of her weapon. "I didn't call in reinforcements," he said. "Bow Street thought the case was taking too long. They sent the extra men."

"Oh dear, you were certain that you had been unmasked." Charlotte laughed carelessly. "It seems you were premature, Mama. Jumping at shadows."

Mrs. Curtis' brow folded and her mouth pursed into a tight pucker. "The die is cast, my dear girl; there is no turning back. We need Sophia. Otherwise she'll point her finger directly at *you* when *his* body is found. All will be for naught!"

She raised the knife yet again just as Jeremy stepped forward. The blade slit his vest, shirt and pricked his skin. A spot of red blossomed on his chest.

"Oh dear," she said, watching the blood spread across his shirt. "It seems you have a ruined shirt." She smiled a repulsive grin.

"You do know that murderers are usually hanged," Jeremy said, holding absolutely still. "It is a most unpleasant death."

Mrs. Curtis smiled her repulsive smile again. "Only if they are caught." She glanced back at Charlotte. "You must stop Sophia. Send her up here and then get back down to the fair and make a great cake of yourself so that everyone will remember that you were there."

Jeremy's heart beat twice its normal rhythm. This conversation was surreal.

He frowned at the housekeeper, rubbing his thumb across the

rough edge of the stone in his hand. As weapons go, it was rather lackluster, but at least it was something.

"Why?" Jeremy asked. "Why did they all need to die?"

There was no reply for several moments, as if he had not spoken at all.

Charlotte and Mrs. Curtis shared a look, one of superiority and condescension. "Charlotte's life should not be made small because of an accident of birth," Mrs. Curtis said. "She deserves all the comforts promised to her by a feckless boy pursuing his own pleasures at her expense."

Then she shoved Charlotte with her free hand toward the stairs. "Go!" she yelled. "Get Sophia!"

Charlotte glanced at Jeremy. "Beg your pardon." She offered a bobbed curtsy and a resigned shrug, as if murder were a small affair. An inconvenience. A slight faux pas.

Jeremy snorted in disbelief. With no sense of remorse or contemplation of what was right and what was wrong, Charlotte had accepted his murder as inevitable. Such a cold and calculating soul.

Watching Charlotte pivot and head down the stairs, Jeremy listened to her footfalls as she turned the corner of the second flight and the echo of her steps became softer.

"I didn't want Charlotte to see this," Mrs. Curtis said.

She suddenly lunged, catching Jeremy unawares. He jerked away, turning as he did so. The knife cut into his sleeve, leaving a gaping hole across his forearm.

Using the stone for extra heft, Jeremy smashed his fist against the knife hilt, trying to knock it from her hand.

It almost worked. Almost.

Mrs. Curtis jumped back, taking a ragged breath that turned into a chuckle. "You think you can escape."

"I'm certainly going to try."

The housekeeper stared at Jeremy for a moment. "By all means, Mr. Fraser. That is your prerogative."

And then she thrust the knife at his chest.

CHAPTER TWENTY-THREE

Learning to Fly

Jeremy's arms were up before he even thought to move. He crossed them in front of his body, pushing out against the knife before the lethal blade reached his neck or his chest.

Had Mrs. Curtis never killed before, he might not have been alarmed; it took self-control, determination, and a hard heart to slit someone's throat or stab them in the gut. But Mrs. Curtis knew what she was about—how much pressure was needed, even how it would feel to slice into flesh.

It was horrifying, all the more so because he did not sense any mania in the woman, just resolve—a cold, cold heart. Like mother, like daughter.

The knife bit into his coat and through his shirt. The slice across his bicep was almost anticlimactic; quick with only a slight sting. But Jeremy knew—he had been told—that the sharpest of knives cut deep and painless . . . and bled profusely. His coat sleeve and vest were soon soaked with blood.

Reaching through the swing of the blade, Jeremy tried to

deflect Mrs. Curtis' aim, paying for it when she nicked his hands, and then dragged the blade over his other arm.

An image of Sophia formed in his mind's eye, her laughter echoed through his head, and anger coursed through his veins. Mrs. Curtis was a threat to Sophia, and she meant to end Sophia's life as well as his. Fury nearly drove him blind, until reason prevailed.

He held his stone above his head in as threatening a manner as he could devise—considering it was a lumpy rock against a finely honed knife. Punching her in the head no longer seemed ungentlemanly—there had to be some justice, some retribution.

Mrs. Curtis shifted her gaze to his eyes, then to the stone in his hand. As he thought would happen, the knife slowed its thrashing.

He stepped back and lowered his stone—it really was a pathetic weapon. "Might I know why you wish to kill me?"

"I thought you would have worked most of it out by now."

Mrs. Curtis leaned away, even going so far as to change the aim of the knife to just above his collarbone. She placed both hands on the hilt. Her intention was clear; she was preparing for a final assault.

Jeremy looked at his puny stone and nearly dropped it. "Is my knowledge that you killed Andrew enough? Or are you simply enjoying yourself now—enjoying the power of holding someone's life in your hands?"

Mrs. Curtis snorted. "I most certainly am not enjoying the violence. What a terrible suggestion. I'm merely the hand of justice. Andrew deserved to die. He was a selfish boy, toying with Charlotte's affections."

"Does Charlotte *have* any affections?" Jeremy asked sarcastically.

He regretted it immediately when Mrs. Curtis lashed up at his neck. Had Jeremy not lifted his arm in time, the knife would have run along his collarbone.

. . . As it had in Howard Tuff's murder.

Jeremy frowned. "These murders didn't begin with Andrew, did they? They began with Howard Tuff, twenty years ago. You rolled him into the hunting trap and left him to rot."

Mrs. Curtis shrugged. "Have you figured out why?"

Jeremy glanced over his shoulder, more to turn his ear toward the stairs than to see if anyone was coming. He could hear the sounds of Charlotte jumping into his carriage and the slow clip-clop of his horses as they started off.

Jeremy shifted as if uncomfortable with his thoughts, when he was, in fact, decreasing the distance between them and planning his attack. "Charlotte called you 'Mama,' and you did not react in surprise or correct her. I would think that Howard was not happy about being a father."

Mrs. Curtis snorted, and a frown flashed across her face. "That is quite a leap of thought. But you're right; Howard was *not* pleased." Her mouth curled up in disgust. "He was not interested in becoming a father. He decided to go back to sea—to sail away. Away from me, away from his responsibilities . . . Hardly the act of an honorable man."

"But was it worth killing him over?"

"I thought so." She smiled—the sight turned Jeremy's stomach sour. "I stabbed him, dragged his body into an old poacher's trap and got rid of his belongings. It wasn't easy. Howard was not a small man." Mrs. Curtis' tone was plaintive, as if she were expecting sympathy.

"Indeed," Jeremy said.

Mrs. Curtis stared into the space above Jeremy's left shoulder, seemingly unaware of his sarcasm. "It was Mrs. Dewey who helped me deal with the complications."

"Mrs. Dewey helped you? With the baby or the murder?"

"Don't be ridiculous," she snapped. "Mrs. Dewey would not be involved in a murder; the baby, of course! I became her companion on an extended holiday, and when we returned, Charlotte was hers. And I was offered a promotion to housekeeper."

"It must have been difficult to watch another woman raise your daughter."

"I saw Charlotte at church; that was enough. I hardly cared for her, or thought I didn't . . . until Andrew came into the picture. He told Charlotte that he adored her while chasing other skirts. *Several* other girls. It was monstrous." She stared off into the distance. "It was Howard Tuff all over again. And so, Andrew met his fate much the same way as Howard. It was easier the second time. Curious, don't you think, how these things circle around?"

"Poor Charlotte. She must have been devastated by Andrew's death."

"Why? William is much more suited to her. Charlotte's biggest obstacle now is Daphne. Charlotte could be mistress of Allenton Park if it weren't for Daphne. I tried to eliminate Daphne as well, but the girl didn't cooperate."

"So inconsiderate." Jeremy tightened his grip on the rock, focusing on the hair above Mrs. Curtis' left ear. A knock with the stone and then a twist of her arm should do the trick. He would throw her to the ground, use his neckcloth to tie her hands together, and march the woman down the stairs.

"Was that why you sent Daphne poison chocolates?" he asked,

continuing to play for time. He gripped the stone and slowly cocked his arm behind him—he would need the extra momentum. "Why you tried to kill her? So the estate, when it was passed on, would not be divided between heirs?"

He tried to keep the derision from his tone—to no avail.

"Naturally." Mrs. Curtis shrugged. "It was all for Charlotte . . . Charlotte and William."

"Then why kill Stacks, or Bertha Tumbler?"

"Gracious, your questions! Too many! It's been grand chatting, but I know you're delaying. It's rather pointless. There's nothing you can do. I'm going to kill you and then Sophia. All I can promise is to do so quickly. You're half gone as it is. I can see you're starting to shake from the loss of blood." She smiled, looking thoroughly satisfied. "I really didn't want to kill anyone after Andrew, but you would not *let it go*."

"Catching murderers and seeking justice is my job."

"Yes. Annoyingly so."

"Do you even realize that you've killed four people?"

"Four and counting," Mrs. Curtis said with a most unpleasant smile.

Jeremy stared, astounded that someone would not care about taking *one* human life, let alone four. As he considered his next move, Jeremy heard voices echoing up from the churchyard. He could not understand the words, but he recognized one voice.

Sophia.

———— • ————

Sophia stared at the approaching carriage and then waved her arms in a wide arc, trying to get Charlotte's attention. The horses shied and pulled the carriage off the path; one of the wheels fetched up on a large rock, bringing the vehicle and its driver to a sudden halt.

Charlotte leaned to the side, likely trying to see beyond the rumps of the horses. She met Sophia's gaze with a look of surprise but it quickly disappeared.

"Oh, Sophia, I'm so glad you're here. I was worried that you would be nearing town by now." Charlotte glanced around the field as she spoke. "I need your help! Mr. Fraser needs your help."

"Where *is* Jeremy, Charlotte?" Sophia asked with a calm she did not feel. Her heart was pounding a mile a minute, and she felt sick.

Charlotte gestured halfheartedly behind her. "If you could help me free the carriage, I'll show you where he is."

"Damn the carriage, just tell me about Jeremy!"

Charlotte sighed—*sighed*, as if *she* were deeply burdened. "He slipped on one of the rocks in the tower and he can't get up." Charlotte squinted at Sophia, almost daring her to doubt her word.

"Slipped?"

"Yes. He hit his head, blood streaming into his eyes. He looks awful. I'm afraid he's going to die, and *you* won't help me get the carriage back on the road. I need to get a surgeon." She pushed herself to the edge of the bench and then used the hub of the wheel to step down. "I thought you cared," she shouted as she examined the wheel. "If he dies it will be on *your* shoulders!"

Sophia ignored the girl, looking past the carriage to the ruined church. Movement on the top floor of the tower caught her eye. Through the crenellations, she could see two figures. Only one faced her.

"Jeremy," she said in a whispered gasp. Then turned her head to yell over her shoulder. "Make sure she does not get away!"

Sophia ran to the church and through the front opening. She heard the rush of feet behind her and Charlotte's scream—a shout of protest and outrage. Sophia would have praised the poachers for being fleet of foot had she not been so terribly worried about Jeremy.

Lifting her skirts to her knees, Sophia took the stairs two at a time. When she reached the top, she found Jeremy standing with Mrs. Curtis near the tower's edge—too close to the edge, and too close to each other. Jeremy was covered in blood. His blood.

Mrs. Curtis glanced over her shoulder, met Sophia's gaze, and raised her arm. The knife in her hand glinted in the sunlight.

Sophia moved before a single thought passed through her mind.

She slammed into Mrs. Curtis, knocking the woman sideways. The knife sliced through the air and across Sophia's arm.

Mrs. Curtis fell hard against the crumbling wall, sending mortar and bricks cascading into the churchyard below. A shout echoed through the glen. It was muddled and unintelligible and Sophia ignored it, turning instead toward Jeremy.

Jeremy stood a few feet away, a horrified expression on his pale face. He reached out, grabbed Sophia's hand, and jerked her away from the wall. The momentum pulled Sophia in a skid across the floor.

At the same time, Mrs. Curtis was attempting to rise. She braced herself against the wall, her knife was once again poised to strike a deadly blow . . .

But with her whole weight pressed against it, the crumbling wall gave way.

Mrs. Curtis fell into the emptiness.

Sophia cringed, expecting to hear a hideous crunch as the

housekeeper's body hit the hard-packed earth. But it never came. Instead, there was a shout and a thump, and then the sound of a woman screeching. Mrs. Curtis had survived the fall, but not unscathed—nor unconscious.

Jeremy helped Sophia to her feet, and they approached the edge of the tower to carefully peek over the side.

Below, Mrs. Curtis lay on the ground screaming, her skirts twisted around her knees. As they watched in amazement, the woman struggled to sit up, reached toward her right foot, and fell back with a yelp of pain.

Charlotte, on the other hand, bucked and pulled, and tried to break free of Glen Phillips' grasp as they stood a few feet away from the fallen woman. She shouted rude words that Sophia rarely, if ever, heard, and finally was allowed to drop into a squat beside Mrs. Curtis.

"Are you all right?" Jeremy asked.

It took a moment for Sophia to realize that Jeremy was addressing her. She pulled her eyes away from the drama playing out below and turned toward him, taking a deep breath to calm her wobbly knees.

"Me?" she said, finally. "*You* were the one being menaced by a deranged killer."

"I actually don't think she is deranged," Jeremy said, lifting Sophia's arm. "And this is why I asked." Her sleeve was a ruin, cut open and soaked with blood. "Mrs. Curtis had no qualms about slicing and dicing." He pointed to his own coat sleeve and ruined waistcoat, still oozing.

Quickly undoing his neckcloth, Jeremy wrapped it around Sophia's wound. "You need a surgeon."

"Strange . . . it doesn't hurt."

"That's good to hear. But, unfortunately, as soon as you start to relax, the pain will make itself known."

Sophia glanced at his bloody waistcoat, knowing that he was speaking from experience. She watched as he wrapped the cloth around her arm, ending at her wrist.

"Is this something they taught you at detective school?" she asked. "How to bind wounds and capture felons?"

"Yes, actually, it was." He paused, staring down at her with a deep frown. "Why were you not more careful? The woman could have killed you—and would have done so cheerfully. She was so intent on securing Charlotte a place in society that she didn't care a wit for anyone who got in the way."

"*Why?* Why was *I* not more careful?! You are asking in all seriousness?"

Rather than step closer to Jeremy—which would have been closer to the drop, as well—Sophia tugged him away from the opening in the wall.

"For an investigator, *Mr. Fraser*, you're rather obtuse at times. I have not hidden my admiration of you and your skills, and I would miss you terribly if Mrs. Curtis had made you into a minced Bow Street Runner."

It was a huge understatement, of course. Sophia, in the space of minutes, had come to realize that her admiration of Jeremy Fraser was much deeper than . . . well, deeper than admiration.

"I could not stand by and let it happen." She clicked her tongue. "*Why* indeed."

Jeremy chuckled, and he brushed a coil of hair out of her eyes. "Being sliced and diced is not my favorite part of the job, either. But you should not take such chances; you could have gone over the side, too. You might not have fared as well as Mrs. Curtis." He lowered his head. "No need to rearrange your features. I quite like you just the way you are."

And then he bent his head and pressed his lips to hers.

At first, it was a tentative kiss, as if Jeremy was as surprised as she was. But when she curled her arms around his neck, Jeremy wrapped his arms around her waist and lifted her to her toes. Their bodies pressed together in the most delicious manner and Sophia forgot to breathe. She was aware of Jeremy and of him alone: his strength, his gentle lips, and his growing passion. Never before had she felt so intoxicated by the presence of another. She was lost in all the sensations coursing through her body. It was exhilarating and filled her with an energy that she had never experienced before.

The sounds of the churchyard drifted away . . . until a pounding noise interrupted them—footsteps rushing up the tower. They broke apart.

Panting as if *they* had been the ones running up the stairs, Sophia stared at Jeremy in wonder. He stared back in much the same way . . . and then he smiled. It was a grin, really. It was saucy and joyful and offered wonderful things to come.

"Miss Thompson, are you all right?" someone behind her asked. "Miss Thompson?"

Sophia continued to stare at Jeremy, and then she started to laugh. She reached up to touch his lips but he grabbed her hand, placing a kiss on her palm. It sent a shiver up her spine. A most delicious shiver.

"Yes, never better," Sophia whispered.

Miss Sophia Thompson was stubborn, frustratingly so.

Try as he might, Jeremy could not convince her to take the hired carriage and go back to Allenton Park. She insisted that she needed to stay at the ruined church until all the loose ends were tied up; *he* insisted that she needed to see to her wound. Unfortunately, she countered that by pointing out his own wound. And round and round they went, until Mr. Hayter tapped Jeremy on the shoulder and passed him a bucket of clean water.

"Got it from the Hummels. Their place is at the top of the road," he said, pointing somewhat uselessly in that direction— but then, he did not know that Jeremy and Sophia had visited the Hummel cottage just a couple of hours earlier and knew exactly where it was. "It seems that neither of you are goin' anywhere in a hurry and best clean your wounds afore they start ta fester."

Sophia thanked the man prettily. Jeremy grumbled; he now had no leverage to insist that Sophia return to her aunt and uncle's home. Still, he unwound the neckcloth on her arm and washed her wound as best he could. It was still bleeding freely, so he rewrapped it with the sash from Sophia's gown.

Sophia returned the favor, washing the wound on his arm. The cut was not as deep as hers—the thick wool of Jeremy's coat had acted as a barrier to the steel. It would not require stitches, so she said. Better yet, it was no longer bleeding.

Sophia also tried to clean Mrs. Curtis' wounds, but the woman slapped at Sophia whenever she approached. The woman gasped in pain with each lunge. Jeremy put an end to it by splashing the water from the bucket over the housekeeper's head; it cleaned her wound *and* cooled her temper.

Waiting for a wagon to carry Mrs. Curtis and her accomplice, Miss Dewey, back down to West Ravenwood took a fair amount of time. Sophia had suggested going to Allenton Park for this purpose, as it was nearby and it took care of two necessities: transportation and information. The family needed to know that Sophia was safe and soon to return.

The three hunters were instructed to say little at the big house—just to request the wagon but not state the reason. Unfortunately, a surgeon was also needed, and Jeremy had no doubt that it was this requirement that brought the family rushing up the hill.

Mr. and Mrs. Waverley, along with William, Daphne, and Mr. Thompson, arrived before the surgeon and the constable. They alighted from their carriage and rushed to where Sophia and Jeremy were seated on the church stairs.

Shocked by their explanation, the Waverleys called the accusations of murder against Mrs. Curtis outrageous. Mr. Thompson was silent in his condemnation; only his shift to stand beside Sophia, shoulder to shoulder, showed his solidarity with his daughter. Mrs. Curtis did not help her case by mocking and deriding her defenders for giving her such little credit. Clearly, pain was clouding the woman's better judgment.

Mrs. Curtis ignored Mrs. Waverley when she knelt beside her, even going so far as to turn her back on her employer . . . former employer. It was sad to watch. Not just because of the pain Mrs. Curtis was inflicting on herself—Jeremy thought broken ribs a possibility besides the broken foot—but the sadness and stillness of Mrs. Waverley that showed her heartache, memories of her eldest son still raw.

Finally her sense of mother's rage flared, and Mrs. Waverley flailed at the housekeeper, smacking and slapping the woman until the hunters pulled her off.

William, however, was a surprise. He did not go near Miss

Dewey, despite her entreaties. He shook his head, and simply shouted, "No!"

Sophia left her father's side and stood next to her cousins for some minutes, saying nothing. She laid her uninjured hand on William's arm, and still they stood in silence. Eventually, William sighed, so deeply that Jeremy heard it across the yard, and after a quick word to Sophia, William turned and walked up the road.

"William is going to walk back to Allenton," she said, turning to her father. "He's not comfortable with the situation and prefers to take himself out of the equation. Might you keep him company?"

Miss Dewey, having heard Sophia's words, jumped to her feet, and would have run after William had not Mr. Phillips grabbed her shoulder. "William!" she screamed after him. "I love you!"

William's step faltered, but he didn't turn around, continuing down the path. Mr. Thompson nodded to Sophia and followed his nephew down the road.

Sophia turned to Miss Dewey. "Perhaps being party to his brother's murder is not a good demonstration of that love." Her tone was smooth, but her words were shards of glass.

"It was Mother's idea." Charlotte lifted her chin, sounding defiant. "*I* did not kill anyone."

"You might want to work on your defense," Daphne said coldly. "That one will not impress the jury."

The surgeon arrived in a rush just before Constable Marley and the Allenton wagon. His examination was brief and confirmed Jeremy's expectation; Mrs. Curtis was inflicted with several broken bones. The criminals would be patched up and then transferred to the town prison to await trial.

Jeremy and Sophia were the last to leave the church clearing, and did not rush to follow the others.

"And so this ends our adventures together, Miss Thompson," Jeremy said with a tight throat as he unwound the reins from the hitching post.

He knew that they would have little time together before he headed east. He would have to write his reports, give his evidence to the magistrate, and then join his fellow Runners on the long journey back to London.

This was not what he wanted. He wanted to pick Sophia up and kiss her until her toes curled. He wanted to spend his days laughing and teasing with this wonderful young lady. *All* his days might be enough—but only just.

"Miss Thompson? You kissed me not an hour ago. You can hardly call me Miss Thompson now. Besides, we agreed to use first names."

Sophia lifted her hand to Jeremy's cheek, and he leaned closer. So close that he could feel her breath on his lips . . . lips that were itching to find hers.

Jeremy stared at Sophia's mouth for a moment before he realized that she was waiting for him to say something. "Yes, yes, we had agreed to first names but . . . I'll be heading back to London soon—"

"Yes, and I will as well. I'm going to plague Sir Elderberry until he accepts me as a Bow Street Detective."

"Sophia . . ."

She cupped his chin and stretched up on her toes. "We make

good partners," she said. "I'm almost certain that Sir Elderberry will not want to separate us."

And then, before Jeremy could argue, Sophia pressed her mouth to his in a kiss that made his heart sing. It took his thoughts away from death and criminals, and left him wondering about the wonders of life and the magical appeal of a young lady called Miss Sophia Thompson.

After

Sophia was miserable.

Not with Jeremy and their planned future together. Absolutely not! In fact, Sophia was of a mind that Jeremy was handsomer, kinder, funnier, and more loving every time she saw him. He was no longer a novice detective but a freshly minted sergeant, one who was touted as being of a superior variety, and cited as having a great ability to reason.

Yes, all was well.

Except for one . . . tiny . . . little . . . problem.

Sir Elderberry was without a doubt the most belligerently unreasonable gentleman that Sophia had ever had to deal with! Despite countless letters explaining the value of a woman detective at Bow Street and stacks of letters from various lords and ladies lending their support to Sophia's ambitions, Sophia had not been able to convince Sir Elderberry that she was Bow Street material.

But now, at last, she had cornered the man at the Frasers'

London townhouse. It was a small gathering of friends and associates—just forty or fifty persons—enjoying the dulcet tones of an operatic soprano in the spacious drawing room.

Sophia was prepared, having studied *Investigating Murder and Mayhem* from cover to cover. She could quote from the book and even cite various laws. Yes, she was ready with arguments and salient points about the value of women in policework. As planned, Jeremy had instigated the conversation and then signaled for Sophia to join them.

"Ah yes, my dear," Sir Elderberry said as Sophia approached and was introduced. "I'm not surprised to find you here. Oh no, worry not, Fraser, I'm not displeased. It's good actually to be able to speak to you in person, Miss Thompson."

"Oh?" Sophia said with great intelligence and hope. "Do you have good news?" She glanced at Jeremy, giving him a bright smile.

"No, I'm so sorry, my dear, no. But I wanted to explain to you face-to-face. I have to be official in my letters; I never get a chance to say what I mean." He, too, glanced at Jeremy. "Shall we walk? The soprano will be back in a minute, and I'd best say what needs to be said quickly."

Sophia's hopes plummeted, but she still followed Sir Elderberry and Jeremy to a quieter corner of the entrance hall.

"First," Sir Elderberry said, "I would like to say that I agree with all your arguments about the need for women in the police force."

"Wonderful!" Jeremy said, bless him.

Sir Elderberry shook his head. "No, not wonderful, there is a but. *But*, I'm afraid we are a long way away from that day. Wives of the present detectives would string me up by the toes if I allowed a woman in among the men—and an unmarried young lady at that."

"That will be rectified soon, sir. I'm to be married in February."

Glancing toward Jeremy, Sir Elderberry nodded and then grinned. "So I understand. Congratulations. However, you will still be a young lady."

"But that can't be helped, sir. My career choice can't be thwarted simply because I'm a girl."

"It *is* really, gone for that very reason. Not only would there be trouble at home for my detectives, but we would have to be careful which cases you worked on—"

"But—"

"A Bow Street Detective has to be able to travel to other parts of the country, all alone—wherever we are hired. You would encounter sleazy people and be required to visit sordid places. And while we would try to keep the ugliness at a minimum, there would be times . . . It's not a pretty picture, you see. And hiring a woman would make me a man short. So, you see, there is a great dilemma here.

"I *have* thought this through. I've considered the welfare of the force, and you, naturally. And no matter how I consider it, the likelihood of me placing a woman in harm's way is slim to none. Unless you decide to open your own agency, I don't see you ever being a detective. Don't look so crestfallen, my dear. Did you really want to stand in the cold, staring at a mutilated body?"

"No, that would not be my favorite part of the job," Sophia said hotly. "But apprehending the murderer or returning a stolen item, finding a lost child . . . *those* moments would make up for the others."

"Yes, I can see that you have thought this through, too. But, my dear, my mind is made up. You're welcome to continue plaguing me with letters, but I will not change my mind."

And then, after having stomped all over Sophia's hopes, Sir Elderberry looked up and tipped his head. "We must be getting back. The soprano has returned."

Sophia watched Sir Elderberry disappear into the drawing room again as the first notes of a beautiful aria drifted into the cavernous entrance hall.

"I'm so sorry, my love." Jeremy looked as crestfallen as Sophia felt.

As she *should* have felt. But she . . . didn't.

"Did you hear it?" Sophia asked. She whirled around and grabbed both of Jeremy's hands. "Sir Elderberry's suggestion? Casually dismissed but, in truth, a marvelous idea."

Jeremy grinned, looked about, and then kissed her right on the mouth—in the middle of the entrance hall, where anyone could have seen them.

"I did, indeed," he said, pulling away. "Will you call it the Thompson Detective Agency or the Fraser Detective Agency?"

"I think the Thompson-Fraser Detective Agency has a nice ring to it, don't you?" Sophia lifted her eyebrows and bounced them up and down. "If you ever get tired of Bow Street, we could be partners."

Jeremy grinned. "The Thompson-Fraser Detective Agency does have a very nice ring."

And again he kissed her full on the mouth—in the middle of the entrance hall, where anyone could have seen them.

Acknowledgments

I would like to express my great appreciation to the many people who helped make *Deadly Curious* a reality. This book was written while I was dealing with significant health issues, and as a result, it experienced some delays. A big thank-you to the entire Swoon Reads team for their patience and guidance throughout the process.

I would especially like to thank Emily Settle for her support and encouragement as well as her finely honed skills as an editor. Many thanks to Kat Brzozowski, who made sense of my first draft. Liz Dresner and KB, who created the cover: superb artwork conveying a mysterious atmosphere with lots of drama. Wonderful! Thank you, Mandy Veloso, my production editor; Kelsey Marrujo, my publicist; and Lauren Forte, my copy editor. And, of course, many thanks to Swoon Reads authors and readers for their interest and support.

As always, I would like to thank my friends and family—

particularly my husband, Mike, who deals not only with *my* woes but those of my characters as well. Christine and Deb, my beta readers who are not afraid to let me know when I have gone astray. And Dan, who thinks everything I write is great.

Check out more books chosen for publication by readers like you.

BEWARE THE NIGHT
JESSIKA FLECK

If You Only Knew
PRERNA PICKETT

A SOLDIER AND A LIAR
CAITLIN LOCHNER

Gone by Nightfall
DEE GARRETSON

ROGUE PRINCESS
B.R. MYERS

Shani Petroff
Finding Mr. Better-Than-You

THE KING'S QUESTIONER
NIKKI KATZ

How to SPEAK BOY
TIANA SMITH

MIND GAMES
SHANA SILVER

THE SOUL KEEPERS
DEVON TAYLOR

WE ARE THE GHOSTS
VICKY SKINNER

How the Light Gets In
KATY UPPERMAN

DID YOU KNOW...

readers like you
helped to get this
book published?

Join our book-obsessed community and help us
discover awesome new writing talent.

1

Write it.

Share your original YA manuscript.

2

Read it.

Discover bright new bookish talent.

3

Share it.

Discuss, rate, and share your faves.

4

Love it.

Help us publish the books you love.

Share your own manuscript or dive between the pages
at **swoonreads.com** or by downloading the **Swoon Reads app**.